Even though she'd been telling herself it didn't matter one way or the other if Quint hired her, she hadn't quite convinced her heart.

It was beating far too fast as she punched the accept button and placed the phone against her ear.

"Hello, Quint."

"Good morning, Clementine. Have I caught you at an awkward time?"

His voice pierced something inside her and sent every ounce of air rushing from her lungs. Quickly, she covered the phone with her hand and sucked in a deep breath before she replied, "No. I'm just finishing breakfast at a little restaurant across from the hotel."

There was a short pause and then he said, "I realize it's still very early, but I wanted to let you know I've thought the situation over and decided that I—and the rest of the family—will be glad to have you as our sheepherder. That is, if you still want the job."

She hadn't realized just how tense she'd been until now. She could feel her body sagging with relief, which hardly made sense. There were other jobs, other places to live. Her life didn't hinge on Quint Hollister or Stone Creek Ranch. Yet a nagging voice had been whispering in her ear that this job was important...

Dear Reader,

Being the youngest son of the Hollister family hasn't always been easy for Quint. While his older brothers held important positions on Stone Creek Ranch, he'd done the chores of a hired hand and constantly complained. Then his father gave him the lofty position of managing the sheep production and now he's working hard to show his family he's worthy of the job.

Recently, Quint's main objective has been to hire a sheepherder to care and guard the flock, while he tends to other ranching responsibilities. But a dependable sheepherder is difficult to find. Then he interviews Clementine Starr for the job. Her qualifications say she's ideal for the tough, lonely task of herding his sheep through the mountains. And soon after he hires her, Quint begins to see that she's not only the perfect sheepherder, but also the perfect woman for him!

Clementine is a nomad, moving from ranch to ranch, and has pushed aside all hopes of having a family of her own. But Quint is convinced his beautiful Clementine is also his Christmas star, and the holiday is all about miracles and the gift of love!

I hope you'll enjoy reading how Clementine finds her forever home on Stone Creek Ranch and that your holidays are filled with hope and joy.

Merry Christmas! And God bless the trails you ride,

Stella

The Rancher's Christmas Star

STELLA BAGWELL

HARLEQUIN

SPECIAL
EDITION

HARLEQUIN®
SPECIAL
EDITION™

Recycling programs
for this product may
not exist in your area.

ISBN-13: 978-1-335-59434-1

The Rancher's Christmas Star

Copyright © 2023 by Stella Bagwell

For questions and comments about the quality of this book,
please contact us at CustomerService@Harlequin.com.

Harlequin Enterprises ULC
22 Adelaide St. West, 41st Floor
Toronto, Ontario M5H 4E3, Canada
www.Harlequin.com

Printed in U.S.A.

After writing more than one hundred books for Harlequin, **Stella Bagwell** still finds writing about two people discovering everlasting love very rewarding. She loves all things Western and has been married to her own real cowboy for fifty-one years. Living on the south Texas coast, she also enjoys being outdoors and helping her husband care for the animals on the small ranch they call home. The couple has one son, who teaches high school mathematics and coaches football and powerlifting.

Books by Stella Bagwell

Harlequin Special Edition

Men of the West

His Texas Runaway
Home to Blue Stallion Ranch
The Rancher's Best Gift
Her Man Behind the Badge
His Forever Texas Rose
The Baby That Binds Them
Sleigh Ride with the Rancher
The Wrangler Rides Again
The Other Hollister Man
Rancher to the Rescue

Montana Mavericks: Lassoing Love

The Maverick's Sweetest Choice

Montana Mavericks: Brothers & Broncos

The Maverick's Marriage Pact

Visit the Author Profile page
at Harlequin.com for more titles.

To Roy and Pam Cox,

With love from your Texas friends!

Chapter One

Quint Hollister was wasting his time. He'd come to that conclusion even before he made the half-hour drive from Stone Creek Ranch to the small town of Beaver, Utah. But he'd promised the woman he'd meet with her, and he wasn't a man who broke his word.

Yet now as he sat at a small table in the Wagon Spoke Café, waiting for her to arrive, he wondered again what had possessed him to pick up the phone two days ago and call her. She wasn't what he was looking for, or needed. But he was desperate. Yeah, he could admit that much. Desperate to prove to his family and himself that he'd grown into a responsible man.

"How about a piece of pie while you're waiting, Quint? It's Tuesday. That means rhubarb is on the menu."

Quint glanced up at the middle-aged waitress with salt-and-pepper hair pulled into a tight ponytail at the back of her head. "Maybe later, Laverne. I'll take a little warm-up on the coffee, though."

"Sure." She tilted the glass carafe over his coffee cup. "You or your brothers haven't been around in the past few days. Been busy at the ranch?"

"Always. Dad just made a deal for the property joining our north boundary, so come next week we'll be taking over the C Bar C ranch."

Surprised flickered on the waitress's weary face. "The Carters sold out? Guess that news is slow making it here to the café."

"Yeah, the family is moving to Montana. Dad is like a kid with a new toy. He's eyed that property for years."

"Good for him. Next time Hadley comes in I'll congratulate him on his new toy."

Quint chuckled. "He'll like that."

She moved on to the next table and Quint picked up his coffee cup, while his gaze slipped toward the front of the café where a wooden door painted a bright green served as the entrance. With only five minutes to spare before their two o'clock meeting, he expected the woman to show any moment now.

Ten minutes later, he was taking another long sip of coffee and pondering the idea of signaling Laverne and telling her to go ahead and get the pie, when the cowbell over the door clanged.

Above the busy tables of afternoon diners, Quint watched a woman enter the busy café and walk over to a long bar located on the left side of the room. From his angle, she appeared to be somewhere in her thirties, and she was dressed in jeans and a faded yellow shirt. A long black braid hung over her right shoulder.

No. False alarm, Quint decided. This lady was the right age, but the rest of her didn't fit his expectations.

Even so, he continued to watch as she moved down the bar to where Ruby was wiping down a spot on the counter. After a brief exchange of words, the redheaded waitress pointed directly at Quint.

His mind whirling, he watched the woman slowly weave her way through the tables until she reached him. By then he'd accepted the obvious and quickly jumped to his feet.

Politely sweeping off his gray Stetson, he greeted her.

"Hello. I'm Quint Hollister," he introduced himself. "Are you Clementine Starr?"

"I am," she replied.

He extended his hand to her while thinking he had to be dreaming. This couldn't be the same woman who'd sent him a résumé for the sheepherding job on Stone Creek Ranch.

"Nice to meet you," he said, while hoping he didn't sound as dazed as he felt.

"I'm pleased to meet you, Mr. Hollister."

Her hand closed around his, and even though her palm wasn't soft and pampered it was far from the hard calloused skin he expected from someone in her profession.

He said, "You can drop the Mr. Hollister. I'm Quint to everyone. Especially with there being six Hollister men in my family."

He released her hand, then jamming his hat back onto his head, he rounded the table and pulled out a chair for her. After helping her into the worn wooden seat, he returned to his own chair and tried his best to look cool and casual.

She said, "I apologize for keeping you waiting. I thought I'd started early enough this morning to be here by two, but I ran into highway construction."

Smiling had always come naturally to Quint. Especially when he was around women, but now his face felt oddly twisted as he attempted to smile at Clementine Starr.

It's the shock, he tried to reason. When a man was knocked off-kilter, he couldn't expect to instantly get his senses back together. Especially when he was looking into a pair of dark brown eyes fringed by long black lashes.

He said, "Yes, I've heard the interstate is being resurfaced in places. No need for you to apologize, Ms. Starr. I've only been here a few minutes. And sitting in the Wagon Spoke and drinking coffee is hardly a pain."

"Please call me Clementine," she said, then glanced over at the waitress, who was still making rounds with the coffee carafe.

Following her gaze, he said, "I'll get Laverne's attention. Have you had lunch? The food here is great. I'll be glad to buy your lunch."

"Thank you. I've already had lunch. But I would like coffee," she told him.

Laverne suddenly glanced in his direction, and he waved a finger at her. She immediately crossed the room to their table.

Inclining his head toward Clementine, he said to Laverne, "This is Clementine Starr, and she's just made a long drive from Idaho. So bring her the freshest, hottest coffee you have."

"I'll make a fresh pot just for you two," she said to Quint, then turned her attention to Clementine. "Welcome to Beaver, Ms. Starr. Would you like a menu with your coffee?"

"No, thank you."

Quint said, "You can bring me that pie now, Laverne. Make it the rhubarb. It might be a while before I'm back in here on Tuesday or Wednesday."

"Gotcha covered," she told him. "I'll be back in a few."

Laverne scurried away, and Quint turned his attention back to Clementine. "First of all," he said. "I want to thank you for making the long drive down here. I'm sure it was an inconvenience for you."

Those dark, dark eyes scanned his face, and Quint had the uneasy feeling that she could see right into his brain. If so, she'd already realized that he was totally mesmerized by her smooth olive complexion, black hair and full pink lips that had yet to get remotely close to a smile.

"Not really. I enjoyed the drive through Utah. Like I told you on the phone, I'm in between jobs. And I've been wanting to find work away from Idaho."

"Why do you want to leave the state?"

He was trying not to stare, but she was so unlike anything he'd pictured in his mind. Being a sheepherder was a damned hard job. In fact, she was the first and only female one he'd ever heard of, and he'd instinctively assumed she'd be a rough, muscular woman with large hands, leathery skin and hair that was dulled and dried from working in the elements. Instead, she was soft and earthy and downright feminine.

Her expression remained stoic. "I've had an urge to see a different set of mountains and valleys. Especially when they'll be my home for several months out of the year."

Why would a woman who was as young and pretty as Clementine Starr want to bury herself in the mountains for two-thirds of the year? he wondered. From her résumé he knew she'd been sheepherding for the past eight years. She was now thirty-four, which made her seven years older than Quint. And for some odd reason, the age difference made him feel a bit of a greenhorn.

"To be honest, Clementine, I can't imagine myself doing what you do. When I was twenty-six, I sure as heck didn't want to be alone with nothing but sheep, dogs and horses for company."

Her gaze slipped over his face. "And how long ago were you twenty-six?" she asked.

He chuckled. "A year ago."

The corners of her mouth bent slightly upward. It was the first congenial expression she'd shown him since they'd met.

"Well, I'm a solitary kind of person," she explained. "The reason I do what I do is that I love being with the sheep and my dogs and horses."

Solitude was nice, he thought. And so was being around the animals. But a woman who looked like her— were those things all she needed in life?

"Sure," he said with a wan smile. "Animals often make better companions. They don't ask much from us, and in return they give us their devotion and love."

"Yes. It's a fulfilling job. At least, it is for me," she said. "But as for moving on from Idaho—the last rancher I worked for lost his grazing lease, and because he didn't own enough private property to run his sheep year-round, he was forced to sell out."

"That's too bad."

She nodded. "Unfortunately, it's a situation that's happening more and more."

He said, "I'm happy to say Stone Creek has plenty of acreage to run sheep year-round. We don't have to lease."

"Lucky you."

Was that a touch of bitterness or sarcasm he heard in her voice? Because she'd been forced to move on from the last ranch she'd worked? No. From the way her résumé had read, she was a typical sheepherder, a nomad living in one place for a while, then migrating to another. She was accustomed to moving on.

"I'll be honest," he told her. "For the past several months I've been searching for the right, uh, person for the job. I've gone through a stack of applicants and actually interviewed three of them. None felt like the right fit for Stone Creek. So here I am at the late end of grazing season without a sheepherder."

She was about to reply when Laverne arrived with the coffee and pie.

"I brought two pieces of pie," the waitress explained as she placed the orders on the table. "Just in case Ms. Starr decides she'd like a bite. If not, I know you can eat two pieces, Quint."

He gave the woman a grateful grin. "Without batting an eye. Thanks, Laverne."

"Let me know if you need anything else."

As she moved away from the table, Quint looked over to see Clementine was studying him closely. Was she thinking he was too young to be in charge of the sheep production on Stone Creek? Or too young to be her boss?

Hell, Quint, Clementine Starr's opinion of you has nothing to do with anything. You're the one in charge of this whole matter. Not her.

Mentally shaking away the taunting voice in his head, he pushed one of the servings of pie toward her. "You were about to say something?"

"Only that we're in similar positions. Earlier in the year I had a job offer on a ranch over by Boise, but it didn't exactly fit what I wanted. So here I am without a job and the season is nearly over. Frankly, I'm surprised you want to hire anyone for only a couple of months or so."

He sliced his fork into the pie while his gaze slipped from her face to her yellow shirt. The fabric was soft and faded from endless washings and molded to the lush curves of her breasts. A tiny silver cross rested in the hollow at the base of her throat while small silver hoops hung from her ears. She was sexy without even trying to be, he thought. And she was also waking up every male cell in his body.

He took a bite of the pie in hopes the taste would distract his rattled senses. "I've had plans for a long while now to increase the flock on Stone Creek, but I can't do that until I get a sheepherder. I was hoping whoever I hired would be willing to pick up the job again in early spring. Or perhaps stick through the winter—if I can afford the extra salary."

"How are you currently taking care of your sheep?"

"With dogs, mostly. Two Great Pyrenees. They never leave the herd. Then someone makes a daily check. Usually me or one of the ranch hands. But now that the flock is up in the mountains that takes up a huge hunk of time. And we all have to deal with other ranching chores."

"I imagine you have bears and coyotes," she said. "What about wolves? Any problem with those?"

"Wolves are practically extinct in Utah, although there are a few sightings from time to time. We have plenty of bears, coyote packs and rattlesnakes. But our ranch has run sheep and cattle both since it began back in 1962, and my father can tell you that over the years we've not lost many animals to predators. Blizzards and diseases are far more deadly to the herds."

She nodded. "I understand. And just in case you're wondering, I always carry a Winchester with me—just in case I have to deal with predators. As for diseases, I can spot and treat most ailments that sheep have."

She named off several health issues she commonly encountered and how she normally dealt with them. Quint had to admit he was impressed with her knowledge. But did wisdom and experience make up for her physical disadvantage? Not that she was fragile by any means. Just guessing, he'd say she was close to five foot five. As to her weight, he decided it wasn't too much or too little. It was just right and in all the places it should be.

"Whatever made you want to be a sheepherder?" he asked.

Shrugging, she glanced away from him, and Quint's gaze instinctively slipped over her profile. In the past several minutes, since she'd joined him at the table, he'd noticed that very little expression showed on her face. Whether she wanted to keep her feelings hidden, or simply didn't express them outwardly, he could only wonder.

"I've always loved sheep. My father always kept a flock on our ranch and that's how I learned to care for them. Most people think sheep are dumb and docile, but the old saying 'as gentle as a lamb' isn't always right. Some can be downright aggressive. But that's just a part of nature. Every living thing has to be tough and smart to survive."

He smiled at her. "My grandfather would love hearing you say that. He's the reason we raise sheep. Does your father still run sheep on his ranch?"

"No. He's dead. The ranch is under different ownership now."

Her voice was stiff, and Quint realized he'd touched on a sore spot. But how was he to know? Up until the phone call he'd had with her a couple days ago, he'd never spoken to this woman. Still, with each passing minute, he was growing more and more intrigued with her.

"I'm sorry. He must have died a young man."

"Yes. Too young."

Clearing his throat, he pointed his fork toward the pie. "Go ahead and eat it. You'll be glad you did."

She looked from him to the pie. "Is this part of the job interview?"

The question was the closest thing she'd come to humor, and he couldn't help but chuckle. "It is. So eat up and enjoy."

She pulled the small plate with the pie toward her and forked into the flaky crust. As he watched her slip the bite between her lips, he felt like he was watching an erotic film. One that he couldn't tear his gaze away from.

"Pardon me if I'm getting too personal, but do you have Basque in your family ancestry?"

Her gaze lifted from the pie and settled on his face. "Not that I'm aware of. Why do you ask? Because I work as a sheepherder?"

His question had nothing to do with her being a sheepherder. No, it had everything to do with the dark mystic aura that swirled around her. As though she'd ascended from those great European mountains.

"No. It was just a thought. That's all." His gaze traveled to her hand that was holding the fork. The back, along with her fingers, was tanned brown with the nails clipped short. There were no rings on either hand, and he wondered if she ever wore jewelry. More specifically had she ever had a wedding band encircling that important finger on her left hand?

Why that question should be entering his head, Quint

didn't know. At twenty-seven, he was years away from wanting a wife. Besides, his taste didn't run toward older women. His date book was filled with names and numbers of women who were far younger than him. Even so, something about Clementine was certainly waking up his libido.

"How much longer do you expect the grazing to last in the mountains on Stone Creek? If you usually have early snows, there's no use in hiring anyone. Unless you want the flock to be guarded while they're down on the lower flats."

Her remark pulled him out of his erotic thoughts, and he purposely downed a swig of coffee to give himself a moment to collect his senses.

"It's hard to predict the weather here. Sometimes we get early snows and lots of them. Other times it's dry and warmer than usual. Presently, I'd guess there might be two or two and a half months of grazing left in the mountains. And like I said, hiring someone to shepherd year-round is a nice idea. I'm just not sure I can swing the extra cost. Stone Creek sheep are only produced for their wool. None are sold for meat purposes. And I'm not sure how the market will be faring come spring and shearing time."

"But in spite of the current market, you want to increase your herd?"

A grin twisted his lips. "I'm contradicting myself, aren't I? But to answer your question, yes. In spite of what the wool market is doing I want to increase the number of sheep on Stone Creek. The way I see things, you have to have ample product in order to make a decent profit."

"Yes. And I imagine you're smart enough to know that ranching involves risk—of all sorts."

Like hiring a woman who had a man thinking of hot nights and sweaty sheets. Yeah, being near Clementine would be a risk, he thought. But even if he hired her— and that was still a big if—he wouldn't be around her long enough to be tempted. Besides, he got the impression she wasn't interested in striking up any kind of relationship with a man.

"Ranching is never easy," he replied as he sliced the last bit of pie on the saucer into two bites. "I don't think you mentioned this in your résumé, but do you have a camp trailer, or wagon to live in? The ranch doesn't have anything suitable for portable living quarters, but I suppose I might come up with something. That is, if we come to terms and I hire you."

"That won't be necessary," she said abruptly.

His eyes widened. "Oh. You've already decided this job isn't for you?"

A slight frown creased the space between her black brows. "I didn't say anything of the sort. I said it wouldn't be necessary to supply me with living quarters. I use a pack horse to carry my tent and other supplies. I'll have everything I need."

If she'd reached over and shoved him out of his chair, he couldn't have been more stunned. He glanced around him as if he needed to reassure himself that he wasn't hallucinating. "You're not joking are you?"

Her expression went blank as she stared at him. "No. Why would I joke?"

To lighten the moment? To make both of them feel easier? Or just to simply be happy in the moment? He wanted to toss the suggestions at her, but he knew none of them would go over well. No. Clementine Starr was not only the dark mysterious sort, she was also the serious sort.

"Sorry," he said. "You took me by surprise, that's all. For me, a tent would be roughing it. And if a bear did happen to come along at night, you wouldn't have any protection."

"Like I told you, I'll have my Winchester. As for roughing it, I don't need luxuries. Just a shelter."

Certain his mouth was gaping, he reached for his coffee in hopes of hiding his reaction. "Have you always worked this way?"

"Always. Except one time. A ranch I worked for already owned a sheepherder's wagon and the manager insisted I use the thing. I didn't like it. I felt boxed in. And it was a pain to move whenever I needed to drive the sheep to another meadow."

"I see," he said, but frankly he didn't understand. Not completely. This beautiful woman preferred to sleep on the ground and cook over a campfire. She'd have to bathe from a basin or in a nearby creek. No electricity or phone service. No Wi-Fi or TV. If she was lucky a tiny portable radio might pick up a weather report or a bit of music, but the mountain ranges usually knocked out the signal. No, he thought, it would be just Clementine, the animals and nature.

She said, "Doubt is written all over your face. And I'm getting the feeling that I'm wasting my time and yours."

Annoyed now, he frowned at her. "I didn't say that, you did."

"Look, I came here not expecting much. Some ranch owners just can't handle hiring a female sheepherder, and that's okay with me. I understand their thinking." She put down her fork and looked directly at him. "Furthermore, I'd hate to think you might feel obliged to hire me just because I am a woman. So either way I can't see this meeting turning out well for either of us."

"Listen, Clementine, you're assuming far too much. Yes, because you are a woman I do wonder about you being able to handle the job. I think that's only fair. It's not like I'm hiring you to knit me a blanket."

A grimace tightened her lips, and Quint was actually glad to see her showing some real emotion.

"No. I'm the person who guards your sheep in order for you to have the wool to make a blanket," she said flatly.

Hell, she had him there. "Okay, Clementine, I apologize for questioning your ability. It's not even your ability that I'm doubting. I've carefully read your résumé. Every rancher you've worked for has glowing words for your work." He shrugged, and to his surprise he felt warm heat climbing up his neck and onto his face. "I guess I'm having trouble picturing you in the role of sheepherder because of my mother and three sisters. They're all hardy women and not afraid of work. Including outdoor work. But none of them could handle your job. Heck, I'm not sure I could handle it."

She eyed him skeptically. "I'm different, Quint. I learned how to be tough a long time ago."

Why? he wondered. And why did he have the ridiculous urge to reach over and cover her hand with his? Why did he want to see her smile? Hear her laugh. None of those things had anything to do with her job experience or his need of a sheepherder.

He released a long breath. "All right. If it's agreeable with you, I'll talk it over with my family tonight and give you my decision in the morning. If you need a place until then, you're welcome to come out to the ranch."

"Thank you, but I already have a hotel room reserved

here in town." She rose to her feet, and once he'd followed suit, she reached to shake his hand.

"I appreciate your consideration, Quint. I'll be waiting for your call in the morning."

Without saying more, she dropped his hand and walked away. Quint stared after her until she stepped through the green door and disappeared from his sight.

"Hmm. You don't see that too often."

Laverne's comment penetrated his whirling thoughts, and he glanced blankly up at the waitress.

"You don't see what too often?"

She pointed to Clementine's partially eaten pie. "A person leave pie behind," she answered. "Guess your lady friend wasn't in the mood for dessert."

Shaking his head, he asked, "Laverne, do I look like a fool?"

"I've seen a few in my day, but I wouldn't put you in that category just yet. Why? The lady from Idaho got your goat?"

It wasn't his goat he was worried about, Quint thought. It was the welfare of several hundred head of sheep.

Slanting the woman a wry grin, he said, "No. She didn't make me angry. I'm just wondering, that's all."

Laverne said, "Me, too. Wondering why she seemed so sad."

He looked curiously at the waitress. "Is that the way you saw her? Sad?"

"Well, let's just say she isn't the jolliest person I've seen in this café," she said, then lifted the coffee carafe. "Need another warm-up?"

"No thanks, I need to get back to Stone Creek." Rising to his feet, he tucked a nice tip into the pocket on her apron. "See you later, Laverne."

* * *

While Quint was on his way home, Clementine was across town in her modest hotel room, sitting on the side of the bed, tapping out a text message to her brother, Kipp.

Have met with Mr. Hollister. He's nice, but seriously young. Not certain he wants to hire me.

After pushing the send arrow, she placed the phone to one side, then lay back against the mattress.

If Quint Hollister decided not to hire her, she could certainly live with his decision, Clementine thought. On the other hand, if his call in the morning turned out to be positive, how was she going to react?

What in heck is wrong with you, Clementine? You've driven nearly four hundred miles to see the man about the job. Now you're wondering whether you want it? You're not making sense.

Closing her eyes, she pressed fingertips to the burning lids and tried to block out the nagging voice in her head. She supposed she wasn't making sense, but something had happened to her back there in the Wagon Spoke Café. The moment the waitress at the bar had pointed out Quint Hollister, she'd been knocked off-kilter. She'd been expecting an older, grizzled rancher, not a young, hunky cowboy seven years her junior! Especially one with a killer grin and eyes that were bluer than the sky. Working for him might be risky business.

Who was she kidding? There was zero chance of Quint Hollister making any kind of a play for her. One look at him was enough to tell Clementine that he had girlfriends running out the ears. Young pretty women with soft skin and pampered hands, who dressed in feminine frills and lace, who no doubt welcomed his attention with open arms. No. He'd never look at her in a romantic way. Which meant she'd always be safe around him. That is, if she could be around the man for a few minutes at a time without losing control of her common sense.

Lying next to her, the phone dinged with an incoming message. She picked it up and read Kipp's reply.

If the man doesn't hire you, he's a fool. But not getting the job would give you a good reason to come home.

Grimacing, Clementine quickly tapped a response.

I have no home.

The phone dinged again, and Clementine's frown grew deeper as she read her brother's remark.

You will have. Some day.

With a heavy sigh, she put the phone aside and closed her eyes. She didn't want to think about the Rising Starr. Not today or any day. Letting her mind surf through the memories of the beautiful family ranch where she and Kipp had resided for nearly all their lives was too painful. And it was even worse to think how their home had fallen into other hands.

How Kipp could stay there and work as a regular ranch hand was beyond Clementine's comprehension. But he insisted that he needed to stay close to watch and wait for Andrea to make a mistake. One he could use for evidence in a court of law. And perhaps his strategy was right, she thought glumly. If Kipp had run from the

Rising Starr the way Clementine had, there would be no chance of ever getting their home back.

With a rueful sigh, she pushed herself up from the bed and reached for her shoulder bag. It was going to be a long wait until morning and Quint Hollister's call. She might as well use the rest of the afternoon to get some fresh air and look over the town. After all, if Quint decided against hiring her, she thought, this would be the one and only time she'd see Beaver, Utah.

Chapter Two

Later that night at the kitchen table on Stone Creek Ranch, Quint was sitting with his older brother Flint and their mother and father, Claire and Hadley. With his twin sisters, Bonnie and Beatrice, attending a function in town, there were only the four of them sharing the evening meal. His other three brothers each had their own homes on the ranch, while another sister lived on a nearby ranch.

Now, most of the beef stew and sourdough bread Claire had prepared for dinner had already been consumed, but everyone continued to linger around the table and discuss Quint's dilemma about hiring Clementine Starr as the ranch's sheepherder.

"Quint, you've been searching for several months for a sheepherder and coming up empty," Flint said. "If you ask me, you'd better snatch this one up."

"I'm with Flint," Claire said.

Quint looked across the table at his mother. At sixty,

she was still an active and attractive woman, with short blond hair that held only a few streaks of silver and eyes that Hadley described as bluebonnet blue. His father, a tall, muscular man with dark hair and rugged features, was only a year older than his wife and still physically capable of doing any job his five sons could do. The couple had been married for more than forty years, and Quint, along with the rest of the family, understood that even though Hadley was the driving force behind Stone Creek Ranch, Claire was its heartbeat.

"You've surprised me, Mom. I didn't expect that from you," Quint told her.

"Why? It's not like you can find a sheepherder on every street corner. From what I understand they're very hard to come by. Even the men who come over from Peru with work visas are becoming scarce. Ms. Starr is available, and you said yourself that she has very positive references. What more do you want?"

Hadley reached over and gently placed a large hand over his wife's delicate one. "He'd prefer to have a man for the job. We've raised Quint to be protective of all females. Not throw them out to the bears or coyotes. Clementine is a woman. He'd be worried about her being alone in the mountains."

Flint grunted. "Quint knew she was a woman before he met with her. Besides, Dad, you're being an old fogy. We have two female deputies on the force, and none of us male law officers do any extra worrying about them being in danger. Because they're just as capable as we are, and I figure the same goes for Clementine. If she's been doing this job for eight years, she should be experienced."

Two years older than Quint, his brother Flint had worked as a Beaver County deputy sheriff for the past seven years. The job consumed most of his time, but he did help out on the ranch whenever his schedule allowed. He was an excellent deputy and equally good at cowboying, and Quint respected his opinion. But his brother hadn't met Clementine. He didn't know she was like a mountain flower. Beautiful and strong, yet vulnerable enough to be crushed.

Absently tapping a finger against his water glass, Quint said, "You'll have to call me old fogy, too. Because Dad put his finger on the problem. I would worry about Clementine. And you're right, I did know she was a female when I granted her an interview. But I was expecting—well, if you could see her, Flint, you'd understand. She's not some rough, tough cave woman."

Claire slanted Quint a look of disapproval. "Now you're being unfair, son. I'm not rough and tough, but I hold up to my job."

Hadley patted the top of her hand. "Yes, you do, honey. You hold up very well to being my wife."

"Hadley, be serious," she scolded her husband. "Quint needs advice. Can't you see he's tormented over this decision he has to make?"

Giving his wife a loving glance, Hadley said, "I can see quite clearly. You're looking at Quint as though he's still our little boy instead of a grown, responsible man. Stone Creek's sheep are his responsibility now. It's his duty to make the final decision concerning their care and welfare, then live with it."

As usual, his father was right, Quint thought. For a long time, he'd wanted the job of overseeing the ranch's sheep division. Now that he held the position, the task of making smart decisions lay on his shoulders. But would hiring Clementine be a wise choice for the ranch? For himself? That was the crux of his concerns.

Leaning back in his chair, he swiped a hand over his face. Damn it, he wouldn't be having this indecision if any other woman had been sitting across the table from him this afternoon in the Wagon Spoke. He would've already hired her. But the moment Clementine had walked up and shook his hand, a strange tremor had rocked his senses, and he still wasn't sure he was thinking clearly.

"You're right, Dad. This is something I have to do myself."

Flint leveled a meaningful look at him. "So what are you going to do? Send the woman back to Idaho?"

Quint let out a heavy breath. "I'm going to sleep on it before I make my decision."

"Good idea, son. Everything looks different once a person has rested," Claire said, then rising from her chair asked, "Now, do any of you want a dish of apple cobbler and coffee?"

All three men didn't hesitate to let her know they wanted dessert, and for the remainder of the meal, the subject of a sheepherder was dropped. But later, as Quint climbed the stairs to his bedroom, which was located on the second floor next to Flint's room, his brother caught up to him.

"Going to bed?" he asked as they walked side by side across the balcony.

Quint nodded. "It's a bit early, but I figured I needed extra time to clear my thoughts. I have a feeling sleep isn't going to come very easy tonight."

Flint gave Quint's shoulder a reassuring squeeze. "You're worrying too much. Trust me, everything will work out."

Quint wished he had his brother's confidence. "Tell me, Flint, do you ever wonder about the female deputies?"

The two men paused at Quint's bedroom door.

A perplexed frown furrowed Flint's brow. "Wonder? In what way?"

"I'm talking about why these women want to do such a dangerous job."

Flint responded with a shake of his head. "No. It's fairly obvious to me that they do their job because they love it. Don't you imagine Clementine is a sheepherder because she loves it? Why else would any woman take on a hazardous job?"

Quint supposed his brother was right. Yet he instinctively felt like there was more to Clementine's choice of profession than merely loving the job.

"I wish I knew the answer to that question," he told Flint, then opening the bedroom door, he added over his shoulder, "See you in the morning."

Clementine was sitting at a small table in a fast-food restaurant, drinking the last of her morning coffee, when her cell phone buzzed inside her handbag with an incoming call. Setting her cup aside, she pulled out the phone and immediately spotted Quint's name on the caller ID.

Even though she'd been telling herself it didn't matter one way or the other if Quint hired her, her heart wasn't quite so indifferent. It was beating far too fast as she punched the accept button and placed the phone against her ear.

"Hello, Quint."

"Good morning, Clementine. Have I caught you at an awkward time?"

His voice pierced something inside her and sent every ounce of air rushing from her lungs. Quickly, she covered the phone with her hand and sucked in a deep breath before she replied, "No. I'm just finishing breakfast at a little restaurant across from the hotel."

There was a short pause and then he said, "I realize it's still very early, but I wanted to let you know I've thought the situation over and decided that I—and the rest of the family—will be glad to have you as our sheepherder. That is, if you still want the job."

She hadn't realized just how tense she'd been until now. She could feel her body sagging with relief. Which hardly made sense. There were other jobs, other places to live. Her life didn't hinge on Quint Hollister or Stone Creek Ranch. Yet a nagging voice had been whispering in her ear that this job was important.

"I'm here in Beaver because I want the job, Quint."

This time she could hear him releasing a heavy breath, and she wondered why he might have thought she'd changed her mind. She was far from flighty or indecisive.

"Good. Then if you'd like to drive out to Stone Creek, I'd be happy to show you around and get you acquainted with the area where you'll be working."

"I'd like that. What time should I be there?"

"It takes about thirty to thirty-five minutes to make the drive from town. Just let me know when you'll be leaving and I'll be waiting for you at the main ranch house with a couple of horses. Do you need directions to get here?"

"I'll figure it out. So look for me in about an hour," she told him.

"Fine. I'll see you then."

"Thank you, Quint."

"That goes both ways, Clementine. I appreciate your willingness to take the job."

His voice was low and masculine, yet there was a

softness to it that slid over her senses like warm rain upon her skin. The odd reaction had her swallowing hard before she replied, "I'll be there shortly."

She ended the call, and twenty minutes later, she was in her truck driving to Stone Creek Ranch.

Quint was standing at the side of the horse trailer, adjusting the brow band on his horse's bridle when Cordell's voice sounded behind him.

"Hey, Quint, does it take two horses for you to check on the sheep these days?"

Quint turned to see the middle of the five Hollister brothers walking up with a teasing grin on his face. As the foreman of Stone Creek Ranch, Cordell probably worked the hardest of any of the Hollister men and Quint had always idolized him.

"I've already sent Jett on that job. I'm waiting on my new sheepherder. The horses are to show her around the ranch a bit."

Surprise crossed Cordell's face. "Oh, so you hired Clementine Starr? No one told me."

Quint shrugged. "It only happened thirty minutes ago. Mom and Dad are the only ones who know I decided to hire her."

Cordell fondly clapped a hand against Quint's back. "Well, congratulations, little brother. Your dreams of increasing the flock are getting closer to coming true."

"I'm not going to be in any hurry, Cord. Dad hasn't allotted me any extra money to purchase more sheep yet. Besides, I'm going to be patient and watch the market. I figure as fall grows near it will be better for buyers," Quint told him. "That way I can get more for my money. Or I should say, the ranch's money."

Cordell's expression turned thoughtful. "A year ago

I wanted to kick your butt for all the complaining and whining you did around here. And look at you now. Doing a man's job because you want to. Not because me or Dad gave you an order."

A sheepish grin crossed Quint's face. "Yeah, I guess for a long time I was a headache to everyone around here. I think—well, you remember how shocked I was when you told me Dad was promoting me to overseeing the sheep division. I couldn't believe he'd trust me to shut the barn door at night, much less manage the care of five hundred head of sheep. I don't think you've ever doubted yourself, Cord, but me—it made a heck of a lot of difference to know someone trusted my abilities. That all of you were willing to hand me an important task."

Cordell's smile was wry. "You aren't the only one around here who had to learn a thing or two about responsibility. You remember how I was before Maggie came into my life and gave me a beautiful daughter."

Quint grunted. "Yeah, you were the biggest playboy in three counties. And I figured you'd be a bachelor until you reached the age of forty, at least."

Cordell laughed. "Only three counties?"

"Well, maybe four," Quint joked. "But I'm not looking for a wife or child. Finding a sheepherder is plenty enough for me."

Amused by Quint's declaration, Cordell said, "One of these days when you meet the right woman, you won't remember any of the girlfriends you have stashed around the county."

"Yeah, yeah," Quint said with a roll of his eyes. "You and Jack can be the old married men of the family. I'm just fine like I am."

Turning to go, Cordell gave Quint's back another affectionate slap. "I'm headed over to the big barn. Brooks and I have a pen full of calves to brand this morning."

"If you could put the chore off until later today, I could help."

He waved away Quint's offer. "No worries. Jack is helping."

In the past three years, Jack, the next to the eldest brother, had spent more and more of his time helping their father comanage the ranch, so it wasn't often he had a chance to spend time in a cattle pen.

"Are you sure Jack remembers how to brand a calf?" Quint called out the question.

Cordell climbed into the driver's seat of his truck, then putting the vehicle into motion, he leaned his head out the open window. "If he doesn't I'll give him a quick refresher course," he joked.

As Cordell drove away Quint turned back to the pair of horses. He was finishing the adjustments on the bridle when the sound of an approaching vehicle caught his attention, and he glanced over his shoulder to see a white Ford truck easing down the grassy slope to where he'd parked his own rig beneath a shade tree.

Stepping away from the horses, he attempted to peer through the windshield at the driver, but the glare of the morning sunlight made it impossible to see anything. It wasn't until the truck stopped and the door opened that he realized it was Clementine.

As he quickly strode out to greet her, he noticed a pair of worn jeans clung to her thighs and hips, while a pale green shirt with the cuffs rolled back against her forearms was tucked into the waistband. Her black hair was fastened into a ponytail, and gauging from its length, Quint figured if the glistening mane was let loose it would reach her butt.

And that has something to do with the job you're hiring her for? Quint, you are one messed-up dude. Get your eyes off her body and your mind on the purpose of her visit.

Shaking away the voice of warning in his head, he crossed the last few steps between them and offered her his hand.

"Thanks for coming, Clementine. I hope you enjoyed the drive here to the ranch."

She gave his hand a brief shake. "I was beginning to think Stone Creek Ranch was only made up of sweeping valleys," she told him. "Then all of a sudden, I spotted the mountains in the distance. From what I've seen so far, your ranch is very beautiful."

Her dark eyes were gazing toward the north and west where evergreens forested the ragged peaks, and Quint got the impression that those high ranges were where she felt truly at home.

"I think you'll like the rest of it, too," he said, then gestured toward the house. "Before we take off on our ride, I'd like for you to meet my parents. They're very pleased that you've agreed to take the job."

"I'd be happy to meet your parents," she said, then glanced over her shoulder to her parked truck. "Is my truck in the way there? I'll move it if need be."

"It's not in the way," he assured her. "And the horses should be fine right here until we get back."

They began walking toward the house, and Quint noticed she was wearing sturdy black cowboy boots. Her stride was long and sure-footed, her shoulders straight and strong. He figured if she ever put her arms around a man, he'd know he was being held.

"The ranch house looks huge," she said. "Do you live here with your parents?"

"Yes. Me and my older brother Flint, along with our younger twin sisters, Beatrice and Bonnie. The rest of my siblings live here on the ranch in their own houses. Except my older sister, Grace. She and her husband live on the Broken B, a ranch just a few miles east of here."

She glanced at him. "Your family sounds huge. How many siblings do you have?"

"Four brothers and three sisters. Altogether, there are eight of us."

"I can't imagine."

The hollowness to her voice made him wonder if she had siblings, or moreover, had she ever had a husband or children. A husband, perhaps. But not children. No, he thought. If she had children she wouldn't be taking a sheepherding job. She'd be taking care of them.

"Do you have siblings?" he asked.

"One. A brother, Kipp. He's in Idaho working as a ranch hand."

"Older or younger than you?"

"Older. But only by two years," she said. "I don't see him very often. But we keep in touch."

He gave her a faint smile. "It would feel strange not to be constantly surrounded by family," he said. "I think I'd get lonely."

She looked at him in disbelief. "You, lonely?"

"Why, yes. Don't you think it would be possible for me to get lonely?"

She opened her mouth to make a reply, but she hesitated as though she'd decided against what she'd been about to say. "I suppose everyone gets lonely once in a while—even you."

Even you.

He was trying to decide what she meant by that when they reached the wooden steps that climbed up to a wide covered porch that ran the width of the house. Several pieces of lawn furniture built of cedarwood and padded with bright yellow cushions were grouped together on both ends of the planked flooring. Pots of green ferns and blooming verbena lined the south edge, where the plants would receive several hours of sunshine.

"This is nice."

He glanced over to see she was taking in everything about the porch, as though the homey touches were something she wasn't accustomed to.

"Thanks. Mom does all this. She likes to grow plants. When it gets deeper into fall, she'll take them all inside so the frost won't kill them."

"I see the house faces the east. Do you ever sit out here and watch the sunrise?"

Yes, this woman would notice such a thing, Quint thought. But he'd bet his last dollar none of his girl-friends would know one direction from another. Not unless they were looking directly at a navigational map on a phone or computer screen. Strange that he'd never thought about such a thing before.

"Sometimes," he answered. "Not often. I'm usually over at the big barn before the sun rises."

He stepped up to open the door, but before his hand closed around the knob, the wooden panel swung open and his parents stepped onto the porch.

"We saw you coming," Claire explained to Quint, then turned her attention to Clementine. "Hello, Ms. Starr. I'm Claire and this is my husband, Hadley."

Hadley smiled broadly and reached to shake her hand. "Nice to meet you, Ms. Starr. Guess there's no need for me to explain that we're Quint's parents."

Clementine shook his hand and then Claire's. "I'm

pleased to meet you both," she said, her glance vacillating from Quint to Hadley. "And I can see the resemblance between you."

Hadley looked at his wife and winked. "She can see the Hollister stamp," he said proudly.

Claire slanted him an indulgent smile. "Yes, dear. She can also see we're keeping her standing here on the porch instead of inviting her into the house."

Hadley chuckled. "You'll have to excuse me, Clementine. It's not often we get a visitor from Idaho."

"We've never had a visitor from Idaho," Claire added. "And we've certainly never had a sheepherder on the ranch. So this is exciting for us."

"Right. Let's all go in. Do you two have time for a cup of coffee, Quint?"

"Sure," Quint told him. "There's no way I can show Clementine over the whole ranch today, anyway."

Hadley opened the door and ushered Clementine into the house, and as Quint followed her over the threshold, he wondered what she was thinking about his parents. More important, what was she thinking about him?

During the past eight years that Clementine had worked as a sheepherder, she'd been employed by a few large ranches, yet she could truthfully say none of them compared to Stone Creek Ranch. Before she'd agreed to drive down here to meet with Quint, she'd studied the ranch's website. However, the site held limited information, most of which was directed at cattle sales. There had been a few pics of their Angus cows and bulls and one photo of a flock of merino sheep. But none of the house or working facilities. She supposed they chose to keep those private.

Now as she sat in a huge den located on the backside of the enormous two-story house, drinking coffee and trying to appear relaxed, she was inwardly trying to absorb the magnitude of the Hollister family.

"I imagine Quint has probably already told you about his wanting to increase our lamb production," Hadley said.

"Yes, he has," Clementine replied. "He also informed me that the sheep are only raised for producing wool. I know some ranchers are strictly wool producers, but I've never worked for one."

"I'm sure it's not the most profitable way to go, but it's our way," Hadley told her, then cast a loving glance toward his wife. "You probably noticed on your drive out here that we're mainly cattle producers. Having sheep on the ranch began with my father, Lionel, and we're happy to keep on with the tradition. We like having them."

"I see," Clementine replied, but frankly she didn't understand. Not completely. In this day and age, most people boiled everything down to money. The profit and loss of any endeavor mattered the most. But the Hollisters considered their sheep a family tradition. One that they obviously enjoyed.

"From the time Quint was a little toddler, he's been our little sheep man," Claire said from her seat in a leather armchair angled close to her husband's. "Have you always been around sheep, Clementine?"

Clementine looked over at Quint's mother, who was a picture of feminine daintiness with her blond bobbed hair, ivory smooth complexion and pink silk blouse. Her left hand was adorned with a huge diamond wedding ring, while her right wrist was encircled with a cuffed silver bracelet set with turquoise stones. She was far different than Clementine's mother, who'd let her fig-

ure go years ago and rarely ever bothered with makeup.
Yet for some unexplainable reason, she felt comfortable
in Claire's company.

"Yes. My dad raised Hampshires and Rambouillets. I
was only a small girl when he began teaching me about
sheep. How to spot the diseases they can develop and
how to treat them. How to move a flock from one range
to the next—the sorts of things a sheepherder has to
know."

From the corner of her eye, Clementine noticed Quint
was regarding her with a watchful eye. Was he trying
to get a sense of how knowledgeable she was about her
job? Or was he simply looking at her as a man looks at
a woman?

*Don't start thinking foolish thoughts before this new
job of yours ever starts, Clementine. Look around you.
Quint has the best of everything and most likely that in-
cludes women. When he looks at you he sees a woman
seven years his senior and a plain one, at that.*

Thankfully, the sound of Hadley's voice interrupted
her runaway thoughts and she looked across the short
space to where the elder Hollister was sitting next to
his wife.

"Forgive me if I sound like a parent, especially since
you're a self-sufficient adult. But with eight children of
my own, I've learned you never quit being a father. So
just in case your dad worries about you, I hope you'll
assure him we'll be a fair employer."

Nearly nine years had passed since her father had
died. Anyone would think she'd be over the pain, but she
wasn't. It was a palpable thing that continued to gnaw
at her. Now she could feel the blood draining from her
face and a cold emptiness sweeping through her.

"I appreciate your thoughtfulness, Mr. Hollister. But my father died several years ago. He and the sheep are—no more."

"I'm sorry," Hadley said. "But even though your father is gone, everything I said still goes. And, you know, he just might be listening in right now. If he is, I hope he approves."

For the first time in years, a mist of tears formed in Clementine's eyes, and she was struck with the urge to leave her seat and go throw her arms around Hadley. She somehow knew the rancher would pat her back and assure her that everything was going to be okay. Something no one in her own family had ever bothered to do. Her brother was too consumed with getting vengeance to think about grief, or what it might be doing to his sister. And her mother—she'd quit caring a long time ago.

"You're very kind," she told him.

"Now, any of my eight children might argue that point," Hadley said with a chuckle.

"Don't let my husband kid you," Claire said as she cast a gentle smile at Clementine. "He's a big teddy bear. But then, he's not the one you'll have to worry about. Quint will be your boss."

Clementine glanced over to see Quint was scowling at his mother.

"Mom, Clementine will hardly need for me to boss her. She knows more about her job than I do," he said.

"I appreciate your confidence, Quint," Clementine told him. "But I think your parents are just trying to make me feel at ease."

Claire gleefully clapped her hands together. "Thank you, Clementine! I can already see we're going to be great friends."

"Of course we're going to be great friends," Hadley

spoke up. "And anytime you need anything, even if you have a gripe, just come to us and we'll see that it gets fixed. Okay?"

Feeling a little overwhelmed by the couple's warmth and generosity, she was momentarily lost for words. "Thank you," she finally said. "You've both been exceptionally kind."

Quint suddenly drained the last of his coffee and rose to his feet. "I think we'd better be going, Clementine. We have a lot of ground to cover."

Seeing he was set on leaving, she placed her cup on a nearby end table and stood. At the same time, Claire rose and walked over to her.

"I'll show you to the restroom," Claire told her. "I imagine you'd like to freshen up before your long ride."

"As a matter of fact, I would." She glanced at Quint. "I'll be right back."

"Certainly. Take all the time you need."

Claire wrapped a hand around Clementine's arm and promptly led her out of the large den. As the two of them walked down a long hallway, Clementine noticed the gleam on the oak floor and how Claire's kitten heels tapped gently against the polished wood. Every now and then the faint scent of her expensive perfume drifted to Clementine's nostrils, and for a second or two, she wondered how it would feel to live like Quint's mother. To be loved and pampered and protected.

Who are you kidding, Clementine. After a day or two the walls would be closing in and you'd be pacing around like a caged lion, searching for a way to escape. You don't need a home built of wood and stone. You don't need dresses and perfume or a diamond on your finger. Especially one that connected you to a

*man. All you need is you, your dogs and horses and a
flock of sheep.*

Clementine shoved at the mocking voice in her head
as Claire suddenly stopped at a door to their right.

"Here we are," Claire said. "This particular bath-
room is only used by me and my daughters. We call it
our powder room. The guys are off-limits so they don't
mess things up with dirt and manure and all that sort
of thing. Do you think you can find your way back to
the den? If not, I'll wait on you."

Clementine gave her a faint smile. "I've been told I
have an inner compass. I'll find my way back."

"Then I'll see you in the den," Claire said, but she
didn't make a move to go. Instead, she reached for Clementine's hand and gently patted the top of it. "I just
want to make sure you understand how glad I am that
you're taking this job. Quint probably won't ever tell
you this, but he needs you. He has big dreams and I feel
certain you can help make them come true for him."

Completely puzzled by Claire's comment, Clementine said, "But I'm just a sheepherder, Mrs. Hollister. I
can't make your son's dreams come true."

The smile Claire gave her was a knowing one. "You
underestimate yourself, Clementine. And please call
me Claire. Like I said, I know we're going to be great
friends."

She patted her hand once again, then left her standing at the door to the powder room.

Clementine stared after her, but only for a moment.
She didn't have time to ponder Claire's remarks or figure out what they could possibly mean. Quint was waiting to show her a part of Stone Creek Ranch and that
was exactly what she needed to jerk her thoughts back
to reality. Once she was out in the wide-open spaces

with a horse beneath her and the wind in her face, she'd remember exactly why she was taking this job.

And it had nothing to do with making Quint Hollister's dreams come true.

Chapter Three

Ten minutes later, Quint and Clementine were riding the horses past the old barn located some fifty yards north of the ranch house. Built with a large loft and a loafing shed to one side, the outer walls were made of faded red boards and the roof was constructed of corrugated iron. Recently Hadley had hired a couple of men to paint the rusting roof and replace a few supporting timbers inside the barn.

"This barn looks empty," Clementine remarked.

He looked over at her and was struck once again at how at home she looked in the saddle. Before they'd mounted, she'd donned a black felt cowboy hat and pushed the leather stampede string tight beneath her chin. In spite of the hat being sweat stained and the brim bent in places, it matched her personality perfectly.

He cleared his throat before he said, "We don't use the old barn on a regular basis. Sometimes we stall a horse or two in it. Or maybe a sick ewe or lamb. The major barns and ranch yard are located over the hill to our right. I'll show it to you once we get back. Right now, I want you to get an idea of the area where you'll be working," he told her. "The sheep are kept on the west side of the ranch. It's the most mountainous part of the property, but there are plenty of grazing meadows, too. And a couple of creeks run from the higher elevations all the way through the property."

"Do the creeks usually have water?" she asked. "Or only in the spring and winter?"

Her deep olive complexion made her teeth flash white whenever she talked. So far she'd not shown him or her parents a wide-open smile, but Quint figured if she ever did, the sight would knock him loopy.

"Depends on the snowfall. Most of the time there's enough water in the creeks to keep the flock watered. If not, there are a couple of wells pumped by windmills."

She nodded. "In case you're interested, I didn't take the job near Boise because of the water situation. The ranch was located mainly on desert land and water had to be hauled to many of the grazing areas. I want my sheep to be able to drink whenever they want and as much as they want."

My sheep. He supposed he could've reminded her that these would be Stone Creek sheep and not hers. But he didn't. The idea that she felt that close to the animals merely assured him that she'd be taking meticulous care of them. And that was exactly the reason he was hiring her.

"I don't expect you'll encounter any problems finding ample water supply. Even during a drought, the wells keep going. Of course, that's not to say the forage won't dry up. Right now there are plenty of grasses on the lower slopes and down in the valleys. And some in the higher meadows. But as we get deeper into fall those begin to dwindle."

She glanced at him. "I've never started a job this late in the season. And you haven't exactly told me how long you expect me to work. Until the snow runs us out of the mountains?"

For hours last night, as Quint had been weighing the idea of hiring Clementine, he'd been asking himself how long he could employ her, but his wants and his means were at odds. Which made him hesitant about giving her a definite number of weeks. But it wouldn't be right to keep her in limbo, either.

"Frankly, Clementine, I need for you to work all year-round. But I'm not sure the ranch can afford you." He grimaced. "See, most of our gains go back into our cattle operations. And no, if you're thinking I resent that, you'd be wrong. Cattle are our bread and butter. The sheep are—well, as Dad said, they're more of a tradition than anything. That's not to say Dad or Jack wants to limit my spending toward the flock. They just expect me to be sensible."

"I only ask to be paid the standard sheepherder wages, plus supplies, like food and other necessities."

Her gaze remained straight ahead on the ridge of mountains in the distance, and Quint could plainly see that she was a no-nonsense kind of woman. She'd never be guilty of standing around chewing indecisively on the tip of a fake fingernail while a lamb stood stuck in a muddy arroyo, crying for its mother.

"That sounds perfectly fair," he said. "So I'd like for you to stay on until winter hits, at least. If that's acceptable to you."

"It's acceptable. That is, if the snow doesn't get too

deep. I have the well-being of my dogs and horses to consider. They come before me."

"I understand," he replied, then drew in a deep breath and let it out. "But I—there's something else I wanted to mention to you."

She glanced in his direction, then turned her attention back to the horse she was riding as the animal suddenly decided to pause and nip at a twig of sage. Deftly reining the gelding away from the shrub, she asked, "Something concerning my job?"

"Yes. I don't exactly feel comfortable with you working out of a tent. While you're gone to Idaho to collect your things, I need to come up with a wagon for you."

She looked at him, and Quint was surprised to see a faint arch of her brows. "Don't concern yourself, Quint."

"You need to have sturdy shelter."

A short laugh burst past her lips. It was the first real emotion she'd displayed since he'd met her yesterday, and all he could do was stare at her in fascination.

After a moment, he said, "I can't see how that could be funny."

Her expression instantly turned serious, and Quint was sorry he'd made the comment. It would've been nice to have heard her laugh a bit more and see her express some happiness.

She said, "I'm sorry. But you're concerning yourself for no reason. A tent is all I want or need. It's light and easy to move around the mountains. See, I like to take my flock where a wagon can't go."

Quint still couldn't fathom how this woman lived for months out of a tent. "I—uh, I get that you want to be mobile, Clementine. But how do you sleep? What do you do about cooking food? For light at night? And excuse me if I'm getting too personal, but keeping yourself clean?"

"Your questions don't offend me. They're very legitimate. But you needn't concern yourself. I can do all those things without living in a box. I have a portable mattress that's plenty comfortable. And as long as I can gather firewood, I cook over a campfire. Otherwise, I carry a small propane burner and use it. I clean myself and my clothes, just like you do. With soap and water. Whether it be out of a creek or a wash pan. As for light, I have one propane lantern and a couple of flashlights for emergencies. I've done this for a long time, Quint. Living outdoors is second nature for me. But I'm not a fool. Deep snow and subzero temperatures would send me back to the ranch yard. Like I say, my main priority is to protect my animals."

Ever since she'd responded to his job ad, he'd been wondering how a woman would survive in a tiny sheepherder's wagon. To imagine her living out of a tent, roughing it, not for just a few days, but for weeks and months was incredible. In all of his young life, he'd never met a woman who was anywhere close to being like Clementine. And he didn't know what to think or how to deal with her.

When he failed to reply, she asked, "Is this causing you a problem? If so, there's no reason for you to continue showing me around the ranch."

The problem wasn't her, Quint thought. It was him. His father believed he was just generally protective of all females. And he supposed that was true, to a certain degree. But this protectiveness he felt toward Clementine was far different. It was downright unnatural.

"No. There's no trouble," he told her, while mentally crossing his fingers. Yeah, he was fibbing a little. But by the time she actually went to work, Quint was going to make darn sure he didn't feel anything toward Clementine Starr. Except relief at knowing his sheep would have a round-the-clock guardian.

During the past few years, Clementine had worked on some beautiful ranches. Idaho was full of majestic mountains, and the leased land near Craters of the Moon had been especially striking with its lava formations. But she had to admit Stone Creek was like a green paradise in the high desert.

As Quint had mentioned, they'd already forged two fairly wide creeks—Bird Creek and Stone Creek, for which the ranch was named—and one smaller stream meandering down from a rocky cliff. There were meadows with thick grasses, wildflowers, big sage and paintbrushes. The mountains rose up like emerald sentinels decorated with rock formations and evergreens. There was just enough brush to offer the sheep adequate shelter, but not so much that the trails were hampered.

The deeper they rode, the more Clementine fell in love with the ranch. A fact that should have left her uneasy. It wasn't smart to like a place or person too much. When a woman formed attachments, she was setting herself up for trouble. Because more often than not, the bonds would end up broken. But now as she gazed around her at the beauty of the Hollister ranch, she felt the dark curtain of indifference she kept around her heart slowly slipping.

"I see one of the dogs," Quint said. "The flock should be close."

Standing up in the stirrups, she peered ahead to where the trail they were riding began to curve up the side of a foothill. Birds chirped and ground squirrels scurried away from the sound of approaching horse hooves. Above their heads, the breeze whispered softly through the pine boughs and scented the air with evergreen. A few yards to their right, sheep bells tinkled, and in that moment, a strange sense of homecoming pierced the center of Clementine's chest.

Easing her bottom back into the seat of the saddle, she gave herself a sharp mental shake. What was she doing? She couldn't let herself get soft and sappy now, or ever. Quint would probably only ask her to work for a couple of months, and after that, he'd probably send her packing. Not because her work was inferior, she thought, but because she was a woman. She didn't have to be a mind reader to know he wasn't keen on hiring a female. He'd only caved to the idea because there was no one else available for the job.

Glancing over at her, Quint said, "There's a little meadow right over this rise. The sheep are probably there."

"The flock is a far distance from ranch headquarters," she commented. "You obviously spend lots of time riding back and forth to check on them."

"I do. And Jett, one of our hands, usually tries to alternate days with me. Presently we only have three full-time ranch hands and two more who come in to do day work whenever we need extra hands. Out of all those, Jett knows the most about sheep. I'm sure you'll be meeting him, soon."

"What about your brothers? They don't contribute any of their time to caring for the sheep?"

He shook his head. "Hunter, he's the oldest of the bunch—he owns and operates a rodeo company, the Flying H. So he's rarely home. Jack is mostly tied up with helping Dad manage the ranch, and Flint's time is mostly consumed with his deputy job. And, of course, Cord has his hands full being foreman and taking care of the cattle end of things."

"I see," she said thoughtfully. "And Jett isn't interested in becoming a full-time sheepherder?"

Her question caused him to let out a short laugh. "Jett? No. He's younger than me and enjoys the social life in town. He'd go bonkers if I told him I wanted him to stay one week out here with the sheep, much less weeks on end."

Clementine had heard those same types of remarks many times before. "Most people can't take the isolation."

The look in his eyes as he searched her face made her think he was probably sizing her up as a weirdo or an antisocial person.

You can't say he'd be exactly wrong, Clem. People bother you because you don't trust them. Not any of them. Walls and roofs make you feel cornered and threatened. It's been a long time since you've felt like a normal woman. And you never want to go back to being her again. Think about it, Clem, that's weird.

She was pushing against the jeering voice in her head when Quint said, "Obviously, it doesn't bother you to be alone."

She shrugged. "You have to like your own company. And that of your dogs and horses."

"But they don't talk."

Smiling faintly, she said, "Oh, yes they do. You just have to learn their language."

She didn't wait for him to reply. Instead, she nudged her horse forward, and a moment later, she emerged from a canopy of pines and into a meadow where a large flock of merino sheep were grazing at a carpet of tender green grass. Two white Great Pyrenees were slowly circling the sheep, while keeping a close watch on Clementine's movements.

Instantly enchanted, she reined her horse to a stop

and quickly slid down from the saddle, then leading the horse behind her, she walked into the milling herd.

At first glance, the merinos appeared to be in great shape, and from the size of the lambs, they'd grown rapidly since the winter birthing season. A few of the animals lifted their heads to peer curiously at their visitor, but for the most part, they appeared to be comfortable with human company.

"We sheared them in April. The wool crop turned out to be fairly substantial."

Quint's voice came from a short distance behind her, and she glanced over her shoulder to see he'd followed her into the meadow.

"They appear to be in great shape," she said, then asked, "Do the dogs always stay with them?"

He came to stand beside her, and Clementine was shocked to find her attention drawn to him rather than the sheep. Men didn't interest her. Not since she'd fallen for Marty, and that had been years ago. But something about Quint made her forget that the majority of men were basically users, liars and cheats.

"They weren't much more than half-grown pups when we put them on the sheep. From that time on, they've never gotten far from the herd," he said, then asked, "Will they cause a problem with your own dogs? I ask, because I think these two would mourn themselves to death if we took them away from the flock."

Clementine shook her head as she eyed the two white dogs. Their coats were a bit raggedy, but other than that, they looked like pictures of health. Clearly Quint took as good care of his dogs as he did his sheep, and she certainly admired him for his devotion. "I would never want you to do such a cruel thing. My dogs won't bother them, and once yours see that mine are here to help guard the flock, not hurt it, the four of them will be fine with each other."

"I'm glad you think the dogs can be friends. So tell me your impression of this side of the ranch?"

Why did he have to be so tall and strong? So darned good-looking? Not that he was one of those pretty boys, she thought. No, from the jut of his chin to his hawkish nose and slanted cheekbones, his rugged features were pure masculinity. Frame them with dark rakish hair that waved over the back of his collar and around his ears, add a pair of sky blue eyes, and he was the perfect image of one hot dude.

"I can't imagine the east side being any more beautiful," she told him, then hoping to calm the fast thud of her heart, she turned her gaze back to the sheep.

"So you think you can be happy here?" he asked.

She'd never had an employer ask her that exact question. She supposed none of them had really cared whether she was happy or miserable. All that concerned them was whether she could do her job and how much she expected them to pay her. But as for her being happy? Well, she couldn't imagine herself feeling true happiness ever again. Yes, she could admit that was a jaded outlook. But she'd found it was better to face reality than to dream about things that could never come true.

"I'm sure I'll like working here. If that's what you're getting at."

His features softened and the faint indention of a dimple appeared in his right cheek. The sight of it caused her stomach to take a funny little flip.

"I'm glad," he said. "I was afraid you might change your mind about the job. Especially after meeting my parents."

Surprised, she asked, "Why? Your parents are lovely people."

"Thanks. That's the way I see them, too. But they can be—well, they're the type that likes to gather their chicks under their wings, and it can be a bit overwhelming at times. Back at the ranch house I was getting the impression you were feeling a bit smothered."

He'd noticed that about her? Dear Lord, what else had he noticed? That she'd like to know, just for a second or two, what it would feel like to be wrapped in his long, strong arms? To know how his lips would taste as they crushed down on hers?

Shaking her head, she latched her gaze on to one little lamb bounding happily around its mother. "I enjoyed your parents, Quint. But if I seemed—smothered as you call it, then just put it down to being indoors. If I'm in a house for very long I begin to feel like a fish out of water."

Now, why had she told him that? She didn't go around revealing personal things about herself to anyone. Especially not a young man like Quint. The guy already figured she was a bit eccentric. Why give him more evidence?

"Oh. Well, I'm glad my parents weren't making you uncomfortable."

Clementine could've told him that *he* was the one making her uncomfortable. But not for anything would she ever want him to guess the womanly reactions he'd caused in her.

She turned a solemn look on him. "Be grateful you have them, Quint. Someday you won't be so blessed," she said, then held up the reins to her horse. "Will he stay ground tied if I drop the reins?"

"Both horses will stay ground tied. Why? You want to walk around?"

She nodded. "I'd like to walk out and take a closer look at the flock if you don't mind."

He nodded. "Certainly. I'll go with you."

After dropping the reins to the ground, Quint stepped close to her side and cupped a hand beneath her elbow. Sure, she was accustomed to walking over rough terrain on her own, he thought. But she wasn't alone right now. He was with her and his father had taught him to be a gentleman no matter if he was in a cattle pen or a ballroom.

"Are any of the ewes in this herd aggressive?" she asked.

"Not really. But I do keep my eye on the rams. Not that they're aggressive. I just don't want to push my luck," he told her. "And you can see for yourself that they totally trust the dogs. By the way, the female dog's name is Zina and the male's is Lash. They're not overly sociable and we don't encourage them to be. But we do give them treats and a pat on the head occasionally. Just to let them know we appreciate them. And they enjoy the attention, but then it's like they know it's time to get back to work."

She nodded. "Most folks don't understand there's a fine line between having a pet and a guardian dog. You can't give them so much attention that it draws them away from their work of guarding the flock. Nor can you ignore them completely. I try to let mine know I'm their partner, but that I also expect them to hold up their part of the job. So don't worry. I won't spoil Zina and Lash."

"The thought never crossed my mind," Quint told her. And then, as his eyes drank in the soft glow of sunlight on her cheeks and lips, he suddenly wondered why she didn't have a husband or children of her own to spoil. Had she ever wanted to be married or been in love? She'd only been twenty-five when she'd begun sheepherding. At that age, most women were planning a family or a career in the workplace. But Clementine had set out for a life in the wilderness. Why? Was she simply a nature goddess? Or was she hiding away from something? He was shocked by just how much he wanted to know the answer.

She glanced up, and for one brief moment their eyes clashed before she quickly darted her gaze to a spot across the meadow. "If you don't mind, I'd like to head back and get a look at the ranch yard."

"Sure. I'll show you where we do the shearing and doctoring and that sort of thing," he told her. "And if we time it just right, Mom will have lunch ready."

"I couldn't impose."

He chuckled. "You'd rather insult her by not eating?"

She let out a heavy breath, and Quint sensed that she really wanted to tell him she'd seen enough and needed to be on her way. And if he wanted to show her that he could be a nice guy, he wouldn't push her to stay for lunch or any other reason. But he didn't want her to go. Not just yet.

"You're twisting my arm," she said.

In spite of the solemn look on her face, he grinned at her. "Trust me, Clementine. It won't hurt for long."

By midafternoon the next day, Clementine drove through the small town of Shelley, Idaho, and on to the northern outskirts where a small wood frame house sat on a few acres of rich farmland. Because her job usually kept her away ten months out of a year, Clementine had never bothered with buying or renting a place of her own. Instead, for those few weeks she lived with

Nuttah, a Blackfoot woman in her early sixties, who'd worked as cook and housekeeper on the Rising Starr for fifteen years. That is, until divorce and death had splintered the Starr family and landed the ranch in the greedy hands of Clementine's stepmother.

From the first day Trent had brought his second wife home to the ranch, she'd disapproved of Nuttah, and over time her attitude toward the woman hadn't improved. Andrea had reasoned that Nuttah simply couldn't cook the type of food she wanted served, but Clementine had known otherwise. Andrea resented the close relationship Nuttah had with Trent. She also didn't like the fact that Nuttah could see everything that was going on around the ranch and shrewdly sum up the situation.

But none of that made much difference now. After Trent died, Nuttah moved here to Shelley and took a job cooking in the school cafeteria, while Clementine had basically become a nomad, moving from one ranch to another.

After parking her truck in the shade of an aspen, Clementine grabbed her duffel bag and started toward the house. As she walked across the yard toward the porch, she spotted Nuttah in the vegetable garden, bending over a row of snow peas. Clementine's sheepdogs, Jewel and Jimmy, were lying on the grass a few yards away.

The moment the dogs caught sight of her, they jumped to their feet and wagged their tails, but they didn't run and greet her with happy whines and slobbery kisses. Instead the dogs stood obediently in the same spot, while she dropped the duffel bag to the ground and walked to the backyard.

"Hello, Nuttah."

The petite woman with long wavy black hair straightened to her full height and shaded her eyes with one hand.

"Clem, is that you back already?"

"Yes, it's me. I made good traveling time today," she told her.

Clementine walked over to the dogs and gave them a few pats on the head before she finished crossing the distance to the garden.

Nuttah walked out of the carefully tended rows of vegetables and came to stand next to Clementine. "I'm glad you made it safely," she said as she wiped a forearm against her brow. "That was a long distance for you to travel alone."

"You're forgetting, Nuttah. Except for the time here with you, I spend most all my days alone."

"Yes, but the highway is full of bad people."

"I can't argue that," Clementine replied.

Nuttah gestured toward the house. "Let's go in. I made fry bread this morning and I'll brew a pot of tea to go with it. While we eat, you can tell me about Mr. Hollister."

After Clementine collected her duffel bag from where she'd dropped it, she joined Nuttah in the kitchen. The room was built at the back of the house, and presently, the door leading out to the porch was open to allow a breeze to blow through the wood-framed screen door. Across the small space, at a single porcelain sink, Nuttah was filling a red granite tea kettle with water from the tap.

More like a mother to Clementine than her actual mother, Nuttah Running Crow was still very beautiful with smooth brown skin, high cheekbones and slanted eyes the color of a dark coffee bean. She'd been married once, years ago, but her husband had suffered a horse accident while the couple was living on the Fort Hall Indian Reservation. A few weeks after the accident, he'd died from his injuries, and Nuttah had never remarried. Her one child, a son, had moved away some years ago to work in the oil fields in Alaska.

During the fifteen years Nuttah had worked on the Rising Starr, she'd grown very attached to Kipp and Clementine and they to her. And thankfully none of the tragedies surrounding Trent Starr had broken the bond between the three.

"So how did your meeting go?" Nuttah asked. "Have you taken the job?"

Sinking into a chair at the farm table, Clementine rubbed fingers against her burning eyelids. She'd slept very little last night, and the long drive back to Idaho had drained her.

"Yes. I agreed to take the job," she answered.

Nuttah carried the kettle over to a gas range and lit a burner beneath it. "You don't sound pleased," she said. "But since you never sound pleased, I guess there's nothing different about this job in Utah. Except you'll be farther away from me."

There were plenty of things different about this job, Clementine thought. But did she want to go over them with Nuttah? Did she want to keep thinking and thinking about Quint Hollister? Hadn't she done enough of that on the four-hundred-mile drive she'd just made?

"It will be different in the fact that it's already into September. I'll probably only be there for a couple of months or so. Unless Mr. Hollister decides to keep me on through the winter months. But I don't expect that to happen."

The woman turned away from the cookstove to cock an inquisitive brow at her. "You mean through January and February? Those are lambing months. The sheep will be kept near the ranch. You wouldn't want to stay in a bunkhouse with men. Or in a cabin. And by then it will be too cold for your tent."

The mere mention of the word tent was all it took for Clementine to recall the look on Quint's face when she'd informed him she didn't work out of a wagon. It was like he was seeing some sort of crazy fantasy. A part of her had wanted to kick his shins, while the other part had wanted to burst out laughing. She didn't mind him viewing her as different. Heck, she *was* different. But she did very much mind him having the idea that she didn't know how to survive on bare necessities.

"You're right, Nuttah, it would be far too cold for the tent. But I don't expect I'll be asked to stay. Stone Creek Ranch is basically a cattle ranch. Money for the sheep is limited."

Nuttah opened a tin canister and pulled out several tea bags. As she tossed them into a ceramic teapot, she said, "Did you like the people? The man who hired you?"

The Hollisters had been a surprise to Clementine. Usually, owners of the larger ranches never bothered to meet with a sheepherder. Before Stone Creek, a foreman had always showed her the ropes and left the rest up to her. But Claire and Hadley had opened their home to her and treated her warmly. As for Quint, he'd been more than a surprise; he'd been a stunner.

"Yes. He was likable. He was also very young and very good-looking. He made me feel old and frumpy."

Nuttah's grunt was a bit mocking. "And why would that matter to you?"

Clementine grimaced. "It doesn't. Not in the way you're thinking. But it did aggravate me because he made me aware of my age and my looks."

Nuttah placed a plate of fry bread and a jar of blueberry jam on the table, along with a couple of spoons. "Is this man married?"

"No. He's single and proud of the fact, I think. But none of that has any bearing on me or the job," she said flatly. "The ranch is family owned and I met his parents. They seemed like nice, fair people. I don't think I'll have a problem with them or Quint."

"Quint?" Nuttah's dark eyes peered at her. "This is the single man who will be your boss?"

"Yes."

Returning to the stove, Nuttah poured boiling water over the tea bags, then carried the pot over to the table. After she'd collected cups, sugar and cream, she sat down in the chair opposite Clementine's.

"So when will you be going back to Utah? In the next few days?"

"I told Quint I'd be back in two days. And for what it's worth, the ranch is very beautiful. I think I'll like working there."

A faint smile touched Nuttah's face. "As long as this young man doesn't remind you that you're a woman."

"You know, Nuttah, sometimes you talk way too much."

"Ha! Everybody talks too much for you."

She poured the tea and Clementine thoughtfully stirred sugar into the hot drink.

"Have you heard from Kipp lately?"

"He called last night. From what I can tell, nothing has changed with him or anything else on the Rising Starr. I wish he would leave there. I have bad thoughts and dreams about him."

The woman's comments sent a chill sliding down Clementine's spine. Nuttah had always been a mystic soul. Whenever she had thoughts or dreams they often came true.

"I've tried to persuade him to leave, Nuttah. But you know how it is with Kipp. He's determined. He won't rest until he gets the Rising Starr back and justice for Dad's death."

"Yes, and he might die trying," the woman murmured sadly.

"I don't want to talk about it anymore, Nuttah." She sipped her tea and hoped the warm liquid would wash away the uneasy feelings that always came over her when she thought of her brother still living on the Rising Starr. Only there was a big difference now that Trent Starr was no longer living. Instead of residing in the ranch house Kipp had grown up in, he hung his hat in the bunkhouse every night.

She picked up a piece of the bread and slathered a layer of jam over it. "You haven't mentioned Buck. Aren't you going to see him anymore?"

Nuttah lifted her chin to a proud angle. "No. The only thing on his mind is getting me in bed. I'm tired of knocking his hands away."

Buck was a widower who lived in town and worked as a mechanic for a farm equipment dealership. The few times Clementine had talked with the man, she'd found him to be amiable, nice-looking and clearly very fond of Nuttah.

"Have you ever thought he wants to put his hands on you because you're beautiful and he's crazy about you?"

Nuttah snorted. "I don't need that sort of crazy."

"You need someone for company."

She snorted again. "Who are you to talk? You're thirty-four. You need a man and babies."

Clementine looked away from Nuttah as the image of Quint's face paraded in front of her eyes. Now, why had *he* come to mind? she wondered, ruefully. He was the furthest thing from husband and father material that she could imagine.

"That's not for me, Nuttah."

With a sad shake of her head, Nuttah tore a piece of the fry bread in half. "Not all men are like Marty. Or your father. Some of them are good."

"Like Buck?" Clementine couldn't help asking.

The woman shrugged. "Buck is good. I'm just not sure he's good for me."

At one time in her life, Clementine had very much wanted the love of a man, to have children and a regular home. In spite of all the painful drama she'd seen going on between her parents, she'd still believed things could be different for her. When Marty had come along, she'd jumped headfirst into a relationship with him. And perhaps, if her father hadn't interfered, things might have worked out well for them. As it turned out, Marty hadn't cared enough to fight for Clementine's love. He'd left the area, and she'd never seen or heard from him again.

Sighing, she wearily swiped a hand through the curtain of hair falling against her cheek. "I'm not sure this job at Stone Creek is going to be good for me, either."

Nuttah frowned at her. "Why? You said that you liked the Hollisters and the ranch."

Unable to stop another sigh from passing her lips, she looked helplessly over at the woman. "Yes, I did say I liked them. But a little voice in the back of my head keeps telling me I might be getting myself into something I've not counted on."

"Something bad?"

"That's just it, Nuttah. I don't know. It's just a feeling." She cast Nuttah a wry smile. "After all these years I think you're rubbing off on me. I'm starting to have *thoughts*."

Nuttah gave her a clever smile. "You're a wise woman. If you don't like what you get yourself into, then you'll know how to get yourself out. Besides, you'll be all alone in the mountains. The only thing you'll be getting into is a flock of sheep."

"I'm glad you think so, Nuttah. Because a flock of sheep is all I want in my life now."

Grunting, Nuttah leveled a pointed look at her. "What about getting the Rising Starr back?"

Clementine shook her head. "That isn't going to happen. Not any more than me having a man and babies."

"Then you're always going to carry around this sadness you have."

Glancing away from the woman's all-seeing gaze, she said, "I'm not sad, Nuttah. I'm practical."

The Blackfoot woman finished the last of her tea, then carried her cup over to the sink. "I think I'll call Buck and see if he'd like to go out dancing. It's Friday night and a band will be playing at the VFW."

Surprised, Clementine stared at her. "Why are you going to call Buck? You told me a few minutes ago that you're unsure of him."

"Yes. But I just figured out that I'd rather be unsure than practical—like you."

Chapter Four

"Wow, Quint, you're home early tonight!"

The exclamation came from his little sister Beatrice as she and her twin sister, Bonnie, stood at the cabinet counter, dishing up bowls of bread pudding. The scent of freshly brewed coffee permeated the air, and he sniffed with appreciation.

He said, "I smelled the coffee brewing all the way into town, so I turned around and came back."

Bonnie frowned at him. "We thought you had a date. What did you do? Stand the woman up?"

Shaking his head, Quint walked over to his sisters. "I would never stand a woman up. Actually, we'd only agreed to meet for drinks and a bit of chitchat. But I decided I wasn't in the mood for either, so I sent her a text and told her I couldn't make it."

"I'd call that standing her up," Beatrice told him.

"We're only friends, Bea. The woman wasn't cut up

over it. I imagine she's already found another guy to chat with over a drink."

Beatrice pulled a face at him. "I'm so glad none of my boyfriends are like you."

Bonnie rolled her eyes. "Quint, did you notice how she pluralized boyfriend?"

Quint grinned at the both of them. "I sure did. Nothing about Bea has changed. So how many boyfriends do you have, Bonnie?"

Beatrice let out a loud laugh. "Are you kidding? She hasn't had one of those since high school!"

The blond-haired, blue-eyed twins were twenty-five now. Beatrice worked as a sales clerk at Canyon Corral, a boutique in town, while Bonnie kept the books for the ranch and dealt with all their father's business correspondence. From the time Beatrice was eight years old, she'd been labeled as boy crazy, and through the years she'd had dozens of boyfriends, but hadn't regarded any of them seriously. As for Bonnie, the shy, reserved sister had always been very picky about her dates. Quint could only recall a handful of times he'd seen her leave the house with a male caller.

"That's because she won't settle for anything but the best," Quint said.

"Thank you, dear brother." Bonnie kissed his cheek, then turned her attention to gathering coffee cups from the cupboard.

Snorting, Beatrice said, "How will she ever know the best if she doesn't do any sampling?"

"Don't worry about me, sissy. I'll know the best whenever I see him." She glanced over at Quint. "Bea and I were just talking about you. We were wondering when your new sheepherder is going to start work."

"Supposedly tomorrow. When you're hauling horses you never know how things will go."

Beatrice looked at him with surprise. "She's bringing her own horses? Why doesn't she use some of ours?"

He shot her a droll look. "Think about it, Bea. Would you rather ride your own horse, or someone else's?"

"Oh. Sorry, Quint. Sometimes I'm not thinking."

"That's because she can't think of anything—except men." Bonnie placed the cups on a tray, then turned a curious look on her bother. "Mom says Ms. Starr was nice, but a little different. Bea and I are eager to meet her."

"I doubt either of you will get a chance to meet her," he said. "Unless you're around whenever she arrives. I don't think I could get her back in the house. I had to practically twist her arm to make her have lunch with me and our parents yesterday."

Quint watched the twins exchange quizzical glances.

"Why? She didn't like the house? Or our parents?"

Rubbing a hand against the back of his neck, he tried not to think about the stoic expression on her face as the four of them had eaten lunch yesterday, or the blank look she'd given him when he'd told her to have a safe journey back to Idaho. To his sisters, he said, "She liked them. I just think —well, she's all business and not too keen on socializing."

Beatrice shot him a droll look. "It's not like meeting your twin sisters would be the same as asking her to attend a party!"

Bonnie frowned at her twin. "Don't be judgmental of the woman, Bea. It might be that people make her feel uncomfortable. If so, I understand completely."

Bonnie probably did understand, Quint thought. For a long time she'd been shy and withdrawn and had hardly ever ventured off the ranch for any reason. But once Vanessa had arrived on Stone Creek and eventually married Jack, Bonnie had begun to emerge from her shell. Now she mixed and mingled and even went out on the town with her sister from time to time. No one exactly knew why or how Vanessa had made the difference in Bonnie's life. But everyone in the family was grateful for the change.

"Hmm. Maybe that's why Clementine isn't married," Beatrice said thoughtfully.

Quint frowned at his sister. "How do you know she isn't married?"

Before Beatrice could answer his question, Bonnie admitted, "We asked Mom and she told us."

Quint shook his head with dismay. "You two are downright nosy. Why are you interested in Clementine's marital status?"

Chuckling under her breath, Beatrice said, "Because we thought—no, let me rephrase that—we hoped you might start seeing her as more than a sheepherder. Like a girlfriend, or something. But from the way you're describing her, I can see that isn't going to happen. You like party girls."

"And that's the whole problem, Bea. Quint will probably be a party guy until he gets gray-haired and carries a cane."

Quint studied both sisters with a look of amused disbelief. "I don't understand you two. Both of you know I have plenty of girlfriends. Why would you want me to consider Clementine in a romantic interest, anyway?"

Bonnie sighed. "Because we don't think any of your girlfriends are that great. We think it would be nice to see you in love—like Cord and Jack."

Beatrice added, "We want you to have one you can get serious about."

Frowning now, he said, "So you two think I ought to get married like Cord and Jack?"

Beatrice pulled a face at him. "Why not? You're heading toward thirty."

"I only turned twenty-seven a few months ago," Quint reminded her. "And why pick on me? I don't want to be a lovesick fool. Why not aim your cupid arrows at Flint? Or Hunter?"

"Flint doesn't have time for love. He's busy being a lawman," Beatrice reasoned. "And Hunter basically lives on the road. He couldn't keep a woman."

Laughing now, Quint started out of the kitchen. "You two are hopeless. And you need to forget about Clementine. She's not looking for the kind of life you girls are dreaming about. She wants to be left alone."

"How sad," Bonnie said.

Sad.

As Quint left the kitchen, he realized that was the second time he'd heard that word applied to Clementine. Was she an unhappy woman? He hated to think so. But he needed to remember her personal life wasn't his business.

Two days later, Clementine arrived on Stone Creek with two horses, a buckskin mare named Birdie and a sorrel gelding she called Peanut, along with a pair of black-and-white border collies, Jimmy and Jewel. Because she had sent a text message to Quint earlier that morning to let him know she'd be arriving, he was waiting for her at the ranch yard when she drove up.

After directing her to an out-of-the-way spot to park her truck and trailer rig, he helped her unload the horses.

"There's a nice pen with a loafing shed directly behind the barn," he told her. "Your horses should be comfortable there until you're ready to leave for the mountains. I'll show you where we store the feed and hay. No need to worry about water. There's an automatic float on the tank inside the corral."

She turned an odd look on him. "Why would I want to pen the horses? I'll be leaving in a few minutes. As soon as I get everything ready to go."

Quint watched her loop the lead rope the buckskin was wearing to an iron loop on the side of the trailer. As before, she was all business, which frustrated him to no end. Why couldn't she loosen up and have a normal conversation with him? As it was, he could hardly tell what she was thinking or planning.

"Why? You and your horses have just made a four-hundred-mile trip. You and they might need to rest," he suggested.

"I broke the trip in half and spent the night in Nephi. They're well rested and so am I. Once we get to where we're going and I make camp, I'll turn the horses loose and we'll all relax."

Since he was hardly in a position to tell her how to take care of her own horses, he conceded. "Whatever you think. If you're set on going, then let me saddle the horse you'll be riding, while you deal with the pack horse."

She slanted him a glance, and Quint could see she wanted to tell him to go about his own business and leave her be. But after a moment, she shrugged. "Thanks. You'll find everything you need in the tack compartment. I ride Birdie." She patted the buckskin's rump. "Peanut is also a good saddle horse, but he doesn't mind packing a load, so he carries all our supplies."

He couldn't help but notice that whenever she spoke of her animals she linked them to her and used terms like we and ours, as though the five of them were a family. And perhaps they were more of a family to her than anyone else, he thought. She'd said her father was dead, but she'd not mentioned a mother. Which made Quint wonder if the woman was also deceased or simply not a part of Clementine's life.

"Plenty of horses don't like to carry packs. You're lucky Peanut will do both."

"Yes. And he's only twelve. So I hope to have him for many more years."

Did she plan to work as a sheepherder for many more years? He tried to imagine her as an older woman still living in the mountains—alone. It didn't fit. Not to his eyes. But no doubt she saw things differently than Quint.

"How old is Birdie? She looks young."

"She's only six. But I've had her since she was a weanling and broke her to ride when she turned two. She's very smart and she's great with the sheep."

"*You* broke her to ride?"

She looked at him. "Sure. Women do know how to start colts, you know."

Yes, Quint knew there were women who trained horses, but he'd never met one. "Where did you learn how to start a colt?"

She turned away from him and reached for the harness and crupper she'd draped over a nearby hitching rail. As she began to tack up Peanut, she said, "A good horse trainer used to work for my father. For hours, my brother and I would watch him work. Kipp is better at breaking horses than me. But I can get the job done."

This was the most she'd talked since he'd met her,

and Quint decided she probably found it easier to discuss horses and ranch work. Obviously those things had always been her life.

Quint went to work saddling the mare, and once both horses were ready to use, she went to the back of the truck and opened the gate on a large dog carrier. The canines immediately jumped to the ground, but rather than race off to explore the new territory, they went straight to the horses and sat waiting on their haunches for Clementine to ride off.

Now that she had everything set to go, Quint's urge to keep her here on the ranch grew even stronger. "Clementine, you don't have to be in a hurry about going out today," he told her. "In fact, I see clouds gathering in the west. It might begin to rain before you can set up camp. You're welcome to stay at the ranch tonight, then head out tomorrow."

"Thanks, but I'd like to be on my way. I have a slicker and I'm used to the rain."

He didn't know exactly what was coming over him, but he suddenly wanted to argue the point. In fact, he felt like ordering her to stay at the ranch. But hell, he knew that wouldn't sit well with her. She'd probably tell him to go jump in the lake and leave, so he kept the urge to himself. Better to have her going off in a rainstorm than to have her leave the ranch entirely, he decided.

"Okay. Whatever you think best," he said.

From the moment she'd stepped out of the truck, Quint had been struggling not to stare at her, but now, as she was about to depart the ranch yard, it was as though his eyes couldn't look anywhere but at her.

Faded denim jeans clung to her thighs and curvy hips, while an equally faded denim shirt was stretched across the fullness of her breasts. She was wearing the same black felt hat she'd worn the day she'd first visited the ranch, and like then, she'd pushed the stampede string tight beneath her chin to hold the headgear firmly in place.

He couldn't deny the ample curves of her body stirred his libido, yet it was her hair that totally mesmerized him. Today it wasn't confined in a braid or ponytail. Today it lay in black shiny waves all the way to her butt, and each little movement she made caused it to swing like a curtain swaying with the breeze. The realization that he wanted to touch it just as much as he wanted to touch her shocked him.

"Yes, it's best that I head on out," she said without looking at him. "A few more hours of sunlight are left. Enough to get me out to the sheep and my camp ready for the night."

He cleared his throat, then said, "I'd be more than glad to go with you—to help you with your tent and whatever else you might need to do."

"I appreciate your offer, but that's totally unnecessary. I've done this plenty of times. It's second nature to me."

She wasn't wearing perfume and yet she smelled utterly feminine. Nor was there a dab of makeup on her face, yet even without it, there was plenty of vibrant color to her lips and cheeks.

A natural. She was that and more, he thought.

"Jett checked on the sheep early this morning. They've moved about a mile west from where you and I saw them. They're in a meadow halfway up the mountain. I figure your dogs will easily find the spot."

"No problem," she said.

Tonight he would sit down with the rest of his family to enjoy a hot cooked meal. What would Clementine eat? he wondered. Something out of a can? Or a bag? The idea bothered him. But not nearly as much as the thought of her asleep with a bear or mountain lion roaming around her tent.

A few minutes ago, when he'd finished tightening the girth on her saddle, she'd walked over and slipped a Winchester in the leather sheath fastened beneath the right swell of her saddle. At least she had some sort of protection, he thought. But what if…

"Is there anything else I need to know before I leave?"

Her question broke into his runaway thoughts, and he gave himself a hard mental shake before he said, "I'll send Jett or Chance out with supplies in a couple of weeks. Will that be soon enough?"

"Yes."

"I keep wanting to say send me a text if you need anything, but you won't have a phone."

No electricity or Wi-Fi. No TV or telephone. Could he handle that? Quint wondered. He'd never tried.

"I have a tiny transistor for getting weather reports. Otherwise, I don't have any way to communicate. But if something serious does occur with the sheep, I'll ride out and let you know."

"What if something serious happens to you?"

The question was out before he could stop it, and she reacted by giving him a dreary smile.

"You won't know about it."

He wanted to groan out loud. He wanted to cradle her face with his hands, to look into her eyes and tell her she was too precious to put herself in that kind of danger. But she'd think he was loony and maybe he would be. These overprotective feelings she evoked in him made no sense.

"The idea doesn't scare you?" he asked.

She looked away from him. "If it did, I wouldn't be doing this job."

He drew in a sharp breath, then blew it out. "No. Don't guess you would."

She moved over to the buckskin and untied the mare's reins, then unwrapped the sorrel's lead rope. As she led the horses slightly away from the trailer, the dogs followed and so did Quint.

"Is there anything else you need to add to the list of supplies you'll be needing?" he asked as she easily swung herself into the saddle. "Jett will bring extra food out for the Pyrenees, so you'll probably see him tomorrow."

"What I've written down is all I'll be needing. After tomorrow Jett won't have to worry about putting out food for the dogs. I'll take care of them."

Quint wanted to tell her that he'd bring the dog food himself. The chore would give him a good excuse to see her again and make sure she had her camp set up and comfortable. But she'd probably get the impression he wanted to see her again, or was checking to make sure she was competent at her job. Either way, she wouldn't be pleased with him. And he didn't want to get started off on the wrong foot with her.

"Thanks. I'll tell him."

She lifted a hand in farewell. "See you."

He raised a hand in response. "Yeah. Take care."

She nodded, then reined Birdie away from him. Quint stood watching her ride off with Peanut following obediently at the mare's side. The collies bounded slightly ahead of the horses, and he watched with faint amusement as the dogs playfully nipped at each other. They knew they were going to a flock and they were happy.

"Clementine is already leaving? She just arrived a few minutes ago!"

The sound of Cordell's voice had Quint's head swinging around to see his brother walking up behind him.

"Yeah, she's on her way. I tried to tell her she should wait until tomorrow. Especially with those clouds gathering. But she wouldn't hear of it."

Both men watched as Clementine and her animals disappeared over the hill that swept downward toward the big house.

"She's doing what she wants to do. Besides, if she hung around here, what would she do?"

Cordell's question pointed out the obvious. Clementine wasn't interested in spending more time with him or his family. Why would he want her to? It was like he told the twins; he wasn't looking for a new girlfriend. And he definitely wasn't looking for love, or a permanent relationship like a wife.

"You're right." He slanted his brother a wry smile. "Guess I should be relieved she's so devoted to her job."

"Yes, you should be." Cordell gave Quint's shoulder a gentle squeeze. "I wouldn't worry myself about her, Quint. From what I understand, sheepherders are a different breed. They aren't like regular folks. If they were, they couldn't do what they do."

Obviously, Cordell could read Quint's mind. Or at least the part that was wondering and worrying about Clementine. He could only hope that his brother couldn't see how attracted Quint was to the woman. He'd probably laugh out loud.

"I'm not worried," Quint told him.

Cordell let out a short laugh. "No. Not much, brother."

Quint frowned at him. "She's a woman," he said defensively.

"Yes. I can see that you've noticed the fact," Cordell said cleverly.

"Can you see that you're getting on my nerves?" Quint asked as he glared at his older brother.

Cordell laughed. "I'm paying you back for all those times you took jabs at me over Maggie."

Quint had the decency to look shamefaced. Before Cordell had married Maggie, a beautiful red-haired nurse from Arizona, Quint had taunted his brother unmercifully. But that was different, he thought. It was obvious to Quint and everyone else in the family that Cordell was falling in love with the woman. In this case, Quint was merely concerned about Clementine's welfare.

Quint grunted. "I don't know why you want to pay me back. You came out the big winner in that deal. You now have a great wife and a precious little daughter."

Chuckling, Cordell patted Quint's back. "You're right, brother. I am the big winner. Now, what are you going to do for the remainder of the day?"

Think about Clementine, that's what he'd probably do, he thought grimly. To Cordell, he said, "I'm not sure. Why? Need some help?"

"Possibly. Chance tells me he spotted a few calves yesterday over on the eastern range that haven't been branded. I could use some help rounding them up. We'll have to take a portable corral."

Grateful for any kind of distraction, Quint said, "I'll go saddle my horse. Will Chance be going with us?"

"No. I've sent him to Beaver to pick up some meds at Mack's clinic."

Mack's clinic was actually Barlow Animal Hospital, their brother-in-law's veterinary services. This past Christmas, their older sister, Grace, and Mack had gotten engaged. Since then they'd married and made their home together with their son and daughter on the Broken B, a fairly large ranch just east of Stone Creek. Grace was the third sibling who'd recently married, and Quint had to admit she was happier now than he'd ever seen her. But Grace was the loving, nurturing sort. And she'd been in love with Mack since her teenaged years. Yes, marriage was good, Quint thought. He was all for it, as long as it didn't involve him.

"Well, I figure you and me can handle the job just fine," Quint told him, then glanced up at the sky. "But I think we'd better tie a slicker onto our saddle. The clouds are growing darker."

The two men turned and began walking in the direction of the big barn where their working horses were stalled.

"Yeah, they're pretty blue," Cordell said. "Looks like Clementine is going to get rained on."

Now, why did he have to mention her again? Quint wondered crossly. "Like you said, she's experienced at the job. She'll be okay."

But come tomorrow and the following days would *he* be okay?

As soon as Jimmy and Jewel located the sheep on the side of the mountain, they returned to Clementine and zoomed circles around her and the horses.

"Okay, you two," Clementine said to the dogs. "Take me to them. And no barking, remember? We don't want the sheep to scatter."

The dogs appeared to understand what she was telling them. They took off in a sedate walk up a dim trail that wound through underbrush, rock outcroppings and tall pines. Thirty minutes ago the drizzle had begun and Clementine had donned a slicker over her shirt and jeans, but now water dripped slowly off the brim of her hat and plopped onto the swells of her saddle. She didn't mind the rain. Actually, it was much better than choking on dust. And the moisture kept the grasses growing, which meant she could stay longer in one spot before she had to move herself and the sheep to a different location.

When she topped a little rise, the pines and aspens opened up to a small meadow filled with sheep. She reined Birdie to a stop, and Peanut halted at their side as she studied the lay of the land. From the size of the grazing area, she wouldn't be able to remain here for long, but that was just one of the nuisances of the job. Moving from one area to the next was essential to keeping the herd well fed and healthy.

Across the meadow, she saw the Great Pyrenees watching her and the dogs intently, while Jimmy made a tiny growl to let Clementine know he knew the dogs were there and he wasn't exactly happy about their presence.

"Jimmy, those dogs are going to be your helpers. I understand you and Jewel don't need helpers, but this herd belongs to them. You're going to have to share responsibilities and be friends. No barking, growling or fighting. Got it?"

Jimmy looked up at her and whined, which meant he understood, but didn't necessarily like the setup. As for Jewel, she appeared to be far more receptive of the other dogs. Her tail was wagging in eager anticipation.

"That's Zina and Lash," she told her dogs. "If you think you can behave yourselves, you have my permission to go over and introduce yourselves."

She rode forward, and the dogs raced ahead of her

until they were about twenty feet away from the Pyrenees, who were standing close together, watching every move the collies made. There was only one other occasion when Jimmy and Jewel had to mix with a ranch owner's personal dogs, which had been a trio of New Zealand Huntaways. Initially she'd been concerned about mixing her dogs with the Huntaways, but they turned out to be friendly and smart and very helpful. Even though they'd been very vocal with loud, noisy barks. As for Quint's Pyrenees, she'd find out soon enough how much they liked to bark.

Once she'd scouted the area and found a spot on a wide ledge of ground, slightly above the meadow, she dismounted and unsaddled Birdie, then went to work unloading all the bags of supplies strapped to Peanut's back. Once she was finished with the horses, she turned them loose in the meadow with the sheep.

By the time she'd finished erecting the tent and rolling out her bed, the light rain had stopped, and she scoured around the edge of the forest until she'd gathered plenty of dead limbs and twigs for a campfire.

Because everything was damp, she dug into a thick bed of pine needles until she had a double handful of dry ones. The needles were enough to act as an accelerant and soon she had enough flames to boil a pot of coffee.

While she'd been exploring the area for a good spot to set up her tent, she'd found a spring of water running from a ledge of shell rock. The water was crystal clear and cold, and even though she doubted it was contaminated with any sort of bacteria, she never took chances. She added purifying tablets to her canteen just to make certain the water was safe to drink.

With water and coffee grounds added to a red granite pot, she placed it on the fire, then gave the dogs their ration of food for the day. Across the west end of the meadow, Zina and Lash were sitting on their haunches curiously watching every move she and the collies made. She figured the dogs had never seen this much activity and were trying to process everything.

Once Jimmy and Jewel began to eat, Clementine measured out a portion for the Pyrenees and walked casually in their direction. She managed to get within twenty feet of them before they both barked and cautiously trotted away from her. Not wanting to pressure them, she placed the food on the ground, then returned to her campsite. It would take a few days for Zina and Lash to trust her, and even then, the dogs would only be her distant friends.

Back at the campsite, while she waited for the coffee to boil, she dug out a can of tuna and a sleeve of saltine crackers for her supper. She'd brought a few fresh foods in her stash of groceries, mostly fruit and potatoes, but if she didn't ration them carefully throughout the two-week period, those would be gone before her bimonthly supply arrived.

She was fairly certain if she sent word to Quint to send more fruit and vegetables, he would gladly oblige. But she wouldn't ask. No. She didn't want him forming the idea that she was needy or demanding. Actually, she didn't want Quint Hollister to think of her at all.

Why not, Clem? The guy is one hot dude. Why not let him know he wakes up the woman in you?

The taunting voice in her ear very nearly made her groan out loud. Thinking of Quint as a man, rather than her boss, was worse than stupid. It was dangerous. Since she'd begun working as a sheepherder, she'd always prided herself in doing good work. She'd strived to be dependable, responsible and trustworthy. She'd never allowed herself to get in a situation that could be misconstrued, whether it be interaction with people or caring for the animals she'd been entrusted with.

When she left Stone Creek Ranch, she didn't want a black mark on her references. She didn't want the reputation of a cougar, and that's exactly what she'd be if she allowed herself to look at Quint in a provocative way. No, she thought. Even though Quint was good-looking and nice, she couldn't be more to him than an employee.

The next day, outside the big barn at the ranch yard, Quint was loading a broken water pump into the back of his truck when Jett returned from his trip to deliver the dog food to Clementine's camp. He quickly shut the tailgate and walked over to where the young ranch hand had dismounted his horse.

"Did you find Clementine at Rocky Meadow?" Quint asked as Jett loosened the saddle girth.

"Yep. Her camp was there, but she wasn't. She and the buckskin were gone so I waited. After about five minutes she rode up," he said. "She'd been out scouting around for more grazing areas."

Relief poured through Quint, and even though he realized his reaction to Clementine's safety was ridiculous, he couldn't help it.

"You gave her the dog food?"

The tall blond man, who was three years younger than Quint, turned an impatient look on him. "Well, sure. That was the whole purpose of my visit, wasn't it?"

Quint huffed out a heavy breath. "Yeah, the whole purpose," he said with a measure of sarcasm. "Except I'd like to hear if everything looked okay. You are my eyes, you know."

Jett used the sleeve of his shirt to mop the sweat from his brow. The day had turned out hot, especially for the last half of September, and the ride back from Clementine's camp wasn't short, or easy.

"Sorry, Quint. I didn't mean to sound curt. Everything looked great. The sheep are fine. The four dogs were all doing their jobs without any sign of problems. Clementine's camp was far better than anything I could make, so you needn't worry about her."

"She looked okay to you?"

"Depends on what you mean by okay. Like nice and pretty? Or healthy?"

Quint wanted to take Jett by the shoulders and shake him. "I mean, did she look stressed? Like she'd been having problems?"

"Not at all. She told me everything had been fine and that in a few days she's going to move the flock on toward Snow Mountain. She expects by then, the small meadow where they are now will be grazed out." Jett's eyes narrowed as he thoughtfully studied Quint's face. "I'm thinking you should've made the trip out there, Quint. To ease your mind about the woman."

Quint could feel a wave of heat washing over his face. He was behaving like an idiot. But damn it, he'd spent half the night imagining Clementine wet and miserable or squaring off against a hungry bear who'd gotten a whiff of food from her campsite. All sorts of harrowing images had gone through his head until he'd finally fallen asleep, only to wake up this morning exhausted and groggy.

"I'm the one who needs to apologize, Jett." Lifting his hat, he raked a hand through his hair, then shook his head. "I think I've made a mistake in hiring a woman sheepherder."

Jett frowned at him. "Look, Quint, your mistake is in thinking Clementine can't take care of herself. She can. So forget about her and get on with doing all the things you need to do around here. That's one of the reasons you wanted to hire a sheepherder in the first place, so it would free you and me up to do other chores. Or have you forgotten that?"

He couldn't forget anything. Not if it pertained to Clementine. And that was the whole problem, Quint decided. He couldn't get her out of his mind and the problem wasn't stemming entirely from worry. No. She was one sexy woman. At least she was in Quint's eyes, and he could admit, if only to himself, that his feelings of protectiveness for the woman were all rolled up in desire and thoughts of how it might feel to make love to her.

Clearing his throat, he said, "You're right, Jett. And I'm going to do as you say and quit worrying."

And stop picturing himself wrapping his arms around Clementine and kissing her bare lips.

Chapter Five

During the next week, Quint's days were busy helping Cordell and the ranch hands with more calf sorting and branding, along with two days of fence repairs. Throughout the long week, he'd done his best to keep his mind occupied and off of Clementine, yet with each day that passed, he realized he was failing miserably. Every day he'd had to fight to keep from saddling up and riding out to see her. Thankfully, each time he'd stopped short of following through on his urges, but he wasn't sure how much longer he could go without seeing her.

"Hey, Quint. Better not make any plans to go to town tonight. Mom and the twins are making a big dinner."

Quint tossed several blocks of alfalfa into a manger before he looked over at Cordell, who'd just turned his horse loose inside the small corral at the back of the barn. The two men had been working all day on the far east side of the ranch and were just now winding down the long day.

"I don't have any plans for a date," he told Cordell. Why bother? he grimly asked himself. None of the girlfriends in his little black book interested him, and he'd been telling himself he needed to find some new women to date. But he just couldn't seem to summon the interest or the energy. "What's the occasion for the dinner?"

"Dad didn't say. He just said that Mom has invited everyone. Other than Hunter, of course. He's up in Oregon right now doing a weeklong rodeo. And then he's on to the next one down in northern California."

Surprised by this news, Quint said, "Wow! A weeklong rodeo? Sounds like our brother is getting big time."

"Well, he's continually adding to his livestock string. And Dad says he's hired a sister act that involves trick riding and shooting. So he has more to offer rodeo committees than just good bucking bulls and horses," Cordell said.

"Hmm. I'm glad to hear it. You and I both know our big brother is happiest when he's on the road."

Cordell grimaced. "It's obvious he's not happy when he's home on the ranch—in that empty house on the hill."

A few years ago, Hunter had been married to Willow, a quiet brunette who'd mostly kept to herself. Expecting the two of them to raise a family, Hunter had built them a pretty log house about a half mile east of the ranch yard. Now, thanks to Willow, the house mostly stood empty. She'd up and left without a word to anyone, and to this day no one really knew the reason she'd deserted Hunter. He'd received divorce papers in the mail and he'd signed and sent them back without putting up a protest. The way he'd explained it, Willow clearly hadn't loved him and that was all the explanation he needed.

"Hunter is the only one who can make that house a

home again. And I'm fairly sure he doesn't want to try that kind of life anymore," Quint replied.

A quiet brunette who'd kept to herself. Hell, was he trying to walk down the same brokenhearted trail that Hunter had traveled? No, Quint thought. He had more sense than to get himself tied to a woman.

"Who knows about Hunter," Cordell said. "He's not around long enough to even guess what he's thinking."

Nodding, Quint moved on from the subject of their absent brother. "Well, no matter the reason for the big dinner. I'll be there with bells on. I missed lunch, so I won't mind if Mom doesn't have anything more than bologna sandwiches."

Cordell glanced at his watch. "Yeah, me, too. I'm going to get on home. Maggie and Bridget are probably waiting on me."

"Lucky you."

Cordell grinned. "Yeah. Lucky me," he said, then cast Quint a thoughtful glance. "Have you heard anything from your sheepherder these past few days?"

Oh, hell. He wished Cordell hadn't brought up the subject of Clementine. Every day he worked to get her off his mind, yet someone in his family invariably mentioned her and then his preoccupation with the woman would start all over again.

"No. I've not sent Jett out to check on her." He shrugged. "I mean, that was the whole point in hiring her. So none of us would have to spend the bigger part of the day riding out to check on the sheep."

Smirking at him, Cordell said, "I was only asking a question. Not scolding you, Quint. If you think all is okay, then there's no need for you to go searching the mountains for her."

Sighing, Quint turned away from the manger and

started walking out of the horse corral. Cordell followed at his side.

"She doesn't want me to concern myself over her welfare," Quint told him. "So I'm trying to keep my distance. But I'll tell you, Cord. It's damned hard."

"Listen, Quint. You're the boss over the sheep. If you want to check on her or the flock every day of the week that's your prerogative."

"Yeah," Quint muttered. "I just don't want her thinking I doubt her ability to do the job."

Cordell slanted a coy grin in Quint's direction. "And maybe you don't want her to get the idea that you want to see *her*."

Quint groaned. He and Cordell had always teased each other. Especially when it came to the subject of women. However, now that Cordell was happily married, the teasing was all one-sided. Only in this case, Quint had to admit his brother had put his finger on the problem.

"Okay, Cord. You got me," he said in a resigned voice. "From the first time I laid eyes on the woman it was like something clicked. Now I can't get her out of mind. You know what I mean?"

Cordell chuckled as the two men walked across the wide ranch yard to where they'd parked their trucks earlier this morning. "All too well, little brother. Trust me, it's like being struck with an illness."

"You know what I'm thinking?" Quint asked.

Cordell let out another short laugh. "I'd be afraid to guess."

"I'll tell you, brother. I'm sick and tired of wondering and worrying about the woman. I think the best way to deal with the problem is just to go see her. That ought to get her off my mind once and for all."

"You think so?"

"It has to," he muttered. "Staying away from her isn't doing the trick."

"Hmm. Well, all I can say is that when I tried getting Maggie out of my mind, I ended up marrying her. So if you're not ready for a wife, then you need to watch your step, little brother."

This time it was Quint who let out a short laugh. "Ready for a wife," he repeated mockingly. "That'll be the day. Sure, I'm thinking about Clementine. But hardly in a permanent way."

Cordell swatted a hand against Quint's back. "Then you don't have a thing to worry about."

Later, as Quint showered and dressed for the big dinner his mother had prepared, he realized the talk he'd had with Cordell had made him feel much better. Now that he'd made the firm decision to ride out and see Clementine in the morning, he felt as if a burden had been lifted from his shoulders, and by the time he headed to the den to join the rest of the family he was whistling under his breath.

The den was located in the back section of the house, with a row of several windows that looked out over a portion of the backyard and covered patio. During the cold months, Hadley usually kept a fire burning in the huge rock fireplace that stretched across one end of the long room, but with the weather still on the warm side, there was no fire tonight. However, there were far more people than Quint had expected to see when he entered the room. Two leather couches, a couple of matching love seats, along with four armchairs and three wooden rockers angled to one side of the fireplace were nearly all occupied with family members. Even

Grace, Mack and their two kids, Ross and Kitty, were among the group.

"Hey, Quint, come over here and sit with us," Grace called to him, then added jokingly, "You look like you need to be sitting next to two doctors."

Quint walked over to where his older sister was sitting next to her husband, Mack. Along with being a veterinarian, the man was also working to build up the cattle ranch he'd inherited from his late father. As for Grace, she was a medical doctor who had a private family practice in Beaver. In spite of being overworked, the couple somehow managed to find time for each other and their children. Which was a good thing, Quint thought, since both had suffered heartaches in the past.

"Don't let your sister talk mean to you, Quint," Mack joked. "You look healthy enough to wrestle a bear."

Quint eased down in the empty armchair situated directly across from where the pair were cuddled together on a love seat.

"Thanks, Mack. I don't exactly have the energy to square off with a bear tonight. But I appreciate the thought." His gaze encompassed both Mack and Grace, who was a taller, much younger version of their blonde mother. "I don't have to ask if you two have been busy. What's going on in town, besides you two caring for sick people and sick animals?"

Grace laughed softly. "I don't have time to listen to gossip in the clinic."

"No. You're too busy jabbing needles in unsuspecting patients," Quint joked.

While she let out a good-natured groan, Mack said, "Actually, Quint, the only gossip I've heard this week was about you and I overheard it in the Wagon Spoke. Laverne and a couple of ranch hands from the Rafter

G were talking about your new sheepherder. They considered having a woman holding the job somewhat of a—novelty."

Quint figured the ranch hands had probably made far snider remarks, but Mack was too considerate to repeat them. The idea burned Quint to no end. Clementine wasn't a coarse woman who chewed tobacco and went around in grubby clothes. She was a lady. One who just happened to work outdoors.

"How would they know? They've never met Clementine," he said sharply, and then it suddenly hit him that he was no different than those gossiping ranch hands. Before he'd met Clementine in person, he'd expected her to be coarse and rough around the edges. "Sorry, Mack. I didn't mean to bite your head off."

Mack exchanged a knowing glance with Grace before he said to Quint, "Forget it. You weren't aiming your frustration at me. Besides, you shouldn't let outside talk get to you. Hadley says you're doing a great job with the sheep and that's what counts. I shouldn't have repeated what I heard, anyway."

Quint felt like a fool. He was being overly sensitive about Clementine and his decision to hire a woman for the job. Gossip was something he usually ignored or laughed at. He needed to keep it that way.

Wiping a hand over his face, he glanced around the room. "Isn't anyone passing around drinks? I need a beer."

"You're too late, dear brother. Mom is about to serve the food," Beatrice said as she walked up behind his chair.

Quint glanced at both sisters, then to Mack. "Do any of you know what this special dinner is about?"

His brother-in-law glanced at his wife. "I don't have a clue. Do you know, honey?"

Shaking her head, Grace looked at Beatrice. "Do you have an idea, Bea?"

The younger twin wrinkled her nose. "Not really. Except that Bonnie says Dad has been on the phone for hours at a time this past week. She believes he's making some kind of big deal, but she's not seen anything about it on paper yet."

Quint glanced down the room to where Hadley was interacting with his three grandchildren. Since Cordell and Maggie's baby daughter, Bridget, had learned how to walk, the little redhead was normally racing around the room getting into one thing after another. But tonight she was sitting contentedly on Hadley's knee, while Mack and Grace's two children were seated on the floor at his feet.

"At the moment, Dad doesn't look like a man who's been wheeling and dealing big business. He looks like a grandfather to me, telling his grandkids a tall tale."

"Could be that Vanessa has discovered some important information about the family tree," Mack suggested.

His brother-in-law's comment had Quint glancing across the room to the tall lovely brunette Jack had met and married after his trip to Three Rivers Ranch in Arizona. For some time now, Vanessa had been digging into the Hollisters' family history, trying to figure out how they were related to the Arizona Hollisters. So far a DNA test had proved the two families were connected. However, no one had evidence of how or when the connection had occurred.

"You could be right," Grace said with a faint smile.

"When Van isn't teaching school, she's usually working on our family genealogy. She's determined—"

The rest of Grace's sentence was suddenly interrupted when Bonnie appeared in the open doorway of the den and announced that dinner was served.

Everyone trooped into the large dining room, and Quint was surprised to see the long oak table set with his mother's best dishes and glassware. Especially the wine glasses. The last time they'd had wine at dinner was back several months ago during the Christmas holidays when Grace and Mack had announced their plans to wed.

"Looks like Mom is going all out tonight," Flint said as he took a seat next to Quint.

Glancing over, Quint noticed his slightly older brother was wearing the uniform shirt he normally wore while on duty.

"Yeah. Maybe we'll find out why in a few minutes. So what's up with the uniform, Flint? Is that all you have in your closet?"

Flint glanced down at his khaki shirt with the county sheriff's department emblems decorating the sleeves and left shoulder.

"I have duty tonight," he explained. "I'm going to have to leave as soon as I eat. The only reason I'm here is because Dad asked me to stick around."

"That's too bad," Quint told him. "Being on duty later means you'll have to skip the wine."

Flint eyed the goblet positioned in front of his plate. "Damn, something big must be going on," he said. "But I don't mind skipping the wine. Better than missing Dad's announcement—whatever that might be."

It wasn't until everyone had a full plate of prime rib

roast and their glasses filled with red wine that Hadley called the group to attention.

"First of all," he began, "you need to thank your beautiful mother for the great meal she's prepared for us tonight. Trust me, she's going to get nicely rewarded for this."

Claire reached over and patted her husband's arm, while down the table, Beatrice said, "Mom has her eye on a diamond bracelet at Weaver's Jewelry in town, Dad. You might keep that in mind."

Everyone laughed, including Hadley.

"Thank you, Bea, for the suggestion. Now, to get down to the reason for this get-together. As you all know, it's been my wish for years now to expand Stone Creek Ranch. I managed to make a step in that direction a few weeks ago when I purchased the C Bar C. Now I'm thrilled to tell you that since the Carter buyout, I've secured even more land to the west of us. The Barkleys are dissolving their farm. As a result, Stone Creek Ranch now owns an additional ten thousand acres."

A few gasps and shocked expressions rippled around table. As for Quint, he could only wonder what was going on with his father. Was he going through some sort of aging crisis?

Bending his head toward Flint, Quint whispered, "What are we going to do with ten thousand more acres? We've not even gotten around to working the C Bar C yet!"

Flint muttered, "God help us, Dad is on a buying binge and it's making him delirious."

At the end of the table, Hadley let out a loud cough. "I can't hear everything Flint and Quint are saying down there, but I have a good idea. They're worried their father is no longer mentally competent."

Quint cleared his throat. "Well, not exactly incompetent, Dad. We're just wondering—what good is all this land going to do us if we don't have livestock on it? And that takes money."

"Lots of it," Jack said from his chair that was located on Hadley's left side. "Frankly, Dad, I'm wondering the same things as my brothers. Yes, currently we have a few cattle to move onto the C Bar C land, but the Barkley place is another matter. How are we going to make that place pay for itself? Yes, Quint is going to purchase more sheep, but even more wool production won't be enough. And we hardly have the time or equipment to raise alfalfa or timothy."

Hadley's expression said he wasn't the least bit worried by Jack's assessment of the situation. In fact, the grin on his face said he knew something his children didn't or he'd already drunk a bottle of cabernet.

"I'm glad you brought this up, Jack. Shows me what a good manager you are. But I want all of you to rest assured that this new venture is not some sort of reckless gamble. Because I've already found a way to not only use and pay for the land, but to also make a profit."

Quint stared at him while thinking this was one time he was glad he wasn't in charge of making business decisions for the whole ranch. "Dad, did you buy a crystal ball? You can obviously see something about the future that your sons aren't seeing."

Hadley chuckled. "Okay, I'll confess. I didn't come up with this idea entirely on my own. I just happened to be talking with Gil Hollister, telling him how much I'd like to have the Barkley land, and that's how it all started."

Gil was the patriarch of the Arizona Hollisters and helped his wife, Maureen, and their children run Three

Rivers Ranch. Since the two families had learned they were related, Hadley and Gil had become good friends. Now it sounded as though the two men had grown even closer, Quint thought.

"And how did this conversation ultimately end?" Jack asked.

"Gil agreed to help finance the cost of the land," Hadley answered. "Which Stone Creek could swing on our own, but with Gil's help it will be much easier on us financially. But that's not all. Gil and Maureen are sending up a thousand head of Red Angus cow/calf pairs to put on the Barkley land."

Quint and Flint exchanged shocked glances, while Cordell practically shouted, "A thousand head! How the hell are we supposed to take care of that many cattle, plus our own? Dad, you ought to know we're already stretched to the breaking point!"

Hadley quickly held up a hand to intervene in Cordell's outburst. "Calm down, Cord. We have that figured out with the rest of the deal. Three Rivers Ranch is sending up three of its men—on a permanent basis to take care of the Red Angus. So I figure with three more hands working around here, we can manage the extra cattle."

Jack said, "Gil and Maureen are special people, but I can't see them doing this out of the goodness of their hearts. What's in it for our Three Rivers relatives?"

"Three Rivers and Red Bluff, their second ranch, are both loaded. Neither property can handle any more cattle. This gives them a chance to expand. We're going to split the calf crop down the middle, then after the first couple of years, if neither is happy, we'll renegotiate."

"Cowboys from Arizona? Gosh, this sounds exciting," Beatrice exclaimed.

Seated next to her twin, Bonnie rolled her eyes. "Bea, does everything always come down to men with you?"

Ignoring the twins, Flint said, "I can't see the ranch hands being willing to relocate. They won't be happy with the cold and the snow."

"No. But they might be happy with the women," Beatrice added with a wink at Bonnie, who promptly rolled her eyes and groaned.

"Gil and Maureen will be paying them handsome wages. And a chance to build a calf crop of their own. So they'll have plenty of incentive to stay here on the ranch."

"This sounds like wonderful news to me," Grace added her thoughts on the matter. "The two Hollister families linking up makes good sense."

"Strength in numbers," Mack added to his wife's comments. "Congratulations, Hadley."

"Thank you, Mack. Now, I realize you guys might need to think on this a while before you join me and your mother in the celebration, but it would make us happy if you'd all join in a toast."

Flint said, "Dad, you are and always will be our leader. We trust your decisions."

"That goes for me, too," Quint added. "If you feel good about this, then so do I."

"Thanks, boys," Hadley said. "So what about you Cord? Jack?"

Cordell gave his father a wide smile. "More cattle, more land, more ranch hands. I don't have to keep tossing the idea around. I'm happy, Dad."

Jack's expression remained serious as he rose to his feet. "I'm willing to drink a toast, Dad. But I need to say something first. Just so you'll know how I'm feeling right now."

Hadley's eyes narrowed shrewdly as he studied his son, who was also the comanager of Stone Creek Ranch. Was Jack going to object to the whole deal? Quint wondered. Of course he had a right to express his displeasure. But surely he'd wait until they could carry on a private conversation instead of ruining this evening with an argument.

"Okay, son, tell me. How are you feeling?"

Jack suddenly let out a joyous laugh as he directed a lovingly look at his wife, then over to his parents. "If I was any happier I'd bust. The ranch is growing and so is my family. Van is pregnant. According to Grace, our baby should be here in about six months."

The twins' mouths fell open and Beatrice yelled out, "Grace! You knew about this and didn't tell! You're an awful sister!"

Grace chuckled. "Everyone knows a physician doesn't reveal a patient's medical history to anyone."

"But Van isn't just anyone! She's family!" Beatrice argued.

"Don't blame Grace for keeping the secret," Vanessa told her. "Jack and I wanted to wait about telling everyone. We wanted to make sure the baby was safely on its way."

"Oh, Van, this is such wonderful news!" Claire exclaimed, and with joyous tears in her eyes, she left her chair and went around to give her daughter-in-law a heartfelt hug.

After that, a few minutes of chaos ensued as the rest of the family gathered around Jack and Vanessa to offer congratulations.

By the time everyone returned to their seats, the food was getting cold, but no one really cared. Especially not their mother. She laughed as she sliced off a piece of prime roast on her plate. "I took pains cooking this for Hadley and his celebration over the cattle and land deal. He didn't know his announcement was going to be upstaged."

"And in the best possible way," Hadley said, then picked up his wine glass. "Now I think it's really time for a toast."

"Except that Van can't have alcohol," Grace said with an impish grin. "She'll have to do her toast with water."

"What a bummer you are, Grace," Beatrice complained. "Do you have to be a doctor all the time?"

"Of course she does," Mack said with a little laugh, then smacked a kiss on his wife's cheek. "That's why everyone tells me I look healthier than I've looked in years."

Mack's remark brought on spates of laughter, while Flint said, "Don't feel badly, Van. I can't have wine either. Duty calls. So we're in this together."

Van smiled at her brother in-law. "Thank you, Flint. I don't feel so left out now."

At the head of the table, Hadley glanced around at his family, then lifted his glass high. "Here's to Stone Creek Ranch, our home and especially our family and the new little Hollister to come. May we always be this happy."

"And together," Claire added with misty eyes.

"Yes, my sweet wife," Hadley agreed. "All of us— together."

As Quint sipped the fruity wine, he thought how blessed he was to be surrounded by a loving and happy family.

The realization warmed him, as did the wine sliding down his throat, but then out of nowhere, his mind was suddenly transported away from the happy dinner table. He was seeing a dark, lonely camp in the mountains with

Clementine sitting by a campfire. The only company she had were the dogs, the horses and the sheep. She wouldn't be sipping wine or laughing with her family.

Did Clementine ever laugh? Oh, yeah, once she'd made a sardonic sound that resembled laughter. But it had been far from an expression of genuine pleasure.

And why should any of that matter to you, Quint? Clementine is little more than a stranger. Just someone you hired to watch over your sheep. Her happiness or lifestyle is hardly your responsibility.

No. Clementine wasn't his responsibility. But that didn't keep him from thinking about her and wishing her life was—better.

And what exactly would be better for Clementine, Quint? Who made you an expert on how people should live their lives? What makes you happy wouldn't necessarily put a smile on her face.

"Quint? You aren't eating. Are you worried about Dad's deal and just don't want to speak up and spoil the evening?"

Flint's question was spoken in a low voice not far from Quint's ear and was enough of a distraction to pull him back to the present and the dinner table circled with happy, laughing faces.

He picked up the knife lying next to his plate and sliced off a bite of beef. "Nothing like that, Flint. I was just thinking what a special night this has turned out to be. That's all."

"Yeah. Our big brother is going to be a daddy," Flint mused aloud. "The Hollister family is growing."

The family was expanding and so was the ranch. Things were looking good. So why wasn't he feeling the joy? Why were his thoughts on a lonely campfire and the melancholy shadows in Clementine's brown eyes?

* * *

Nuttah and I both worry about you, Kipp. What good is going to come from you hanging around the Rising Starr and working your butt off for an evil woman? Yes, we understand you want our home back. But what if you end up like Dad? Then I'd have nothing. Oh, sure, Mom is still over in Boise, but it's not the same with her anymore. I don't need to remind you that nothing has been the same with her since she left the family.

Sorry I'm running on like this, dear brother. I guess being so far away has made me start looking at things through a wider lens. Land, money, a house—I used to grieve about losing it all. But that was years ago. I've learned there are more important things. Yes, you want justice and wrongs to be righted, but I hope you won't let your feelings turn into vengeance. The Rising Starr isn't worth the cost. Revenge will only consume you until you're miserable.

I'm doing okay here on Stone Creek. The weather has been especially nice and the grass is still thick. I haven't seen lambs so fat in a long time. There's a nice spring close to my camp so I've been enjoying plenty of water for drinking and washing. I doubt I'll be so fortunate with my next move. The horses and dogs seem to like it here and they have company on this job. Two Great Pyrenees are with us. Their names are Lash and Zina. I'm enjoying having them as they're very smart and helpful.

A ranch hand will be bringing supplies in a couple of days. I'll send this letter out with him. He's a very young guy. Even younger than Quint

Hollister, but he knows a bit about sheep, so I appreciate talking with him. As for everything else, all is well, so don't concern yourself about me.
Your loving sister,
Clementine.

After signing her name, she slipped the letter into a stamped envelope and addressed it to Kipp Starr in care of Rising Starr Ranch. Odd, how writing those words still felt familiar, even though she'd not lived there in eight years. Old habits die hard, she supposed.

She placed the letter safely inside a duffel bag and left the interior of the tent. Bright sunlight washed the camp area, and a quick glance at the sky revealed only a few clouds scudding from the north to the south. A few yards away, below the short ledge where her camp was located, the sheep were ripping at the tender shoots of grass growing among the rocks and short clumps of sage. A few of the ewes wore bell collars, and now and then the gentle tinkles joined the whispers of the breeze sifting through the pines. The peaceful monotony was a sound that normally soothed Clementine, but today she was feeling more restless than she could ever remember.

These past few days she'd been reflecting a lot about Kipp and their lost home. But not nearly as much as she'd been thinking of Quint. She could easily imagine the things that kept him busy throughout his days. She'd lived on a ranch her entire life. The chores, both large and small, were never-ending, and she didn't have to wonder if he did his share. Judging by the perfect upkeep of the ranch, she figured all of the Hollister men were hard workers. But what did Quint do at night? Enjoy entertainment in town? Visit one of many girlfriends?

Damn, Clementine. What does any of that have to do

with you? Marty taught you a hard lesson about men and where their priorities lie. Don't be fooled with the notion that Quint might be different.

Disgusted with the voice in her head, she left the campfire and, after pulling on a ranch coat, started down the sloping ground to where the horses were grazing among the flock. She was nearing Birdie when both horses lifted their heads and stared curiously at the forest outlining the far end of the meadow.

When Peanut suddenly nickered loudly, Clementine knew someone was approaching.

Standing between the horses, she peered in the dense line of pines and aspens. Less than two minutes later, she saw a horse and rider emerge from the edge of the forest and immediately recognized Quint on a sorrel horse with a blazed face.

What had brought him out here today? Was he bringing her supplies a couple of days early? No. Not without a pack horse. Most likely he'd ridden out to make sure the sheep were all well and safely grouped.

Clementine remained where she stood and waited as he rode slowly through the large herd of woolly Merinos. The closer he grew to her, the faster her heart thumped. And the more she wanted to believe he'd ridden all this way just to see her.

Chapter Six

"Hello, Clementine." He climbed down from the saddle and, leading his horse behind him, came to stand directly in front of her.

"Hello, Quint."

Smiling, he inclined his head toward the dogs. "Looks like you have plenty of protection."

She couldn't believe how good it felt to let her eyes drink in the sight of his rugged face and tall, lean body. Today he was wearing a brown denim jacket over a hunter green shirt, and the earthy colors somehow made his blue eyes appear even more vivid.

"Yes. They know their jobs."

He drew in a deep breath and let it out, and Clementine got the impression he was feeling a bit awkward. About what, she couldn't possibly guess. It wasn't like he needed an excuse to show up at her camp, she thought. These were his sheep. This was his land. And she was his employee.

"So how are things going?" he asked.

Very quiet until he'd ridden up, she thought. Now her heart was thrumming loudly in her ears as though just seeing him was enough to cause it to sound alarm bells.

"Very well. No problems."

He glanced out at the flock of sheep. Except for a few frolicking lambs, most of the herd had ignored his arrival and continued to graze.

"The sheep look good."

"No sickness or injuries," she told him. "I've had an easy time of it."

"That's good to hear," he said.

She didn't know what it was about this guy, or why she reacted to him so strangely, but she had to admit that seeing him again was like seeing the sunrise. He lifted her spirits as nothing had in a long, long time.

"I'll just come out and say it, Clementine. I've been worried about you."

Two or three weeks ago, hearing that statement from a man would have irked her to no end. She didn't like her ability questioned. Yet with Quint, she somehow understood that he wasn't doubting her experience or skill as a sheepherder, he was thinking of her as a person—a woman.

"You shouldn't have been. Like I told you before, I'm an old hand at this."

His gaze slowly traveled from the hat on her head all the way down to her boots, and she couldn't discern if he was trying to gauge her capabilities, or merely sizing up her feminine attributes. Either way, the inspection left her feeling exposed in more ways than one.

He said, "Yes. I'm beginning to see that."

She breathed deeply, then gestured up the slope to where her campfire was sending a small swirl of smoke into the air. "Would you like to go up to the camp? There's a bit of coffee left on the fire if you'd like some."

His brows lifted, and Clementine suspected her invitation had surprised him. Frankly, it had surprised her. The last thing she needed to do was get overly friendly with her boss. But having coffee and a few words with the man could hardly be described as flirting, she assured herself.

"Thanks," he replied. "I'd like that. I've not had camp coffee since spring roundup. Cattle roundup, that is."

Clementine gestured to his horse. "You want to leave him here with my horses? Or take him up by the camp and tie his reins?"

"He'll be good right here."

He reached up and slipped the bridle completely off the horse's head, and the animal immediately went to grazing alongside Birdie and Peanut.

With the horse situated, he followed her up a narrow, rocky trail until they reached the wide ledge of ground where her tent and campfire were located.

Clementine gestured to the folding stool sitting a couple of feet away from the fire. "You take the chair," she said. "I prefer my log. I found it a couple of days ago up higher on the mountain. Peanut didn't have any trouble skidding it down here for me."

The log that was positioned directly on the opposite side of the fire ring had once been the fat trunk of a pine. Now the four-foot piece of wood was free of bark and bleached a light tan color. At night, Jimmy had taken to snuggling next to the log, and Clementine figured she'd skid the piece of makeshift furniture to her next camp to make the dog happy.

Quint said, "I don't need to take your one seat. It won't hurt me to stand."

"Nonsense. Sit and I'll pour the coffee."

He did as she insisted, and she filled two red granite cups with the strong, grainy coffee. Nearby, in the branches of an aspen, birds flittered and chirped while down in the meadow a pair of lambs bleated for their mothers, but to Clementine, the sounds of nature were muted by the heavy drum of her heart beating in her ears.

"Do you need cream or sugar?" she asked. "I only have the powdered kind of cream, but it's fairly tasty."

"Just a bit of sugar would be good."

She fetched the sugar from a plastic container and, after stirring a spoonful into the cup, handed him the steaming drink.

As soon as he'd sat down on the stool, he'd removed his leather work gloves, and now he wrapped both bare hands around the warm tin cup.

After taking a careful sip, he said, "This is good."

"It's not comparable to what you'd get in a coffeehouse, but it'll give you a kick," she said as she settled onto the log with her own cup.

He arched an inquisitive brow at her. "You know about coffeehouses?"

She leveled an indulgent little smile at him. "I haven't spent all my life sheepherding. I used to live not far from Pocatello, so I've been to town a few times."

"Sorry if you thought I was implying you were— hayseed. I didn't mean anything of the sort. It's just hard for me to imagine you sitting at one of those little glass tables with an espresso or some sort of frothy drink, while watching a busy stream of people walking up and down the sidewalk."

"Hmm. When I was a teenager and still in high school, my friends and I would drive into the city and do that sort of thing. At that age it's fun. Now I'd rather be sitting right where I am."

He glanced around him. "This is a fine place for a camp. How much longer do you plan on being here? Jett said you mentioned moving the flock on toward Snow Mountain."

"That's right. I'll probably push the sheep onward the day after Jett brings supplies. Right now, they're content, so they're still finding grass. About three days ago, a couple of the rams thought they were going to lead their ladies astray, but the dogs put a stop to their mischief."

"The dogs are getting along okay?" he asked.

Nodding, she said, "The Pyrenees were a little cautious at first, but now they're a part of the family. I think Jimmy and Jewel like the extra company."

He looked down to the meadow where three of the dogs were sitting on their haunches, diligently watching the flock, then to Jimmy. The male collie had chosen to follow Clementine and was now stretched out on his belly some several yards away with his attention carefully zoned in on her and Quint.

"Looks like this one thinks you need to be protected as much as the sheep," Quint commented.

Clementine glanced over her shoulder at Jimmy and the dog perked his ears.

"Sometimes I worry because he likes me too much. I try not to encourage him. But he's been that way since he was a baby. Most shepherds would've already sold him. But I'm soft, I guess." She shrugged and wondered what was pushing all these words from her mouth. Normally she only spoke what was necessary. "Anyway, Jimmy does his job and his sister keeps him in line."

He let out an amused grunt. "My sisters try the same thing with me. But I'm not as compliant as Jimmy."

During the short lunch she'd had with Quint and his parents on the day he'd showed her around the ranch, Clementine had learned he had twin sisters, Bonnie and Beatrice, who were two years younger than him. Along with an older sister, Grace, who was a medical doctor. Usually, Clementine didn't meet any family members of the ranch owners she worked for, but the Hollisters had made it all seem perfectly normal. Yet that day had messed with her thinking a bit too much. It wasn't healthy to let her thoughts dwell on Quint and his family.

She swallowed as the urge to sigh struck her. "I'm not surprised," she said. "My brother isn't compliant, either."

He smiled faintly, and for the next couple of minutes he seemed content to drink his coffee and survey the flock. Clementine tried to concentrate on everything but him, but it was hard not to take note of his rugged face, broad shoulders and long legs encased in worn denim. He was the perfect image of a working cowboy and she was drawn to him in ways that shocked her.

Eventually, he broke the silence by asking, "What about coyotes? Had any trouble with them?"

"No. I've heard them in the far distance but not seen any. I'd be surprised if a pack wanted to take on four dogs. But I won't let my guard down. Neither will the dogs. They sleep with one eye open," she told him.

A lopsided grin twisted his lips. "And you? How do you sleep? With one eye open, also?"

"No. With one hand on my Winchester."

His brows lifted. "Guess that's the safest way of getting a restful night."

She felt a smile spreading over her lips, and the spontaneous reaction took her by surprise. How was this guy managing to make her do things she normally didn't do? She was being silly.

"Actually, I don't sleep with my hand on my rifle," she admitted. "But I do keep it near."

"So you were only joking?" he asked.

She very nearly laughed at the skeptical look on his face. "Yes. I do know how to joke."

He let out a long breath, then gave her one of those grins of his that made the pit of her stomach do funny little jig dances.

He said, "Well, we do see bear signs around the ranch from time to time. Especially up near our grandfather's old cabin."

She looked at him with interest. "You have an old cabin on the ranch? Where is it?"

"East of here." He twisted around on the canvas stool and pointed toward a line of sharp mountain peaks. "It's near the top of the middle peak. Once you get up there you can see for miles."

She gazed at the spot he was pointing to. "Wow! That's getting on up in high elevation. Is it a log cabin?"

He nodded. "Logs were the only material he didn't have to haul up the mountainside. But it does have two little glass windows. How he managed to get those up there without breaking them is a good question."

Turning her gaze back to his face, she said, "I suppose you and your brothers probably use the place for a hunting cabin."

"No. None of us hunt. But our grandfather did. At least, that was his excuse for going up to the cabin. Although, we never saw him return to the ranch with any game."

As she studied his face, she realized this was the first time in years that she'd found herself interested in a man's conversation. And her fascination wasn't brought on by the simple fact that he was darned good-looking.

No, there was something about the way he had of looking at her whenever she spoke. As if he was listening intently to every word and considered what she had to say important to him.

She sipped her coffee, then forced her gaze on the low flames of the fire. "Is your grandfather still living?"

"No. Lionel Hollister died eight or nine years ago."

She lifted her gaze back to his face, and judging from the faraway look in his eyes, he was reflecting on something in the past.

"Did he always live here on the ranch, too?"

He nodded. "Grandfather did more than live here. He built this ranch from nothing but untamed land and a dream. Without him there wouldn't be any Stone Creek Ranch."

"He must've been quite a man," she replied. "What about your grandmother? Is she still living?"

He cleared his throat, then grimaced as though he was trying to swallow a chunk of green persimmon. "We don't know. His wife left the family a long time ago. She'd be pretty old now. But it's possible she could be living."

Clementine didn't miss the fact that he'd avoided calling the woman his grandmother. Which surprised her somewhat. After meeting Quint's parents, it was hard to imagine the Hollister family going through such discord. But she supposed they were like any regular family who'd suffered through troubles and trials.

"Sorry. I shouldn't have asked," she said.

"Why? Nothing wrong with asking. And it's not like we've ever tried to keep their split a secret. Divorces happen in plenty of families. I guess in my grandfather's case, what made it so exceptionally awful was that they had three very young sons, and once she left, she never saw them again."

The revelation shouldn't have surprised her. After all she and Kipp had gone through because of their father's divorce, she'd learned just how selfish and uncaring a parent could be. Especially when it came to their children. But deserting them completely was a whole other matter.

"That's tough." She gestured toward the sheep. "Not one of those ewes in your flock would leave her babies behind. If you do have one that rejects her babies, then you need to ship her to the sale barn and get rid of her as fast as you can. Because I can promise you she won't develop a heart."

"Yes, that's a hard lesson I learned when I was a young boy. We had a mare who refused her baby. Dad didn't get rid of her. But he never allowed her to have another foal. It was sad."

He drained the last of his coffee, then set the cup on one of the stones that made up the fire ring. "Speaking of babies, our family got some news last night," he said. "My older brother Jack and his wife, Van, are expecting a baby in March. They're both pretty much on top of the world. So are my parents. They've been wanting more grandchildren."

If Clementine's father had lived, she supposed he would've enjoyed a grandchild or two. That is, as long as she and Kipp had married spouses of his choosing. But who would've ever lived up to his standards? When it had come to his family, Trent Starr had been a controlling type of man. He'd wanted to dictate both of his children's personal lives. So much so that Clementine had ended up losing the only man she'd ever grown close to. She supposed her father's domineering behavior had stemmed from their mother divorcing him. Naturally, he'd not wanted the same heartache and mistakes for his own children. But Trent's failed marriages had been his own fault. He'd just never wanted to admit his shortcomings.

"That is happy news. I'm sure your parents are celebrating."

"Yeah. We had a big family dinner last night. Everyone was there except our big brother, Hunter." He leaned forward and touched a finger to the handle of the coffeepot to test the warmth of the handle before he poured a measurable amount into his cup. "But we shared the news with him over the phone."

"Sounds like you approve of your brother and sister-in-law becoming parents."

"Sure. Jack really wants to be a father and he and Van have been married for a while now. I think he was beginning to doubt it was going to happen."

Clementine had quit picturing herself as a mother a long time ago. But that didn't mean she thought all women should follow her example. No. She was different. She wasn't cut out for love, or marriage, or family.

"Good for them and your parents."

Across the low, smoky fire, his gaze met hers. "Have you ever wanted to be a mother, Clementine?"

The question was a simple one, albeit a bit personal. Did he feel as though he knew her well enough to talk to her about such private matters? The idea was disturbing. She didn't want any man to know what was going on deep inside her.

"I don't mind you asking the question," she said after a moment. "But I'm curious as to why you wanted to know."

He didn't blink or look away, and she suddenly forgot that he was seven years younger and, along with the age difference, also her boss. This time she didn't have to wonder if he was looking at her as a man looks at a woman. She recognized a glint of appreciation in his eyes, and the sight of it made her tremble inwardly.

"Because when I look at you I see you as a wife and mother. Don't ask me why. I just do."

His words struck her hard. Or was it the low and gravelly sound of his voice that had gotten under her skin? Either way, she couldn't continue to hold his gaze. Before she realized what she was about to do, she stood and walked over to the edge of the ledge.

"You're only seeing the surface, Quint. I'm not like the women in your life. But in a way, you've flattered me. Being a wife and mother are admirable roles for any woman. They're just not for me."

"Why?"

The single word was spoken directly behind her left shoulder, and she realized with a start that he'd followed her away from the fire.

She swallowed. "Some people are destined to be certain things. Like you were meant to be a cowboy—a sheepman. Well, I was destined to be a sheepherder. And this life of mine isn't made for having babies—or a husband."

"I like to think I have a choice about my future, instead of just leaving it to destiny."

She shrugged, even though she was feeling far from indifferent. "Destiny. Choices. I believe the two are intertwined. Anyway, we're doing what we want. And that's the bottom line, don't you think?"

She heard him sigh, and then he stepped forward so that he was standing directly at her side.

"Yeah, the bottom line," he murmured.

A few moments of silence ticked by, and Clementine was wondering what she could do or say to get rid of him. Not that she wanted him to leave. Not really. But she wasn't sure her heart could hold up to this mad race he was taking it on.

"Would you care to go for a ride?"

His question broke the silence and brought her head around.

Staring at him blankly, she asked, "You mean on the horses?"

His lips twitched ever so slightly. "What other kind of ride would I be talking about?"

Oh, my, how had such a stupid response come out of her mouth? As the question dashed through her mind, embarrassed heat washed over her face.

"Excuse me—I was—my thoughts were far away," she attempted to explain her inane response. "But yes, a ride would be fine with me. Was there something you thought I should see?"

"You plan on moving toward Snow Mountain in a couple of days, and I thought we might scout out the area. And there's something south of there that I'd like to check out."

She had no idea what the *something* might be, but it hardly mattered. In spite of her better judgment, she wanted Quint's company.

"In that case, I'll saddle Peanut and we'll ride," she told him.

A few minutes later, as they rode away from the camp, Jimmy followed on Peanut's heels and Clementine immediately called his name and made a hand gesture to send him back to his sister and the herd.

The dog obeyed, but Quint could see the animal wasn't

thrilled about the order she'd given him. "It wouldn't have hurt for him to go with us, would it? I mean, if three dogs can't handle the flock, they're not worth their weight in salt."

He watched her lips press together in disapproval as she nudged the gelding forward. "Jimmy needs to understand his job. And that is to guard the sheep. Not me."

Even though her voice was firm, Quint got the impression it bothered her just as much as it had him, to send the dog back to camp. She just didn't want Quint to guess she had a soft spot.

Soft spot? Hell, what was he thinking? The woman was tough as nails. Tougher than he could ever be. Was he trying to kid himself into believing she could develop a soft spot for him?

Why not, Quint? In the past, you've never had any problem charming a woman into your way of thinking. Why should Clementine be any different?

Because she was different, he argued back at the little voice banging around in his head. And anyway, he was all wrong in looking at Clementine in a romantic way. She wasn't interested in having a relationship with him or any man. She'd more or less made that clear a few minutes ago when she'd talked about sheepherding being her life. He shouldn't be wasting his time on her. And yet, something felt so very right whenever he was near her.

Trying to shake away the troubling thoughts, Quint glanced over at her. "There are several meadows between your present camp and Snow Mountain," he said. "Were you planning on setting up at the nearest one?"

"Probably. It's not far from a creek. So plenty of water will be there for the livestock and me."

"That would be Bird Creek. We have to be in a severe drought for it to go dry. Thankfully this year has been a bit better about snow and rainfall. I didn't think to ask earlier, but where are the sheep currently watering?"

"There's a small pool on the lower slope of the meadow at the edge of the tree line. It stays full from a natural spring several yards above it."

He shot her a guilty grin. "I confess. My brothers and I have covered lots of miles on this ranch, but there are still sections of it that are new to me. I had no idea there was a spring in that area."

"I just happened to stumble upon it."

Quint very much doubted Clementine ever simply stumbled on anything. Whether she was in the mountains or the desert, he figured she was more than adept at finding what her flock needed. In fact, when it came to sheep, she made him feel like a green horn.

"I don't believe luck factors into anything you do, Clementine."

She arched a brow at him. "You're right. I can't rely on luck. Only myself."

Earlier, before he'd ridden up to find her standing out among the sheep, he'd thought he might find her looking more like a typical sheepherder. After all, she'd been out here in the wild for nearly two weeks now. He'd expected her hair to look dull with dust, her lips and skin dry and drawn. Because she'd packed in all her belongings on Peanut, she couldn't have brought but a handful of clothes with her, so he'd definitely assumed her jeans and shirt would be somewhat grimy with soil. He'd been wrong on all counts. A fact that totally amazed him. Everything about her looked fresh. From the long black braid falling over her shoulder, to her faded jeans and melon-colored shirt.

Quint, you've dated all sorts of pretty women. And you'd been physically drawn to each of them in one way or another. Clementine isn't any more attractive or more desirable. She's only stuck in your mind because she's an anomaly.

No. That wasn't true, he mentally argued with the inner voice. Yes, she was intriguing because she was different. But there were so many other things that drew him to her. The way she walked, the sound of her voice, how she went quiet and thoughtful whenever he spoke to her, and the gentleness of her hands whenever she touched the dogs and horses. Everything about her made him want to get close to her.

They rode on westward for nearly an hour before they came to a barbed wire fence that stretched north toward the mountains and south to a stand of evergreens.

"This is something I've not seen on Stone Creek before," she said. "A fence."

Quint reined his horse to a halt and stepped down from the saddle. Clementine did the same, and the two of them walked over to the fence.

"The land beyond this fence was the something I wanted to see," he explained. "Last night at dinner, Dad announced that he'd just purchased this adjoining farm from the Barkleys. It's going to add ten thousand more acres to the ranch."

Her brown eyes turned a skeptical look on him. "Your father must think the land will be profitable. Does he plan to keep it or resell it?"

"Once Dad purchases land, he'd never turn loose of even one acre. No. He's going to use it to run Red Angus. Which should work. There's more grassland on the Barkley place." He turned a knowing grin on her. "When the right time comes, I'm going to point out that I could use some of the grazing area for the sheep I plan on buying soon."

"You believe he's going to go along with that idea?"

"I hope so. There's enough land to share, I think. And Dad knows how much I want to expand our wool production. Actually, there are more things I want besides more land and sheep. I want to build a special shearing barn and another for shelter when the weather gets brutal and the lambs start dropping. Presently, we only have a small portion of a barn set aside for the sheep. But I plan to make changes for the better."

She continued to study his face, and as he looked into her brown eyes, he suddenly struggled to remember what he'd been saying. All he could think was that only the width of a hand separated them. He could smell a flowery scent drifting from her hair and see the sheen of moisture on her bottom lip. A lip he very much wanted to kiss.

"You think Hadley will go along with all your plans?"

"Maybe not all at once. But eventually, he will. He wants me to succeed with the sheep."

The corners of her lips turned slightly downward. "Dreams don't always come true, Quint. I hope yours don't get squashed."

He frowned. "Why would you think in such a negative way? Because you consider me too young and naive and full of pipe dreams?"

She glanced away from him. "No. I'm not doubting your ability. It's just that—well, I've lived a lot longer than you and I've learned that plans don't often work out. Hopes and dreams are just something we have when—"

Her voice trailed away, and as his gaze slipped over

her solemn profile, he wondered what could've possibly gone on in her life to leave her so dispirited.

"When?" he gently urged.

Her sigh reminded him of a lonesome wind whistling across a cold valley. The sound chilled him.

"When there's nothing left to hold on to," she finished.

Her expression remained stoic as she continued to gaze out at the stretch of green pasture, and he realized something or someone had clearly taken the sunshine from her life. He wanted to prod her into telling him everything about herself and why she carried such sadness. But he recognized it was too soon for him to pry into her personal life. He needed to give her time to feel comfortable with him.

Today she'd talked more than he'd ever expected. Which gave him hope that she would eventually open up to him. But would revealing her past heartaches and secrets to him ultimately draw her closer? He couldn't answer that question. He only knew he wouldn't rest until he felt her arms come around him and her lips pressing eagerly to his.

"I'm sorry you feel that way, Clem. Because I'm not a man who gives up on a dream. Not for any reason."

Turning slightly, she looked up at him. "It's nice that you're not afraid to dream. Maybe you'll get all those things you want."

All those things included her, Quint thought. She just didn't know it yet. But she would in time.

He gave one last glance at the land across the fence, then slipping a hand beneath her elbow, he urged her in the direction of the waiting horses.

"We'd better mount up. I have a long ride home," he told her.

* * *

Clementine was quiet as the two of them rode side by side back to her camp. But Quint hadn't really expected her to talk. He figured she'd already said all she intended to say. And she was hardly the sort of woman to chatter on about inconsequential matters.

Yet in spite of the silence, Quint felt connected to her in a way he didn't quite understand. He only knew it was a nice feeling, and when the sight of the camp appeared in the distance, he was almost sorry the ride was ending.

"You might want to write down anything extra you might want added to your supply list. Chance is going into town tomorrow and will pick up whatever you'd like."

"Thanks. I would like some extra fresh fruit."

"That's all?"

She glanced at him. "I've never been high maintenance."

Obviously she was joking in her own dry fashion, yet Quint also knew there was a wealth of truth in her comment. She clearly didn't want for much. At least, not in the form of material things.

Chuckling, he said, "Nice to know I won't be forced to put a cap on your spending."

She didn't reply, but he thought he saw her lips twitch, and the idea that he'd amused her was enough to please him.

A moment later, as they rode into camp, she said, "No need for you to get down from your horse, Quint. I'll be right back with the list."

"No bother. I need the exercise, anyway," he told her.

She shrugged. "Suit yourself."

While she disappeared into the tent, Quint climbed down from the saddle and walked over to the edge of the ledge. The sheep had migrated down the slope but were still safely in the meadow with the dogs watching them from different angles.

The sight of the flock never failed to lift his spirits. Especially when he thought of how proud his grandfather Lionel would be if he could see this year's lamb crop. He often wished the old man was still here to share in the joy of seeing the sheep healthy and growing. His brothers had always been more partial to raising cattle, and his dad, though he liked the sheep, didn't love them nearly as much as Quint. As a result, he'd always felt a bit alone with his sheep project. Until Clementine had come along. Now, as far as the sheep were concerned, he felt as if she was his kindred spirit.

The sound of footsteps alerted Quint of her approach, and he turned to see her walking toward him. She'd left her felt hat in the tent and now the late afternoon sun glinted off the crown of her black hair. If he ever had the chance to slide his fingers into the long strands, he knew it would feel soft and smooth. Just like her skin would feel. And just like her lips would taste.

"Here's the list. And if you don't mind, I'd appreciate someone mailing this letter for me. Every couple of weeks, I usually send my brother an update on how things are going with me. I don't like him to worry."

There were still times that Quint had to remind himself that she couldn't simply pick up a cell phone and call whomever and whenever she wanted. Even if she could get a signal out here in the mountains, there was no way to keep the phone powered.

He took the envelope along with a small square of paper from her and stuck them into a pocket on the front of his Western shirt. "I'll make sure it gets in the mail," he promised, then added, "You know, Clem, if you'd like to call your brother, it's perfectly fine with me if you want to ride into the ranch. The dogs will take care of the sheep while you're gone."

She shook her head. "No. He doesn't expect any more than a letter from me. If I called while I was on the job, he'd think something was wrong."

So she corresponded with her brother by letter twice a month. It wasn't much communication, but more than he'd expected from her.

"Okay. Just thought I'd offer."

Glancing away from him, she said, "Guess that sounds odd to you. But we're not like you Hollisters. Kipp does his thing and I do mine. But we're close. We don't forget we're siblings."

From where they were standing, the sunlight was filtering through the limbs of an aspen, and as the leaves flickered in the breeze, so did the patches of light and shadows on her face. And as he studied her slanted cheekbones and the line of her lips, he wondered if she ever longed for a man to kiss her, make love to her. Had she ever felt passionate about any man?

The questions were unsettling to Quint. Mainly because he didn't want to imagine her making hot, passionate love to anyone but him.

Clearing his throat, he tried to shove away his thoughts. "It's good that you have him," he said, then drew in a deep breath and let it out. "I'd better be going."

She glanced at the lowering sun. "Yes. It's not wise to ride at night. Unless you have to."

"Well, thanks for the coffee. And the company."

"You're welcome."

She turned her brown eyes on his face, and try as he might, he couldn't stop his gaze from dropping to her lips.

"Am I? Really?" he asked.

Her nostrils flared faintly as she drew in a deep breath, and for a split second Quint considered reaching for her just to see how she'd respond. But he didn't want to tear down all the progress he'd made with her today. At least, progress in the way of becoming her friend. And for right now he had to be content with that much.

"What kind of question is that?"

Grinning faintly, he said, "I'm never quite sure about you, Clementine. But I guess a man is never supposed to be entirely sure about a woman, now, is he?"

"Not this woman."

The annoyed expression on her face caused him to chuckle. "Take care, Clem."

She didn't follow him as he walked over to his horse and swung himself into the saddle. But as he rode away, she lifted her hand in farewell. And to Quint that was almost as good as a kiss.

Chapter Seven

Clementine emptied the syringe filled with antibiotic high upon the lamb's neck, then gently massaged the injection spot before untying the small rope securing its legs.

"There you go, little one. By the end of the day you're going to feel like kicking up your heels," she said to animal.

The lamb quickly climbed to his feet, then scurried to join the rest of the flock. She watched until the lamb was reunited with his mother, then rising from her squatted position, she scanned the herd to make sure she'd not missed any other showing signs of respiratory distress.

This past week she'd doctored several of the lambs, who'd come down with what a human would consider the sniffles. So far all had recovered nicely and she hoped the strain was starting to wane. Especially before Quint showed up again. If or when that might be.

Three weeks had passed since the day he'd ridden up

and surprised her with his unplanned visit. And since then she'd not been able to think of much else but him.

Damn the man! He'd ruined everything for her. Normally, she'd be enjoying the brisk fall air, the glorious gold color appearing on the aspen leaves and the coats on the sheep growing long and thick in anticipation of winter to come. Yet instead of getting pleasure from nature's changes, she was constantly thinking about the man and watching for him to ride up again.

Something had happened to her that day he'd arrived at her camp. The moment he climbed off his horse and walked up to her it was like she'd been hypnotized. She'd wanted to walk with him, talk with him and even sit in silence with him. But even more, she'd wanted to touch him, to discover how it would feel if he kissed her, made love to her.

There had been moments during his stay that she'd gotten the impression he was thinking the same things about her. But he'd not reached for her in any way. He'd not implied with words or touches that he wanted her. When he'd ridden away she'd felt frustrated and lonely and very foolish.

Hungering for a young cowboy like Quint was ridiculous, and yet night after night, she'd been tormenting herself with images of him in the arms of a woman ten or twelve years younger than herself. The faceless woman was always wearing soft, feminine clothing with pretty jewelry. Her nails were painted and perfectly shaped, her hair smooth and glossy. No, she thought sadly. Quint wouldn't be out on the town with a woman like Clementine. He didn't want a woman like her, period. Not even for a brief affair.

Don't tell me you'd be willing to have an affair with Quint! Talk about stupid! You'd be asking for an even bigger heartache than what you went through with Marty. Is that what you want? To have your heart torn out and tossed away? Besides, you don't want to be like the women Quint dates. That's not you!

Her thoughts were suddenly interrupted as Lash barked, followed by a high-pitched yip from Jimmy.

"Hey, there, Clementine!"

The sound of Jett's voice brought her head around to see the young man riding out of the thick stand of aspens. She was always glad to see the friendly ranch hand. He liked chatting about the sheep and giving her offhand news about the work going on around the ranch. Yet she had to admit she was disappointed that the rider hadn't been Quint.

"Hello, Jett. What brings you out today?"

He climbed down from the black gelding and pushed his hat off his forehead. "Cord sent me out this way to check on a fence and Quint wanted me to stop by your camp and give you a message."

A message. Apparently it wasn't anything vitally important, otherwise he would have ridden out and given it to her firsthand.

Clementine unconsciously buttoned the top button on her sherpa-lined jacket as a chilly wind swept through the trees and onto the flats where they were standing.

Three weeks ago, she'd moved the flock to the base of Snow Mountain, and so far there was still enough grass to keep the animals sufficiently fed. But if the weather continued to grow colder, she knew it was only a matter of time before she'd have to head them back toward ranch headquarters to make it more convenient to feed them alfalfa.

"He thinks I should turn the flock back east?"

Frowning, Jett scratched his forehead. "I asked him

about that very thing. Not that it's my business," he said, then gestured out at the grazing sheep. "But the grass can't last much longer."

Just hearing this young man voice her own thoughts out loud left a heavy weight on her shoulders.

"What did he say?"

"Said not yet. Said when the time comes you'd know exactly what to do."

The information struck her with a mixture of pleasure and pain. To hear Quint trusted her judgment was nice indeed. And yet in the back of her mind, she knew her time here on Stone Creek was dwindling down. Which was not something she should feel sad about. When she'd taken the job, she'd been aware there was only a short amount of grazing season left.

"Oh," she finally said. "Then what was the message?"

"Quint says you've been back here in the mountains for a good while now. He thought you might want to go out for a couple of days and make a trip to town or something. Just to have a break. I can stay here and watch the flock."

Even if Quint had extended the offer to her in person she would refuse. For one thing, she had no desire to explore the streets of Beaver and shop for things she could never put to use while sheepherding. And secondly, as much as she'd like to see Quint again, she was very much afraid she'd end up making a fool of herself.

"Well, you can tell him that I appreciate the offer, but no thanks. I don't need a day or two off. I'm fine with being right here."

Jett grunted. "I told him that would be your response."

"I'm sorry you wasted your time with the message, Jett. But you're welcome to a cup of coffee while you're here. I made a fresh pot about an hour ago."

He glanced over to her camp, where lately she'd kept a fire burning until she went to bed at night.

"Thanks. It sounds tempting, but I'd better get on with the chore Cord gave me to do. The Red Angus for the old Barkley farm will be arriving soon. Got to make sure the fence in this section is still solid." He gestured toward his horse. "I have a few things for you in the saddlebag. Quint thought you might enjoy some fresh food."

Was that all Quint had been thinking about her? Whether she needed fresh food or rest?

What else would you expect him to be thinking about you, Clementine? Like how attractive and irresistible you are? Damn, a man spends a couple of hours with you for one day out of the past three weeks and you get to dreaming he has the hots for you!

"Uh—that's nice. I can always use fresh food."

She followed him over to his horse, where he untied the saddlebags and carried the leather satchels over to the entrance of her tent.

"Where do you want me to put these things?" he asked as he began to pull out plastic sacks filled with fruit. "There are bananas, apples, oranges, grapes and strawberries."

"I have a food bag to keep everything from bear reach," she told him. "Just a minute. I'll have to shimmy up a tree to fetch it."

He frowned. "Where is it? I'll take Champ and you can stand in his saddle. He won't mind. I've done it before."

She let out a short laugh. "I'd rather climb. I'm not much of a trick rider."

Five minutes later, she came down the tree with the bag and he filled it with the fruit. "Mmm. Smells delicious," she said. "This is going to be a treat. Thanks for bringing it by, Jett. And—please thank Quint for me."

"Sure," he said, then awkwardly cleared his throat. "Uh—Clementine, I probably shouldn't say this and God help me if Quint ever found out, cause he'd want to kick my rear end! But I figure he won't ever hear it from you."

She was staring at him now, her mind whirling as she tried to figure out what was on this young cowboy's mind. "Is whatever you're going to say some sort of secret?"

He shrugged. "Not really. It's just that I know Quint really good—uh, or should I have said really well? I don't know. I never was too good with grammar."

"But you can rope a cow or ewe if you need to, right?" she asked with a faint smile.

He smiled. "Yeah. And what I'm trying to say is that I can tell that Quint really likes you."

Clementine's heart thumped. A silly reaction considering Jett was just repeating his own thoughts, not Quint's.

"Likes me? I—uh—if you're meaning as a girlfriend, then you're way off base, Jett. I believe he trusts me with his flock. And he might like me as just a friend. But the rest—no. I mean—" she broke off as a short, cynical laugh burst out of her. "He's a Hollister."

"So? What's his last name got to do with anything? He's just a man."

Yeah, just a man who could have most any woman he crooked his finger at, she thought dismally. "You're a nice young man, Jett. But none of this—well, even if Quint liked me in that way—I'm not in the market for a guy."

"Oh. I see." He grimaced and shook his head. "Sorry

if I've embarrassed you, Clementine. It's just that Quint's like a brother to me, and I was sort of hoping to put in a good word for him. See, he'd never admit it, but he's kinda shy."

Shy? The urge to burst out laughing hit her again, but this time she managed to stifle the reaction. "You know, Jett, winter will be here before long. It wouldn't be wise for me to strike up a relationship with Quint while knowing I'll have to be leaving before too long."

He looked positively glum. "Gosh, I don't believe Quint would—"

She waited for him to go on, and when he didn't, she decided he'd been about to say something better left unsaid.

Tugging his hat down lower on his forehead, he turned and started toward the gelding. "I'd better be going before I really get in trouble. See you, Clementine."

He mounted the black horse, and as she watched him ride off, she had to wonder just how well the young man did know Quint. And if he was right about Quint liking her, just what could it mean? Nothing, really.

The sooner she pounded that into her brain, the better off she'd be.

Later that night, Quint was staring into a glass of beer while the walls of the bar practically shook from the loud music blaring from a jukebox at the back of the room. On the opposite wall from the long, polished bar where he was sitting, Chance and Jett were playing a round of pool.

When Quint had told the two men he was driving into town for a beer and invited them to join him, they'd happily accepted. But so far tonight, the two men hadn't been much company. Which was probably his own fault. He'd been in a sour mood ever since Jett had returned to the ranch yard and given him Clementine's response to taking a couple of days off work.

She was just fine where she was—she didn't need time away from her work.

Darn it, just what kind of woman was she? Didn't she ever want to be sociable? To live like a normal person?

"Hey, cowboy, how about buying a girl a drink?"

Annoyed at the voice interrupting his thoughts, but trying not to show it, Quint glanced over at the pretty blonde climbing onto the bar stool next to him. He'd known Julie since high school and had dated her occasionally, but never seriously. Tonight she was dressed in a red sequined blouse and a black leather skirt slit up on one pale thigh. Her hair was lying in perfectly ironed waves on her shoulders, while long, false eyelashes fluttered over blue eyes. At one time, he'd considered this woman gorgeous. Now he thought she looked garishly fake. Had she changed or had he?

"Hello, Julie."

She gave the bartender her order, then turned a wide, seductive smile on him. Normally, her suggestive greeting would have sparked his interest. Now the thought of getting close to this woman made him want to run to the hills, literally.

Oh, Lord, even when he was in town at his favorite bar, he was thinking of the mountains. More precisely the black-haired beauty camped in the foothills. No matter how many beers he drank or how many women he dated, her dark brown eyes haunted him. Unlike the constant flash of Julie's come-hither smiles, Clementine's soft pink lips rarely ever curved upward. But when they did, it was like the sun breaking through a bank of storm clouds.

"Is that all you have to say? Just hello?" Julie asked.

He said, "I've had a busy day and have lots of things on my mind."

She sniffed as the bartender placed a wine cooler in front of her. "I thought you'd be happy to see me. We had such a good time when we went to the concert down in Cedar City a couple of months ago. So why haven't you called me? I finally gave up on you and went out with David Lowry. But to be honest, Quint, he was boring. And I…"

Julie's voice turned into a dim drone as Quint's thoughts returned to the base of Snow Mountain and Clementine's camp. Most likely she'd be sitting by the fire right now, trying to stay warm in the dropping temperatures. She'd probably poured herself a cup of coffee from the granite pot and was sipping the hot brew and gazing up at the stars. No doubt Jimmy would be somewhere nearby. The collie adored her and Quint could hardly blame the dog. She was impossible to resist.

He'd not seen Clementine since the day the two of them had ridden to the Barkley boundary fence. Not that he'd stayed away from her camp on purpose. Ever since Hadley had made the land and cattle deal, no one on the ranch had had a chance to draw a deep breath. Each time Quint had tried to make a trip to visit Clementine, another chore had stood in the way.

When Cordell had sent Jett out today to give the boundary fence one last inspection, Quint had jumped at the opportunity to send her an invitation to come out to the ranch for a day or two. After all this time, he'd thought she'd surely like the idea of standing beneath a hot shower and eating food that hadn't come out of a can. But she'd turned down his invitation. Telling Jett, thanks, but no thanks.

Was she that averse to being around people? Or did she simply want to avoid seeing him?

Hell, Quint! What makes you think you made that much impression on Clementine? Just because you thought you saw a glimmer in her brown eyes? Just because she talked to you? Women talk to you every day. That doesn't mean they want you in their bed, their life. "…he brought that new car, you remember, the red foreign thing. He ended up totaling it on the way to St. George when he ran into the back of a mail truck. It was a miracle he wasn't killed, and sometimes I wonder if he'd wrecked on purpose. You know, the insurance and all. Stephanie says he's already burned through his inheritance, but is anyone surprised over that? He's a jerk. I hate that my sister won't divorce him. A woman doesn't have to put up with that kind of crap nowadays. And…"

Pushing his empty beer glass aside, Quint looked over at the pretty blonde. "You're going to have to excuse me, Julie. My friends are waiting on me."

She spluttered in shock as he slid off the bar stool. "But Quint—the night has just started! I thought we'd—"

"Some other time, Julie." Like a million years from now.

He walked to the other side of the room where Chance and Jett were just finishing a game at one of the pool tables.

Chance, a tall man in his early thirties with dark hair and broad muscular shoulders, had worked for Stone Creek ranch for more than ten years. Before he'd come to the ranch, he'd had a wife, but something had happened to end the marriage. Something that Chance refused to talk about. Jett was constantly trying to set him up with a woman, and sometimes he did give in and go on a date. But he didn't want a serious relationship and Quint could hardly blame him.

"Hey, Quint, how about a game? Jett's no match for me," Chance joked.

"Okay, Chance, I'll take you on. Just don't cry in your beer whenever I beat you," Quint told him.

Jett handed the pool stick over to Quint. "What about Julie?" he asked with a clever grin. "She might not want to wait around while you play pool."

Quint muttered a curse word under his breath. "I must have been suffering from some sort of mental lapse to go out with her."

"Why?" Jett asked. "She's a real looker."

Frowning, Quint said, "She has a problem I just can't deal with."

Jett's eyebrows arched in question. "What's that?"

"Her mouth. It never closes."

A knowing expression crossed Jett's face. "I get it. You prefer the quiet type."

Quint shot him a look of warning. "I don't want to discuss Clem tonight."

Jett rolled his eyes. "All I'm going to say is that you better do something fast. She's thinking she'll be leaving in a month or two. In case you've forgotten, winter comes around here whether you want it to or not."

Leaving? No. Quint couldn't handle the possibility of Clementine moving away from Stone Creek. To think of never seeing her again just wasn't acceptable.

His jaw set in a rigid line, he muttered to Jett, "Yeah, but winter isn't here yet."

"Hey, is somebody down there going to play? If not,

I'm going to the bar," Chance called from the far end of the table.

"Rack them up, Chance. I'm coming."

Early the next morning, Quint was sitting at the breakfast table eating the last of a biscuit and washing it down with coffee when Cordell entered the kitchen wearing an oil duster. Raindrops spotted the shoulders and his black cowboy hat.

Quint took one look at his brother and groaned. "Don't tell me it's raining!"

Frowning, Cordell pulled off the duster and headed straight to the cabinet and the coffeepot. "It is. And you should be celebrating, not complaining, little brother."

Wiping a weary hand over his face, Quint said, "Yeah, I understand we need the rain. But I—"

His cup in hand, Cordell walked over and joined him at the table. "You what?"

Blowing out a heavy breath, he said, "I know the cattle are coming today and you guys might need extra help, but I—I need to ride out to the sheep camp. Jett was out there yesterday and said Clementine has been doctoring a few of the lambs for the sniffles. It could just be the cooling weather, but I want to make sure they're not suffering from nasal bots. If so, the whole herd will need to be dosed for parasites."

"If she needed help, don't you think she'd ride in and tell you so?"

Quint frowned. "She'd never put the flock in danger. Not out of negligence. But sometimes these things are hard to diagnose in sheep."

Regarding him over the rim of his cup, Cordell said, "So you want to check the sheep out for yourself. And see Clementine while you're at it."

Gazing into the brown liquid in his cup, he said, "Why do you say that? Why does Jett keep telling me to go see Clementine? You'd think I had her name tattooed on my forehead or something!"

"Oh, come on, Quint. You've made it pretty clear to me that you're infatuated with the woman. Why try to deny it?"

Shaking his head, Quint placed silverware on his empty plate and pushed it aside. "Probably because I have the feeling it's a hopeless thing."

"Why do you think it's hopeless? She told you so?"

Quint snorted. "No! She doesn't even know I'm interested. I can't summon up the courage to talk to her about it."

Cordell groaned with disbelief. "You're joking. Right? This is my little brother Quint? The one who's loved girls since he entered middle school?"

"Yeah, I know it doesn't sound like me. But Clem is—well, she's been alone for a long time. She doesn't want a traditional life with a husband and kids."

"How do you know she doesn't?"

"She told me."

Before Cordell could reply to that revelation, Quint rose and carried his dirty dishes over to the sink.

Behind him, Cordell said, "So that's what she thinks now. It's up to you to change her mind. That is—if that's what you want—a family with her."

Did he want Clementine for the long haul? Could he see himself settling down with her? Incredibly, he could see himself having babies and making a home with her. But she wasn't seeing herself in that role and there lay the problem.

"Cord, I've not even kissed Clementine! How could

I possibly plan my future around something that's just a—thought in my mind?"

"Hell, Quint, what are you waiting on? Grass to grow under your feet?"

Frustrated, Quint walked back over to the table and picked up his coffee cup. "No. I'm wondering how I might look with a red handprint on my face," he said with a wealth of sarcasm.

Grunting, Cordell said, "I'd rather risk being slapped than lose my chance with the woman I wanted. Question is, are you willing to risk going through a bit of pain for her?"

He let out a long breath. A bit of pain? He'd walk through fire if he thought it would open Clementine's eyes to him.

"Yeah, I guess you're right. I need to show her I'm interested or forget her entirely."

Cordell was about to reply when their mother suddenly entered the kitchen from the utility room. As soon as she spotted Cordell, she walked over and gave his shoulders a one-arm hug.

"Good morning, son. How's Maggie and my little granddaughter?"

Cordell beamed at the question. "My beautiful wife is great and Bridget is the smartest, prettiest girl in the world, of course."

"Of course." Claire chuckled. "You wouldn't expect anything else from a child of yours. I'm sure the next one will be just as perfect."

Quint's gaze traveled from his mother to Cordell. "Next one? Is Maggie pregnant again?"

Smiling, Cordell waggled his eyebrows. "Not from lack of trying."

"Cord!" Claire scolded.

Laughing, he kissed his mother's cheek. "Just kidding, Mom. Maggie is loving her job at the hospital for now. But she wants a houseful of kids. Just like I do."

Quint eyed his brother, while thinking it hadn't been too long ago that Cordell was running from the very idea of marriage and kids. But after he'd met Maggie, his opinion on the subject had taken a turnaround. In the past weeks, Quint had felt his own views shifting about having a family. But the change in him didn't mean much without Clementine.

"We'd all love that, Cord," Claire said with a smile of approval, then changing the subject, she asked, "Are you ready for the new cattle to arrive?"

"More than ready," Cordell told her. "Maggie says I've been acting like a kid with Christmas coming."

Claire laughed lightly. "So has your father. I've not seen him this excited since the twins were born."

"Speaking of Dad," Cordell said, "Has he come down for breakfast yet?"

With a playful roll of her eyes, she said, "He left for the ranch yard nearly an hour ago. Said there were lots of things he wanted to do before the Three Rivers hands arrived with the cattle. What things, I don't know. Rearrange a few hay bales?" she joked.

"I'll get right over there." Rising to his feet, he looked over at Quint. "Don't worry about us. Go see after your sheep—and Clementine."

"Thanks, Cord," Quint told him. "I'll catch up with you this afternoon."

"Right," Cordell replied, then grabbing his duster from the back of a chair, he exited the kitchen.

Quint crossed the room and placed his coffee cup in the sink. "Thanks for the coffee and breakfast, Mom. I need to get to work, too."

As he pulled on a jean jacket, his mother walked over to him. "Did I hear Cord say you were going out to see Clementine?"

"Yes. From what Jett tells me, some of the lambs have been puny," he explained. "I want to make sure it's nothing serious. Why do you ask?"

Stepping up to the sink, Claire sunk a dirty pot into the sudsy water. "I know you men have had a lot of things on your mind. In case you've forgotten, the party we're giving Grace and Mack is set for Saturday night. That is, if we can get the barn cleaned out in time. Your father says it will be done, but I'm beginning to worry."

He watched her scrub the pot with a scouring pad. She was all for doing special things for her children, which was well and good. But Quint was hardly in the mood for a party. Sure, he was glad that Grace and Mack were happily married. He was thrilled that Jack was going to be a father. But it was going to be hard for him to get in a celebratory mood when his every thought was on Clementine. Damn it!

"To be honest, I had forgotten about the party. But don't worry, Mom. We'll get things ready. I might not have time to work on things today, though. Maybe tonight I can get Jett and Chance to help—"

His mother frowned. "Quint, I'm not wanting you to go start cleaning on the barn! I was asking about your trip out to Clementine's camp because your father and I thought it would be nice for you to invite her to the party. That is, if you'd like for her to attend."

Quint stared at his mother. "Clementine at a party? I can't see that happening, Mom. But I'll ask."

Smiling with a confidence that Quint was far from feeling, Claire patted the side of his arm. "I'm sure you'll know just the right thing to say to persuade her."

"And what if I managed to convince her to attend, Mom? Don't you think she'd be miserable?"

"Well, there's always that possibility," Claire conceded. "But I'm hoping she'll surprise you and enjoy the evening."

His mother might as well have asked him to sprout wings and fly, but he kept the negative thought to himself.

"Okay, Mom. I'll do my best. But don't expect a miracle."

Claire gave him another wide smile. "Miracles do happen, son. Especially during the Christmas season."

"Christmas is still weeks away!"

"It's the spirit that counts, Quint."

He bent his head low enough to press a kiss to her forehead. "I'll try to remember your advice."

Because it was going to take more than a miracle to talk Clementine out of the mountains.

Chapter Eight

Long before Quint caught sight of Clementine's camp, he could smell frying ham, strong coffee and wood smoke drifting on the cold morning air. What in heck was she trying to do, attract every bear within a ten-mile radius?

As soon as the question darted through his mind, he was ashamed of himself. She couldn't go to the kitchen and cook a meal, or stroll into a restaurant and order whatever she'd like. She had to make herself a decent meal, no matter what kind of wild animals were around to be tempted by the smell.

When he arrived at her campsite, he climbed down from his horse, and after tethering the animal to the limb of a twisted juniper, he walked over to where she was squatted on her heels, tending to pieces of canned ham sizzling in an iron skillet.

"Looks like I got here just in time for breakfast," he said.

Rising to her full height, she greeted him with a faint

smile. "If you're hungry I have enough for two. Especially if you'd like a piece of fruit with your ham. Thanks for sending Jett by with everything."

As his gaze rested on her soft, womanly features he felt something begin to quiver deep inside him.

I'd rather risk being slapped than lose my chance with the woman I wanted.

Yeah, now Quint understood what Cordell had meant with those sage words of advice.

"My pleasure," he said to her.

She reached down and moved the skillet off the fire and on to one of the rocks encircling the flaming wood. "I imagine Jett told you a few of the lambs have had the sniffles. I hope he didn't worry you with the news."

"Not really. My only concern was that the flock wasn't coming down with nasal bots. If so, I knew you'd need help deworming all of them."

She shook her head. "I've been checking for bots and not found any so far. The sheep aren't displaying any signs of parasites. I think it's just the change in temperature. They're all quickly recovering."

Nodding with approval, he said. "Good work. I knew I could trust you."

"Thanks."

He gestured to the sizzling ham. "Go ahead and eat. I've already had my breakfast."

"Would you like coffee?" she asked. "I made plenty."

"I would."

She poured two cups of the coffee, then filled a paper plate with the ham, along with slices of apples and oranges.

Taking a seat on her log couch, she motioned for him to take the stool. "So what brings you out so early? Are you headed over to the new land? Jett mentioned the cattle might be coming today."

"Yes, they're expected to arrive a little later today. But I'm not headed to the old Barkley land. I came out here to specifically see you."

"And the sheep," she added as she forked a bite of ham to her lips. "As soon as I down this food, we'll go have a look. Just so you can rest your mind."

This morning she was bundled in a green plaid coat. A woolen muffler in a mustard color was wrapped tightly around her neck, while the old felt hat she usually wore covered her head. The only time she got any relief from the cold temperature was when she was close to the fire. The idea bothered Quint more than he wanted to admit. And yet he reminded himself that she was living the sort of lifestyle she wanted. Or seemed to want.

He said, "My mind doesn't need resting. Not from worry over the sheep."

Lifting her head, she looked at him. "You came out to talk to me about something?"

"Yes. And I really don't know how to do it," he admitted.

Her brows arched ever so slightly. "You want me to head the flock back toward ranch headquarters, is that it? The need for my services is coming to an end."

Jett had mentioned she was thinking her job here on Stone Creek would soon be ending, but Quint hadn't given that part of their conversation much thought. All that he'd been able to think about was seeing her again and letting her know he wanted her to be more to him than his sheepherder.

"No!" The word burst out of him, causing her to pause a slice of apple halfway to her mouth. "That isn't what I came to talk with you about. But now that you've brought it up, I'll just say this. The sheep stay on the range until snow covers the ranges. If the weather gets to be too much for you, then give me word. After that—well, I'd like for you to stay on and care for them permanently. We'll figure out something about your housing—when the time comes."

"Permanently." She repeated the word in a low, stunned voice. "You mentioned that idea before, but you doubted you could afford a year-round sheepherder. What's changed?"

He'd changed, Quint thought. It was that simple. He wasn't exactly sure what sort of allotment his father would allow him for this upcoming sheep season. He was hoping it would be a larger sum, but no matter. Over the past couple of weeks, he'd decided if he had to pay Clementine out of his own income for the extra months of work, he'd gladly do it.

"We—uh—what's changed is all the new land and livestock that Dad has recently purchased. We expect to make a bigger profit this coming year." Which wasn't exactly a lie, Quint thought. Both Hadley and Jack expected big dividends from the ranch's new venture with the Arizona Hollisters. "It's only right that the sheep division gets an increase in working expenses."

She popped the piece of apple into her mouth and thoughtfully chewed. "That's good. I know how much you want to grow your sheep herd. But I—I'd have to think on taking the herding job permanently."

Quint quickly decided that it was enough for now that she was willing to think about the job offer rather than turning it down outright.

"Okay. We'll talk about that later—when the time comes," he said, then taking a deep breath, he gave her one of his best smiles. "What I wanted to talk with you about today is—inviting you to a party—at the ranch. My parents are throwing a sort of belated wedding party or reception or whatever you want to call it for my sister Grace and her husband, Mack. They got married in a simple ceremony several months ago but have never taken time for any kind of reception. With them both being doctors they're kind of tied down."

The longer he'd talked, the lower her jaw had dropped. Now she was looking at him in sheer disbelief. "A party? Me? You must be joking. I—I've not done anything like that in years! Not since—I—was much younger."

And living a different life, Quint thought. What he'd give to know how she'd lived back then and why she'd turned her back on it.

To her, he said, "I'm not joking. I'd really like for you to come. So would my parents."

Lowering her head, she absently rearranged the food on her plate. "Thank you for the invitation, Quint. It's thoughtful of you, but totally unnecessary."

Exasperated, he said, "I'm not asking out of obligation. I'm asking because it would be nice for me to have you there."

She lifted her head, and as her gaze collided with his, he felt an odd mix of pleasure and pain strike the middle of his chest.

"I almost believe you," she said.

He left the stool and dared to take a seat next to her on the smooth log. When she didn't jump up or scoot away from him, he couldn't help but feel a sense of triumph.

"You should believe me, Clem. By now you ought to know I don't lie about things."

Her nostrils flared as her eyes traveled slowly over his face.

"Yes, I know you're not a liar. But I don't really know your family. I'd feel—like an outsider."

"All the more reason to come to the party and get to know them better." He gave her a faint grin, then because he felt as nervous as hell, turned his gaze to the chunks of burning pine. "I'm sort of glad you brought up the subject of not knowing us. There's something about us Hollisters that I've been wanting to tell you. The time just never seemed right for it. It's probably not right now. Not with me trying to convince you to come to our family get-together, but—"

"Look, Quint, you're wrong if you think I need to hear your family secrets," she interrupted. "I'm not the type to dig into a person's private life."

He chuckled softly. "That's an understatement, Clem. But this isn't exactly a secret. And it isn't really about dirty laundry. Or I should say, we don't yet know if any of it was dirty. It's more like a mystery."

"You've sparked my curiosity."

Seeing she was willing to listen, he reached for the coffeepot and tilted it over his cup. "Do you remember me mentioning Grandfather Lionel and how he got a divorce when Dad was very small?"

"Yes. The way I remember it, she left her three young sons and never bothered to see them again."

"Right. Well, there's something about Lionel that we can't figure out," he said.

"What's there to figure?" she asked. "From what you told me, he built this ranch and lived on it until he passed away."

"True. It's before he came here to Beaver County that has us stumped. But first I need to go back to about two years ago. A family down in Arizona with the same name as ours contacted Dad. We'd never met any of them before, but we soon learned they were very rich, notable ranchers."

"You mean like you and your family?"

With a wry chuckle, he shook his head. "No. Compared to them, we're little fish. Like minnows swimming alongside a whale."

Her expression turned skeptical. "I find that hard to believe."

"If you ever saw their ranch, you'd see the huge contrast. Jack and Cord have been there. They say it's a huge cattle and horse production. But anyway, Maureen, the matriarch of the Arizona Hollisters, had been working on a family tree and she contacted Dad with the notion that our two families might be related. A DNA test proved she was correct. Now we have a bigger question to deal with. How did we become related?"

Her brows pulled together. "The connection should be fairly easy to find. Unless someone had a baby out of wedlock and doesn't want the secret revealed to the rest of the family."

"True. But none of the living family members have had a child out of wedlock, nor would they lie about such a thing. No, we believe the connection had to have happened long ago. That's where Grandfather Lionel comes into the picture. Van has been searching for clues to solve this, but she keeps hitting snags. The biggest issue is Lionel's birth certificate. No one knows his exact birth date. He'd always told his family he was born in a county south of Beaver. But the state of Utah has no record of it on file. Van has also searched for info on Great-Grandfather Peter, who was Lionel's dad. But he's a dead end, too."

"How very strange." Leaning forward, she set her empty plate on one of the rocks that formed the fire ring. "You mentioned Lionel's ex-wife. Even if their divorce was bitter, she'd surely be willing to tell you something about his birth date. That is, if she's alive."

"Yes, Van is hoping the woman might have answers. Trouble is, none of us has any idea where Scarlett might be, or if she's still living." He shook his head. "Grandfather was very bitter about her. In fact, I don't recall him ever saying her name out loud. The few times I heard him say anything at all about Scarlett, he referred to her as *that woman*."

"How terrible—for both of them," she murmured.

"Yeah, it would've been nice to have had a loving grandmother living here on the ranch with us. But that wasn't in the cards."

She was quiet for a long moment before she finally asked, "Why are you telling me this, Quint?"

He squared his knees around so that he was facing her. "Because I—I guess I want you to see that we're not a perfect family."

Shaking her head, she made a sound that was caught somewhere between a laugh and a sob. "Oh, Quint, if you only knew about—"

"About what?" he prompted.

"Nothing," she said, then shaking her head, she looked away from him and swallowed. "No, that's wrong, Quint. There are all kinds of things I could tell you about my family. But then you might not want me to be your sheepherder. Much less attend your sister's wedding reception."

"That isn't going to happen," he said gently.

She suddenly reached over and wrapped her hand over his forearm, and the unexpected gesture surprised him; it also filled him with hope.

"I told you my father had died, but much more happened to my family before his death. When Kipp and I were ten and twelve years old, my parents divorced."

"That's rough. I can't imagine how broken I'd feel if my parents weren't together. Seeing Mom and Dad bonded together with love makes everything better for me and my siblings. Especially when things aren't going as well as you planned."

Nodding, she said, "When my parents split, it was an awful time in our lives. In the end, Kipp and I both chose to stay with our father. Our ranch, the Rising Starr, had always been our life, and Dad had the means to take care of us far better than Mom. Looking back on it, and knowing what I know now, I would've probably chosen to go with my mother. But my brother and I didn't have any idea our father had been a serial cheater. Our parents simply explained they were divorcing because they couldn't get along. It wasn't until we were much older that we learned about his bad behavior."

"I imagine it was probably for the best that you didn't learn about your father's infidelity at such a young age. Especially if you were happy living with him. The truth would've ruined those years for you."

She looked at him, and Quint got the impression she was seeing things in him she'd never noticed before. He could only hope they were admirable traits.

"You're right. I'm glad I didn't know about Dad's cheating back then," she said quietly.

"It must have been a rough time for your mother."

Nodding, she said, "Yes. But she didn't let it get her down. She got married again. To a man she'd known in high school. They moved to Boise shortly after they married and then we rarely saw her. But to her credit she did keep in touch until we reached adulthood. Now, not so much."

Her hand continued to rest upon his arm, and Quint likened her touch to a blowtorch. In spite of the cool weather and the thick denim of his jacket, her hand was shooting heat down to the tips of his fingers and all the way up to his shoulder.

"What about your father?" he asked. "Did he remarry?"

She groaned. "Oh, yes. And that's when the downhill slide began. Andrea was a much younger woman and she wasn't the country type. She was constantly complaining and demanding things that Dad simply couldn't give her. We watched him work himself into the ground to try and please her. I suppose he was afraid Andrea would divorce him like our mother had divorced him. It's hard to figure what was going on inside Dad. He wasn't one to show his feelings."

So Clementine had come by that honestly, Quint thought. Up until today, she'd kept her feelings mostly under wraps. Now that she was sharing her past with him, he could only hope it was the start to letting him see inside her heart.

"Did he and Andrea stay married?"

"Regrettably, yes."

"Why regrettably? If she made him happy…"

"Happy?" Her eyes suddenly turned flat and lifeless. "She killed him. Intentionally and methodically killed him."

Quint stared at her in stunned fascination. "Are you serious?"

She looked away from him, and he could see her jaw was clamped as though she was fighting against emotions she'd rather he not see.

"Very serious," she said in a strained voice. "Kipp

and I can't prove it, but we feel certain she was behind his death."

"How did your father die?"

"Slowly—over several months. At first he simply complained of fatigue, but his weakness progressively worsened. The doctors couldn't diagnose the problem. They attempted to treat the symptoms even though they couldn't detect the underlying cause. Finally, he became so sick he was bedridden and a nurse was called in to care for him."

"What was his wife doing all this time?"

The corners of her mouth turned downward. "Acting like a concerned and loving wife." She snorted with contempt. "Andrea was so concerned she gave the nurse a night off and assured me and my brother that she'd keep careful watch on her husband. That's when Dad took his final breath."

"Damn! Sounds incriminating to me. Surely an autopsy was performed?"

"Certainly. But the cause of death was eventually listed as some long medical name that basically meant his autoimmune system was out of whack. Sure it was out of whack. Ingesting toxins tend to do that to a person," she said bitterly.

"So your stepmother was never seriously questioned by the police about her husband's death?"

"No. It was common knowledge in the small town where we lived that Trent Starr had been ill for several months. Everyone naturally assumed the illness finally took him."

"What happened with Andrea after Trent died? Did she leave the ranch right away?"

Her brown eyes widened, and for one crazy second,

Quint thought she was going to burst into hysterical laughter.

"Leave? Oh, Quint, she's still on the Rising Starr. Dad's will left everything to her! Or I should say, the will that showed up in court stated everything belonged to her. Kipp and I will never believe it's the authentic document. Dad was crazy about Andrea, but he loved us, too. And he knew we were the ones who would keep the Rising Starr going. Not Andrea. Never in a million years would he have willed everything to her."

"It all sounds fantastic, but I believe you, Clem. However, there is one thing I don't understand. You said Andrea wasn't happy living in the country. Why is she still there? If the ranch is lawfully hers now, why hasn't she sold it and moved?"

"Oh, she would have done that very thing if it hadn't been for Dale. He's a ranch hand Dad hired not long after he married Andrea. Over time she caught Dale's attention and the rest... Well, my brother and I figured the guy made her see that getting their hands on the ranch would be the same as acquiring a gold mine. It's a prime piece of land and it's paying off steadily."

Quint frowned as he patched together the pieces of information she'd given him. It made a very ugly picture. "How do you know the property is paying off? Surely you left the ranch after she took over ownership."

"I did leave. That's when I went to work as a sheepherder. I've never been back to the Rising Starr. But Kipp is still there. Working as a hired hand for the woman who killed our father! It's—"

The rest of her words broke off as she bent her head and choked back what sounded to Quint like a painful sob. The idea that she'd been hurt so badly and still continued to hurt over the family tragedy was like a knife right in his heart.

Before he recognized what he was about to do, his arms circled around her and gently drew her forward, until her head was lying against his shoulder.

"Clem, don't cry," he said gently. "I can't bear to see you hurt this way."

Her hands came up and wrapped over the ridge of both his shoulders as though she needed to anchor herself to him. The thought caused his chest to swell with emotions.

"I'm sorry, Quint. I've not cried in years and years. Not until today. And I'm ashamed of myself," she said.

Her voice was muffled against his jacket, but the agony was still wrapped around every word, and the sound instinctively caused his arms to tighten around her.

"Why would you be ashamed for showing you're human?" he asked.

"I don't like being weak. I don't like letting all that happened on the Rising Starr tear at me anymore. I'm so tired of it." Lifting her head, she looked at him. "After Dad died and the will was read, I was consumed with the urge to get revenge. But that was wrong, Quint. Over time I learned to let the hate go and I was much better for it."

He used his forefinger to wipe a teardrop from her cheek. "But you're still carrying the sadness. I wish you could let that go, too, Clem. I'd really like to see you smile. To see sunshine and happiness in your eyes."

She gave him a wobbly smile, then whispered, "You call me Clem. No one does that. Why do you?"

He inched his face toward hers. "Because that's—how I think of you—my Clem."

Her eyes slowly closed and then her face angled toward his. The invitation was all Quint needed to capture her lips with a hungry kiss.

Clementine didn't know how or why it had happened, but all of a sudden Quint's lips were touching hers, transporting her to a strange and wondrous place.

Had she been alone for so long that she'd honestly forgotten what it was like to be kissed by a man? She couldn't remember ever feeling such a wild burst of emotions coursing through her. All she could think was that Quint's arms were holding her tight. His hard, hungry lips were plundering hers in the most delicious way.

In the back of her mind, alarm bells were clanging, while the words dangerous, foolish and heartbreak zoomed through her head. But Clementine was beyond heeding the warnings. For long days and nights, she'd thought of little else but Quint. She'd imagined kissing him and having his strong arms around her. Now that those dreams had become reality, she didn't want to let them go. Not until she'd filled herself with enough passion to last until the next time.

The next time!

The thought was enough to have her easing her mouth from his and dragging in a mind-cleansing breath.

"What are we doing?" she asked in a husky voice. "This isn't supposed to be happening!"

Instead of putting him off, his hands flattened against her back and drew the upper part of her body even tighter against his.

"Why isn't it? I've wanted to do this almost from the very first moment I met you in the Wagon Spoke," he murmured.

"No. You couldn't have."

Smiling, he traced the tip of his forefinger over her

cheekbone, then downward until it was outlining her lips. And the look in his eyes was like she was the most fascinating thing he'd ever encountered in his life. The thought was so heady it caused her senses to spin even faster.

"How do you know what I was thinking then? Or now?" he asked, his voice little more than a whisper.

At some point during their kiss, her arms had circled his neck, and to her amazement, she still couldn't bring herself to lower them to her sides, or to order her hands to stay away from his body. Touching him was a pure gift. It was filling her with warmth and joy and something far more dangerous. Deep inside her, desire was flickering to life and burning its way through every inch of her body.

"You're not thinking," she murmured. "If you were, you'd know I'm not the kind of woman you should be— kissing."

"You're a beautiful woman. Why shouldn't I kiss you?"

She couldn't remember a man telling her she was beautiful. Even Marty, who'd thought of himself as somewhat of a lover boy, had never spoken those words to her. Hearing Quint say them caused a strange quiver inside her and the reaction pushed her to her feet.

"I'm much too old for you, Quint."

Standing, he gathered her into his arms. His hands splayed against her back, then moved slowly down to the curve of her waist. When he pulled her hips forward against his, it was all she could do not to place her lips over his, to thrust her tongue deep into his mouth and let the dark, masculine taste of him fill every pore, every aching crevice.

"Don't you think I should be the one to decide if your

age is right for me? As far as I'm concerned, you're the perfect age for me," he said.

His hands pressed her hips even tighter to his and she was shocked to feel his erection bulging against the fly of his jeans. One kiss had done that to him?

Why not, Clementine? Look what's it's done to you.

Shoving the taunting voice out of her head, she looked into his blue eyes. "Maybe for today or tomorrow. But not for very long."

But then he wasn't thinking about ten years from now, or even ten months from now. His mind was on the present and nothing more. Yet even understanding she was nothing more than a momentary diversion for him wasn't enough to dampen the special way he made her feel, or the pleasure his touch gave her.

"I like how you can see into my mind and know what I'll be thinking when gray starts to sprinkle your hair and wrinkles fan from the corners of your eyes."

He touched his finger to the spot next to her eye, and Clementine fought the urge to turn her face toward his hand, to kiss the hard calluses on his palm.

"What would you be thinking? She needs a facial and a dye job?"

His eyes grew soft as one corner of his lips tilted upward. "No. I'd be thinking how very glad I was that you came into my life."

Bittersweet pain suddenly overwhelmed her, and with a little sob, she eased out of his arms and walked until she was standing beneath the boughs of a pine. Across the meadow, the bells on the ewes tinkled as the dogs herded them away from the tree line. The herd was getting restless and ready to move to better grass. Soon there would be no better grass to move to. When that day came she was going to have to make a major decision.

Before today, before Quint had taken her into his arms, the choice wouldn't have been all that hard. Now she was all mixed up and very afraid her emotions were going to outweigh common sense.

She was blinking at the moisture misting her eyes, when Quint walked up behind her and rested his hands on her shoulders.

"Did I say the wrong thing, Clem?"

She swallowed hard. "No. You said the perfect thing. If you truly meant it."

"I truly meant it."

With a groan of misgiving, she turned and rested her hands against his chest. "Maybe now you do. But I—" She looked at him for long moments, and as she did, something inside her melted and suddenly the future didn't matter nearly as much as this moment, or tomorrow or the next day. "You know, Quint, I think I'd like to go to your sister's celebration."

His eyes widened, and she could clearly see she'd surprised him. She could also see joy on his face and that was enough to convince her that she was doing the right thing in accepting his invitation.

"You do? You really will come to the party?"

The amazement in his voice made her smile. "Yes. I really will. Only I have a huge problem."

"If it's the sheep, don't worry. I'll find a man to come out and take your place for a couple of nights. He might not be as diligent as you, but as long as he keeps the predators away that will be enough."

A pent-up breath rushed out of her, and she wondered if some sort of dam inside her had broken. She felt different. Like all the cold bitterness had slipped away and a warm golden feeling had taken its place.

"I'm glad. I wouldn't want to leave the flock unattended. But that's not the problem." She looked down at her jeans and scarred cowboy boots. "I can't go to a party wearing the clothes I have with me. Your family would be embarrassed to have me there."

"They wouldn't be embarrassed," he assured her with a happy grin. "But no worries. I'll make sure you'll have something nice to wear. I mean, with six women in the house, surely they'll know what you need."

Feeling as if she'd just jumped off a cliff and into a deep pool of water, she said, "Okay. But I don't want any of them to go to a lot of trouble."

He chuckled. "Are you kidding? Bea works in a boutique in town. She loves helping women pick out clothes."

"If you say so."

His hands were still on her shoulders and now they gently kneaded the flesh. "You've made me one happy guy, Clem."

For now, maybe. But then, nothing in her life was permanent. She didn't expect it to be. "So when is this party? I might need to know when to show up."

His laugh was sheepish. "I kinda got sidetracked. It's Saturday night. So I'll send out your replacement Friday. Early enough for you to ride to the ranch before dark. I know you can make the trip by yourself, but I can come out and ride with you—if you'd like."

"Thanks, but that won't be necessary. I'm sure you'll be very busy from now until then. So I'll see you whenever I get there."

Groaning, he pulled her into his arms. "I don't know how I'm going to wait for three long days to be with you again. Maybe I should have another kiss or two before I leave. Just to make the wait more bearable."

Her heart was suddenly thumping. "Maybe you should."

This time as he lowered his lips to hers, Clementine didn't expect to experience the same emotional reaction she'd experienced when he'd kissed her a few minutes ago. This time she expected to have complete control of her senses. But she was wrong.

The instant their lips met, pleasure burst inside her brain and sent signals of joy to the rest of her body. He tasted so good. Felt so good. She didn't want to let him go. She had the sinking feeling that she'd never want to let him go.

Don't think about tomorrow, Clementine. Only this moment. This feeling of being wanted.

He kissed her several times over before he finally lifted his head, and by then both of them were breathing hard and dazed from the intensity of their embrace.

"I, uh, think I'd better be going," he said in a low, husky voice. "Before Jimmy decides he wants to sink his teeth into my leg."

"Jimmy?" She looked behind her to see the faithful dog was sitting a few feet away, carefully watching Quint's every move. Sighing, she said, "Sometimes he forgets who he's supposed to be guarding. I'll give him a pass today. He's never seen a man get this close to me. He's confused."

And so was she. Very confused as to how she'd gone from trying to keep plenty of distance between her and Quint, to falling eagerly into his arms. It had to be a dangerous loss of her common sense.

"He'll have to get used to having me around. So will

you, Clem." He kissed her forehead, then turned and started toward his horse. "See you Friday."

She stood where she was and watched him swing easily into the saddle. As he rode away, he lifted a hand in farewell and she made a single wave back at him.

Jimmy stood on all fours and stared after the horse and rider until the pair disappeared into a stand of gold aspens. Once they were out of sight, he looked at Clementine and made a sound that was somewhere between a growl and a whine.

Clementine shook her head at the concerned canine. "Don't worry, Jimmy. This thing with Quint won't last for long."

Chapter Nine

"If anyone else gets married in your family anytime soon, Quint, I'm going to need a back brace," Chance said as he carried a hay bale across the wooden floor of the barn.

Following right behind him with another bale of hay to be used for seating around the large open space, Quint said, "Don't worry. No one else in the family is contemplating marriage. Unless one of Bea's many crushes turns into something serious."

Chance grunted with amusement as he positioned the makeshift seat near the wall. "I hope Bea gets a wandering eye. We need a long break before we clean this barn out for another wedding shindig." He raised up to his full height, then pushed both fists against the small of his back. "It wouldn't have been so bad if the cattle from Arizona had shown up next week instead of this one. And the fence in the water gap hadn't needed repairing at the last minute. Guess with the Barkleys only raising crops, they weren't all that worried about their fences."

"I agree that it's been a whirlwind around here," Quint replied. "But things are coming together. The cattle are settled, the three new men from Three Rivers are learning their way around the ranch and the mild weather is holding. What more could you ask for?"

A wily grin on his face, Chance said, "I'd settle for a pretty girl to dance with tomorrow night. One that won't talk about wedding rings or baby cribs. I'll bet you won't have that trouble with Clementine."

No. Clementine wouldn't be talking about love or babies. He couldn't see her bringing up any subject that had to do with the future. But at least she'd talked to him about her past and the terrible circumstances that had caused her and her brother to lose their father and the ranch. Quint was glad she'd opened up to him, and yet he was still haunted by the loss and pain he'd seen on her face and heard in her voice. He'd give most anything to take her sorrow away. But how did a person go about righting something so wrong, or remove a pain she'd carried inside her for so long?

Quint looked over at the ranch hand. "How did you know Clementine was coming to the party?"

Chance rolled his eyes. "Jett. How else? He can't keep a secret."

Shaking his head, Quint glanced toward the open double doors on the west side of the building. Ted, a day worker the ranch sometimes hired for extra help, had left early this morning to take Clementine's place at the sheep camp. If all went well, she should be riding up in the ranch yard fairly soon.

"Her coming out of the mountains to attend the party

isn't a secret. It's more like a miracle. I'm still shocked that she agreed to it."

"Hmm. Me, too. From what little I saw of her when she first came to ranch, she seemed distant. But Jett says you're pretty gone on the woman."

He let out a short laugh. "You're right. Jett can't keep his mouth shut."

"So he's right."

Quint flashed him a guilty grin. "Let's just say Clementine is becoming mighty special to me."

"Sure, she's special to you," Chance said with a playful smirk. "She takes good care of your sheep."

She did more than that, Quint thought. She made his life feel purposeful. She gave him a direction he'd never had before. Yeah, he was probably a fool for letting his feelings grow to such mammoth proportions in such a short time. Especially when he had no idea if she would ever have a serious thought about him. But her kisses had felt very real, and that was enough to give him hope.

Quint said, "Yes, she takes better care of the sheep than I ever could. She's an amazing sheepherder."

Chance groaned. "I might as well plan on getting the back brace. Cause it sounds like you'll be the next Hollister to have a wedding party here in the barn."

A wedding with Clementine? A few weeks ago, the thought of getting hitched permanently with any woman would have had Quint laughing hysterically. Now he couldn't imagine himself with any woman other than Clementine.

"You're getting way ahead of things, Chance. I'm just now getting to know Clementine. And she—"

The ranch hand slanted a speculative glance at him. "She what?"

Quint couldn't explain to Chance, or anyone, how much Clementine had lost in the past. Her parents' divorce, her father's death and then her home. She probably believed she wasn't supposed to have anything more than what she had now. In fact, he wasn't sure she *wanted* anything more in her life.

He cleared his throat. "Nothing—just that she has sheep on her mind. Not me."

"I figure you can do something to change that."

Shaking his head, Quint started out of the barn. "Come on. Let's start carrying in the folding chairs. Mom plans on about sixty or seventy people showing up and she wants seating for all of them, plus the tables set up for food and refreshments."

Chance blew out a heavy breath. "Forget about me wanting a pretty girl to dance with. After this, I'll be going to bed with a heating pad."

Chuckling, Quint nudged him out the door. "You're not that old, buddy."

The sun was dipping low behind the mountains by the time Clementine finally arrived at the ranch yard. Quint was there waiting for her and immediately took over the task of unsaddling Birdie and settling the mare into a comfortable pen with a loafing shed and plenty of alfalfa and fresh water.

He'd obviously been very glad to see her, but he'd not greeted her with a passionate kiss. Which was probably a good thing since several men had been milling about the ranch yard, with the majority of them casting surreptitious glances in their direction.

That had been more than three hours ago. Now, after eating a simple meal of beef stew at the kitchen table, Quint had gone to help with the final preparations at the barn, and his twin sisters were escorting Clementine, arm in arm, to a bedroom they'd prepared for her.

"We're so glad you decided to attend the party," Bonnie said as they began to climb a long staircase to the second floor of the massive house. "We rarely ever have house guests. Having you is a treat."

"Absolutely," Beatrice added to her sister's comment. "Back in early summer some of our relatives from Arizona came for a visit. Maureen and Gil are really nice people and they're fun—especially with them being our parents' age. But you're different—in a good way, that is."

Yes, she was different all right. The walls around her, the roof over her head and the chattering voices—to everyone else, those things were normal, but to Clementine they flung her back to a time she desperately wanted to forget.

Clementine gave both twins a wan smile. "You two are being overly gracious. I'm nothing special. But thank you for making me feel welcome."

"Oh, we want you to feel more than welcome. We want you to feel like part of the family," Beatrice happily replied.

"We sure do," Bonnie added. "So while you're here for the party, we want you to be comfortable."

"Anything you want or need just tell us, or our mother. We'll be glad to get it for you," Beatrice said, then added sagely, "But I wouldn't bother with Quint, though."

Clementine looked at her. Was this young woman already trying to warn her to stay away from her brother? If so, it wouldn't be the first time someone had tried to step between her and a man. For more than a year, her father had made Marty's life a living hell, simply because he was dating his daughter.

"Why not bother with Quint?" Clementine had to ask.

Beatrice slashed a dismissive hand through the air. "Oh, because he's a man. He doesn't understand what we women need. He only knows about things like lariats and saddles and horses and sheep—stuff like that. If you told him you wanted some bath oil, he'd say, what's that?"

Clementine smiled, even though she could have told Beatrice that after eight years of basically living away from civilization, all she knew about was caring for livestock and surviving in the wild.

"I'm sure everything will be fine," Clementine told her. "Your home is very luxurious."

"We don't really think of it that way," Bonnie said. "Guess that's because this is the only home we've ever known. It's not fancy, but it's very comfortable."

"Do you have a home you go to when you're not sheep-herding?" Beatrice asked.

A cold weight hit the pit of her stomach, and Clementine hated herself for the reaction. After all these years, losing the Rising Starr shouldn't still hurt. But it did, and she often wondered if the pain would ever go away.

"I don't own a place of my own," Clementine answered honestly. "Since I'm usually away from a flock for only a couple of months out of the year, it would be a waste. I stay with a Blackfoot woman in Shelley. Her name is Nuttah. She's been a widow for a long time."

"Is Shelley in Idaho?" Bonnie asked.

"Yes. Close to Idaho Falls. It's one of many places in the state where potatoes are grown. There are open fields and nearby mountains. It's a pretty place." But it wasn't like Stone Creek Ranch, she thought. Was that because Quint was here and not there?

She was still thinking about the self-proposed question when they reached the second-floor landing, where the twins guided her to the left.

"Your room is over here by mine and Bonnie's. Since Jack and Cord married and moved to their own houses, there are extra bedrooms. But we decided to keep sharing a room." She laughed impishly. "Being twins we've always shared things. Except for boyfriends. Not that Bonnie would want any of mine, anyway. She's far too cultured for my tastes."

"Bea! Stop it!" Bonnie shushed her. "Clementine is here to enjoy herself. Not listen to your silly prattle about men!"

Instead of getting angry with her sister, Beatrice let out a hearty laugh. "I'm sure Clementine has her own ideas about men. And I doubt she goes for the bookworm type—like you."

Rolling her eyes, Bonnie opened the door to the bedroom and ushered Clementine inside. "You'll have to ignore my sister. She's clueless."

Clementine walked to the middle of the room and gazed around her in fascination. The space was furnished with a queen-size cherry wood bed and matching dresser and chest. Moss green drapes hung partially over double windows, while the bed was covered with a flower-printed comforter done with the same green theme. A large shaggy throw rug in off-white protected the oak flooring at the side of the bed, while a padded dressing bench stood at the end of the footboard. A stack of clothing sat on one end of the bench.

"This is very lovely," Clementine murmured, then looked from one identical twin to the other. Didn't they understand that she normally lived out of a tent? "But I—honestly don't need anything this—fancy."

"Oh, Clementine, this isn't anything posh," Beatrice told her. "And like I said, we want you to be comfortable."

"We put some nightclothes here for you." Bonnie pointed to the stack of clothing on the dressing bench. "We know you had to ride in from camp, so we weren't sure you'd have room in your saddlebags for those sorts of things."

She glanced around her as she suddenly remembered the leather bags she carried with her. "I forgot that I left my saddlebags in the mudroom. I'll go get them before bedtime."

"No worries. Before Quint went to help with the last of the barn preparations, he carried them up for you," Beatrice said. "They're in the closet. Along with the things we picked out for you to wear to the party tomorrow night. There are several dresses for you to choose from, but if you don't like any of them, you're welcome to go through our closet. Bonnie and I wear the same size so we share some of our things. Of course, she considers most of my clothes too daring for her," she added with a laugh.

As Clementine looked at the twins, she wondered if things might've been different for her if she'd been fortunate enough to have had sisters. Having more siblings might not have prevented Trent's death, but at least a pair of sisters would've come closer to sharing the depth of her loss over her father and the Rising Starr. As it was, Kipp saw the tragedy through a man's eyes whereas Clementine saw it through her heart.

"I really don't know what to say," she said to the young women. "I'm overwhelmed."

"Gosh, no need for that," Bonnie said, then looping her arm through Clementine's, she urged her toward the closet. "Come on. Now that we're up here, you might as well look at the dresses. We're just dying to see which one you're going to choose."

A few hours later, when Quint finally made it back to the ranch house, the evening was growing late. Except for his parents who were still in the den, the house was quiet, and his mother informed him that Clementine had already gone to her room.

Hoping to see her before she went to bed, Quint hurried up the stairs and was happy when he spotted light shining from the crack beneath her bedroom door.

After a brief knock, she opened the door, and he gawked as she stood across the threshold in a blue robe wrapped over a pair of blue silk pajamas. Her long hair was loose and spilled in thick waves around her shoulders and down over her breasts.

"Wow! Look at you!" he exclaimed with a grin.

Her cheeks turned slightly pink as she glanced down at herself. "Yes, your sisters thought I needed night wear. I didn't have the heart to tell them I—"

She broke off suddenly, and Quint watched her face change to a dark rose color.

"Tell them?"

"I—uh—normally don't bother with nightclothes."

The simple remark instantly conjured up the image of her naked body between the sheets and how soft and smooth her skin would feel beneath his hands.

He cleared his throat and tried to stop a grin from appearing on his face. "Sounds like the perfect way to sleep to me."

She didn't smile, but he could see a glow in her eyes that warmed him through and through.

"Mind if I come in?" he asked.

Her expression turned skeptical. "For what?"

"To do this."

With his hands on her shoulders, he walked her backward until he used the heel of his boot to shut the door. As soon as the latch on the knob clicked, he pulled her into his arms and captured her lips with his.

He heard her tiny moan, and then her mouth opened and her arms slipped up to encircle his neck. Kissing her was like nothing he'd ever experienced. It was a magical journey, and before he realized what he was doing, his hands traveled back and forth across her shoulders, then up and down her back. Beneath the thin fabric of the robe and pajamas, he could feel every little bump of her backbone, the indention of her waist and finally the flare of her hips.

He was quickly becoming lost in the embrace when she pulled away and took a step back. From the dark look in her eyes and the rapid rise and fall of her breasts, Quint knew she was just as aroused as he.

She said, "We—uh—as nice as that felt, Quint. I don't think this is—"

"The right time or place?" he finished for her.

Nodding, she gave him a rueful smile. "Exactly."

"To be honest, I'd just planned on giving you a chaste little kiss to say good-night. But—something happens when our lips get together. It's like striking a match, don't you think?"

Sighing, she looked away from him. "Yes. I'd say we're combustible."

She didn't appear all that pleased about the fact. But he figured she was having enough problems trying to adjust to being here in the ranch house and around his family. She was probably feeling very out of place. She wasn't even accustomed to wearing satin and lace pajamas, much less being cooped up inside four walls.

He said, "I mainly knocked on your door to make sure you're comfortable and have everything you need."

"No worries. Your mother and sisters have been spoiling me as if I'm some sort of princess. I honestly don't know how to feel, Quint. Except that I'm being a bother."

He frowned. "That's awful to think that way, Clem. Mom is thrilled to have you here. And so are my sisters. Is that so hard for you to believe?"

Shrugging, she turned aside and gazed across the room at the double windows. "A little. For a long time, even before Dad died, I felt unimportant. And since then the opinion of myself hasn't changed much."

He closed the short steps between them and rested a hand upon her shoulder. "Funny you should say that, Clem. Because I used to feel the same way. My older brothers all had significant jobs. Hunter with his rodeo company, Jack as manager of the ranch, Cord as the foreman and Flint a deputy sheriff. And for a long time I was just a hired hand. And because I felt unimportant, most of the time I behaved like a jackass. I'm still amazed that Dad and Jack saw fit to put me over the sheep production. I believed they thought I was far from being up to the job."

A wry little smile tilted one corner of her lips. "Obviously they believed in you. I'm not sure what my father saw in me. Like I said, he didn't express his thoughts out loud very much. I worked at his side, day in and day out. But Dad never bothered to tell me that I was anything more than a hired hand. You've been blessed. You've learned your family actually admire and appreciate you. That's good."

"Yeah." His fingers gently kneaded her shoulder. "They do. And they appreciate you, too. So while you're here just lap up the attention and enjoy it. Okay?"

She gave him a lopsided smile. "I'll try."

He bent his head and placed a soft kiss on her lips, then touched his forefinger to the end of her nose. "I'd better say good-night. The twins probably heard me come in. They'll watch the clock until they hear me go out the door."

"I got the impression that the twins adore you."

As his gaze met hers, he cupped his palm against her cheek. "I'd like it even better if you adored me, too."

Her lips quivered ever so slightly. "Ask me that tomorrow night after I see whether you can dance without stepping on my toes."

She was joking, of course. She was also deliberately changing the subject. But before she went back to the sheep camp, he was going to do his best to find out whether he was wasting his time with her, or if her kisses were actually telling him that she cared.

The next morning, Clementine had a few minutes with Quint over breakfast before Cordell had come into the kitchen and asked for his help moving heifers. Apparently it had been a job that couldn't wait until later, and he'd left with his brother, while promising Clementine he'd see her later in the afternoon. However, by midafternoon Jack had snagged him to help set up a temporary stage for the live band who'd be supplying the music for the party.

Clementine decided it was just as well that she'd not had extra time to spend with Quint. The more she was with him, the more she wanted him. And that couldn't be a good thing. The man was far too young for her.

Plus, he was a bona fide bachelor. Yes, he might be all for a brief, passionate affair, but was she? Would the temporary pleasure be worth the eventual pain she'd feel later? Once she had to leave Stone Creek Ranch?

Trying not to dwell on that dismal thought, she leaned toward the dresser mirror and stared at her image. What was he going to think whenever he saw her? That she looked like a weed pretending to be a flower?

The question had barely had time to pass through her mind, when a knock sounded on the door and Beatrice poked her head into the room. "Is it okay if Bonnie and I come in?"

"Please do. I need your fashion advice."

The twins entered the bedroom, and as they walked over to where Clementine stood before the mirror, Beatrice gasped with surprise, while Bonnie stared in wonder.

"Oh, my, Clementine! You look positively radiant!" Beatrice exclaimed, then glanced to her sister. "Doesn't she, Bonnie?"

Smiling broadly, Bonnie nodded. "Perfectly lovely. That dress looks like it's made for her. You made a wise choice, Bea, when you brought that one home from the boutique."

The dress was red velvet with an off-the-shoulder neckline and a fitted bodice. The full skirt flared out from her waist and fell all the way to the floor, where the toes of a pair of black high heels peeped out from the soft fabric.

"I've never had a dress like this," Clementine admitted to Quint's sisters. "I think—I probably look like a tomato trying to disguise myself as an apple."

Laughing, Beatrice came up behind Clementine and gave her shoulders a gentle squeeze. "You're so funny,

Clem. You look beautiful—like you wear heels and velvet every day."

This brought a short laugh from Clementine. "Thankfully, the heels on my cowboy boots are high, so I'm okay walking in the high heels. But the only time I wear dresses is when I go to church with Nuttah. And they hardly look like this one." She turned away from the mirror to look at the two women. "I promise I'll be very careful not to get a rip or stain."

Bonnie shook her head, while Beatrice rolled her eyes. "Listen, you can't have fun while worrying about the dress. And anyway, it's yours now. Bonnie and I want to gift it to you."

"No! It's too much!" When she looked at the twins, her heart grew as soft as butter and she didn't want that. No. Letting herself care about anyone meant losing them later on. She couldn't handle that. Not anymore. "I—it's a lovely gesture from you two. But I couldn't really."

"You could, really," Beatrice said in a no-nonsense voice. "Because we're not taking it back."

Clementine blew out a long breath. "What would I do with it? Dress up for the sheep?" she attempted to joke.

Smiling, Bonnie hurried forward. "You're going to wear it for our Christmas Day party. It'll be perfect!"

Beatrice scowled at her sister. "No way! That's less than a month away. She can't wear it tonight and then again for the Christmas party! She'll need something new!"

"No, girls, I—"

Ignoring Clementine's protest, Bonnie said to her sister, "That's true. But this dress is red and velvet, at that. Christmas always says velvet. We could change this one up with a shawl or a glittery pin."

Clementine opened her mouth to inform the twins that she'd probably be long gone by Christmastime, but she didn't have the chance as a knock on the door interrupted their conversation.

"It sounds like there are a bunch of bees in there," Quint said through the closed door. "Is it safe for me to come inside?"

Bonnie walked over and opened the door for her brother. "A gentleman isn't supposed to go into a lady's room," she said primly. "Unless he's invited."

"It's okay, Bonnie," Clementine told her. "Except for fastening my bracelet, I'm all ready to go."

"Quint can take care of that," Beatrice said quickly, then snatching ahold of Bonnie's arm, the twins hurried past their brother and out of the room.

Clementine drew in a bracing breath and, with her heart pounding heavily in her chest, turned to him.

"Clem!" With an awed expression on his face, he crossed the room until he was standing in front of her. "You look incredible!"

In spite of the makeup on her face being a light application, it made her cheeks feel strangely stiff as she tried to give him a smile. "Thank you. Your sisters gave me quite a bit of help. Beatrice even painted my fingernails to match my dress." With a nervous little laugh, she held out one hand. "Imagine. Me with nail enamel."

"I don't have to imagine anything," he said softly. "I'm seeing it all and you look perfect."

"Thank you, Quint." She reached down and picked up a bracelet encircled with rubies and rhinestones. The piece matched the choker she'd chosen to wear with the dress. Handing it to him, she said, "I'd appreciate you fastening this onto my wrist. I tried but I can't manage the clasp with one hand."

"My pleasure."

Stepping closer, he took the piece of jewelry, and as he wrapped it around her wrist, Clementine was inundated with his masculine scent and the warm touch of his fingers against her skin. He was wearing a dark copper shirt and dark blue jeans. A bolo tie with an oval slide of turquoise inlay in the shape of a thunderbird was pushed to the base of his throat. Three-day whiskers on his face and hair that hadn't seen a barber in months gave him a rakish look that intensified his sexy image.

Did he have any idea what sort of effect he had on women? she wondered. Specifically on her? It was shameless how much she wanted to slide her arms around him and feel his hard body pressed against hers.

"There," he said after a moment. "That should stay fastened."

Instead of releasing his hold on her hand, he lifted the palm to his lips. Beneath the long skirt, Clementine's legs quivered.

"Thank you."

His gaze dropped to her lips, and then just as his head began to slowly descend toward hers, Claire's and Hadley's voices sounded out on the landing.

"My parents are heading downstairs. They must be ready to go." He gave her a rueful grin. "Your lipstick has been spared."

She could've told him that her lipstick was the last thing she'd been thinking about, but she kept the thought to herself. She didn't need to encourage him any more than she already had.

She said, "Then we need to go join them. It's almost time for the party to start, isn't it?"

"As far as I'm concerned the party started the moment I laid eyes on you in that red dress." He curled an arm against the back of her waist and guided her toward the door. However, once they reached it, he paused and looked down at her. "Before we leave this room I want to make sure—well, I understand this isn't your cup of tea. And I feel as if I pushed you into it. If you start feeling too uncomfortable just tell me."

The fact that he was being so considerate about her feelings took away most of the unease she felt over joining a crowd of people. "As long as you're with me, Quint, I'll be fine."

He smiled at her. "Don't worry. I'll be like one of your belled rams—impossible to lose."

Because Thanksgiving had occurred two days before, Claire had decided to combine the holiday with the reception party in order to keep the extra food and preparations to a one-time effort. At the back of the room, a pair of long tables were filled with ham and turkey and several side dishes, while next to them, a dessert table held pumpkin and pecan pies, along with a three-tier wedding cake decorated with pink poinsettias. Beer and champagne were available to anyone who wanted to celebrate with a kick of spirits, while punch and coffee were offered to the less exuberant guests.

The twins had tried to talk their mother out of the holiday food, insisting it was tacky to combine the two celebrations, but Grace had argued that she loved the idea, and since the party was actually celebrating her wedding, she'd had the last word. As for Quint, he was hardly focusing on the food or beverages. Clementine was at his side, looking so beautiful she was practically taking his breath away.

Each time he introduced her to friends and the family members who'd not yet had the chance to meet her, he could see surprise flicker across their faces. Everyone knew he'd hired a sheepherder, but none had expected anything like Clementine. Especially his oldest brother, Hunter. To honor his sister's wedding, he'd left his rodeo stock and the employees who took care of them out in California, where the last of the winter events were taking place, and traveled back to Stone Creek for this one night.

"So you're Quint's new sheepherder. It's a real pleasure to meet you, Clementine," Hunter said as she cordially placed her hand in his. "I've been hearing great things about you."

"I'm sure they were all exaggerated," Clementine said with a modest smile. "Quint tells me that you're a rodeo producer. Is your season winding down now? Or does it ever close?"

"Not completely, but at this time of the year it does slow down. A few of the California events will be going on in December. But I've promised Mom and Dad I'll be home for Christmas this year. Will you still be around for the holiday? Or is Quint giving you the boot?"

There was a teasing note in Hunter's voice, yet there was a curious glint in his eyes as he looked from Clementine over to Quint.

She hesitated, then said, "I'm not sure where I'll be at Christmas. It depends on—a few things."

Apparently she hadn't yet decided about accepting his offer to stay on, Quint thought. Or maybe she'd believed he wasn't serious when he'd talked to her about keeping the job year-round.

Hunter flashed a smile at her, and Quint was reminded of how charming his oldest brother could be when he put his mind to it. Along with the charm, he was tall and muscular like their father, with rusty brown hair that waved rakishly back off his forehead.

"Well, I'm sure by Christmas you'll have it all figured out," Hunter replied.

Awkwardly clearing his throat, Quint said, "Hunter has hired a new trick riding and roping act. Two sisters from Nevada. And from what he says they're a big drawing card."

Hunter slanted him a clever grin. "Beautiful women are usually a good investment."

Quint gestured to his brother's big hand still wrapped around Clementine's. "Uh—Hunter, you can let go of Clementine's hand now."

Chuckling, Hunter gently eased Clementine's hand back to her side, while to Quint he said, "Oh, it's like that, is it?"

The possessiveness Quint was feeling over Clementine wasn't anything new. From the very beginning he'd felt an uncommon need to protect her, and the closer he'd grown to her, the more the feeling had ballooned. And though he didn't like admitting it, he was downright jealous of Hunter.

"As a matter of fact, it is, big brother," Quint told him.

Hunter gestured across the room to the four-piece band that had suddenly begun to play. "Then you'd better take your lady for a dance before I decide to take her for a spin."

Like hell, Quint wanted to bark at him, but didn't. Instead, he clamped a hand around the back of Clementine's waist and promptly guided her to the open area of the room where couples were already starting to dance to the slow song.

"You haven't asked me if I can dance," Clementine said as he drew her close to him.

"I don't need to," he replied as he relished the perfect fit she made in his arms. "Anyone who can ride a horse as well as you can move to the rhythm of music."

She laughed softly. "Quint, I ride a horse every day. I haven't danced in years."

He smiled down at her. "Don't worry. I'll refresh your memory. Besides, I'm wearing steel-toed boots tonight—just in case."

Her eyes were sparkling as she smiled up at him, and Quint decided there had to be something magical in the air. He wasn't sure his boots were even touching the floor.

"I'll try not to put them to the test," she said.

His hand tightened around hers. "You can step on my toes all you want, Clem. You being here at the party is—pretty special to me."

"This might surprise you, Quint, but it feels pretty special to be here."

"With me?" he murmured the question.

Her fingers gently tightened on his. "Yes. With you."

A long breath rushed out of him. "I had to ask. There for a minute I thought Hunter was going to steal you away."

Amusement quirked her lips. "Not hardly. I think your brother enjoys teasing you. But I like him. He reminds me a lot of Hadley. Or the way I imagine Hadley at Hunter's age."

Quint glanced across the room to where Hunter was speaking with an old family friend. For the most part, his brother appeared to be happy, but Quint believed his outward appearance was just a mask to hide the pain he was carrying underneath. Four years ago, Hunter's divorce had shaken Quint. He'd always seen his big brother as strong, wise and unshakable. Seeing him in pain over losing his wife had turned Quint away from the very thought of marriage. But now, Clementine was slowly and surely making him wonder if he could be happy like Jack and Cordell.

"I wish Hunter was as happy as Dad is now," he said, then seeing Clementine's brows arch in question, he realized he'd surprised her with his remark.

"You think he isn't?"

Quint shrugged. Tonight was too special to spoil it with Hunter's heartaches. Eventually, he'd explain how his brother had loved and lost. But for now he wanted her to think only of good things and being with him.

"I don't really get to see him enough to know what's going on in his life." He smiled brightly at her. "But I'd say for sure that Grace appears to be on top of the world tonight. Wouldn't you?"

She glanced around the room until her gaze landed on Quint's older sister. "For sure. And she looks so elegant." Her gaze turned back to his face. "Your mother and sisters are so warm and friendly. You're blessed to be a part of such a big loving family."

You could be a part of my family, Clementine. And then you'd never be alone. Never think of yourself as only a hired hand.

The thoughts were itching to jump off Quint's tongue. Yet he understood it was too soon to say such serious things to her. And he could wait. Like his mother had said, Christmas was a time for miracles. Maybe by then, she'd be ready to hear the hopes and dreams that were beginning to build in his heart.

Chapter Ten

This had to be a fairy tale. As the night wore on, the thought kept revolving through Clementine's head. She couldn't remember any time in her life when she'd talked and laughed so much, danced one song after another, while never growing tired of having a man's arm around her waist, or his hand clasped so tightly around hers. This wasn't supposed to be happening to her. Yet in spite of knowing the evening was all momentary make-believe, she was determined to drink it all in and tuck away the precious memories. Because tomorrow reality would set in and she'd be back with the sheep and the dogs and horses.

But that was a good thing, she told herself. Because with them she felt safe. Her animals were forever faithful. She could trust them to never leave her. Not by choice, anyway.

The song the band was playing suddenly ended, and Quint's voice broke into her wandering thoughts.

"I think we need a little cool air, don't you?" he asked.

She glanced toward the front of the room where coats and jackets hung from a row of coat trees. "It's cold outside. I'll need to get my wrap," she told him.

"We don't have to go outside for a little air," he said. "Follow me and I'll show you."

He led her off the dance floor and past a group of people enjoying glasses of champagne. Clementine had already sipped one glassful, and with Quint's company already making her head buzz, she'd steered clear of adding any more fog to her brain.

At a wide door, partially shadowed by the hayloft above their heads, he opened a slide latch, then led her into the dark room.

"I smell alfalfa. What is this? A room to store hay and grain?" she asked.

He flipped a switch, and a dim fluorescent light illuminated the far end of a room filled with stacks of green alfalfa hay.

"Only hay," he answered. "Actually, this is the hay set aside for the sheep. Think it will be enough to last until spring grasses?"

With his hand against her back, he urged her to walk deeper into the room where tons and tons of hay were stacked from the floor to the raftered ceiling.

"To be honest, I don't think so. You have a big flock. And I suspect when the weather gets bad, you have antelope and deer come down to eat with the sheep."

He chuckled under his breath. "And plenty of reindeer."

Her expression was one of amused skepticism. "I don't think reindeer live this far south, Quint."

"Well, this time of the year, Santa's reindeer need

to stop off from time to time for a snack. So if you see some of them out with the sheep, don't get alarmed."

She gave him an impish smile. "In other words, you feed Santa's reindeer hoping it will persuade him to bring you more gifts."

"Now you're getting the picture," he teased. "But seriously, as for the hay, you're right. This won't be quite enough. When it comes to the sheep I just can't fool you. Or the reindeer."

"It's called experience," she explained. "I've had years of it. Starting when I was just a child helping Dad."

"Apparently you've learned a lot—about sheep." He placed his hands on her bare shoulders and turned her toward him. "I'm hoping you're learning a few things about me—and Stone Creek Ranch."

In this closed-off part of the barn and without her wrap, she should've been cold. But standing close to him with his fingers pressing into her flesh, she was like a flame about to burst into an all-out fire.

"What kind of things do I need to know about you?"

Her voice sounded breathless and she wondered if he possibly knew how much he affected her. It was crazy how much she wanted to press herself to him, how desperate she was to have his lips roaming over hers, tasting the desire that was burning for him.

"Like how glad I am that you answered my ad for a sheepherder."

"You've already told me that."

"Well, I confess that at first I doubted your ability," he said. "But now I've learned how competent you are."

"A girl always likes to hear she's competent."

Smiling, he drew her forward until the front of her body was crushed against his and her head was forced to tilt back in order to look up at him.

"This girl is more than competent." One hand came up to cradle the side of her face. "She's beautiful and desirable. And she makes me very happy."

Like drops of sunshine, his words were spreading warmth through every fiber of her being, and before she could stop herself, she raised up on the tips of her toes and angled her lips toward his.

"Clem. Oh, Clem," he whispered just before he opened his mouth over hers.

While she kissed him earnestly, hungrily, her hands found their way to the middle of his chest, where she pressed her palms against the pads of warm muscles. In a matter of seconds, his tongue was probing against her teeth, begging to take the kiss even deeper.

She gladly complied, and with a guttural groan, he cupped his hands around the bottom of her rear and pulled her hips tight against his. The contact caused an ache to build between her thighs, and she could only think how incredible it would feel if he would lay her on one of the hay bales behind them and make love to her. To be connected to him in every possible way was the only thought in her brain.

Without breaking the contact of their lips, he began to slowly walk her backward, and Clementine realized the very same thoughts must have been rifling through his mind. And with each step they took, she clung to him, while her mind and body surrendered to the magic his lips were creating on hers, to the luscious heat permeating from his roaming hands.

She was unaware of everything but him until the back of her legs finally bumped against the hay, and she groaned with anticipation as Quint started to bend her backward. But before that could happen, the loud burst of a man's laughter accompanied by multiple female giggles could be heard above the dim beat of the music.

The sound was close enough to bring Quint's head up, and he looked at her with regret. "I nearly forgot there's a party in the next room. Sounds like they're right outside the door. We'd better slip out of here before someone walks in."

His words cooled the sizzle in her brain, but it didn't take away the burn on her cheeks. She'd lost all control! Another few seconds and she would've been pulling at his clothes and begging him to make love to her.

"I *had* forgotten!" She stepped aside and quickly straightened the bodice of her dress, then forced herself to meet his gaze. "I'm ready. Let's go."

Frowning, Quint wrapped a hand around her upper arm and drew her to him. "Are you angry with me?"

Confused by his question, she shook her head. "No. Why should I be?"

A smirk twisted his lips. "Because I put you in a— situation that could've been very embarrassing."

The urge to laugh and cry hit her at the same time, making the sound that slipped from her mouth resemble a gurgle. Risky? Didn't he know she was beyond caring about anything, except becoming a part of him? No. To him those were only kisses and the end result would've been only sex.

She said, "Wrong. I did that to myself. So if I'm angry at anyone, it's me."

With a groan of regret, he pressed his cheek against hers. "Clem, it's supposed to be like this for you and me. It's a gift. You're making it sound like wanting each other is a curse."

Wasn't it? she asked herself. Wasn't it a torment to want something she'd never be able to have?

Easing back from him, she reached for his hand. "We'd better get back to the party."

Thankfully, he didn't argue the point. Instead, he pressed a soft kiss against her cheek and walked her back out among the merry partygoers.

"Clementine, you really should let me ride with you, at least part of the way," Quint said as he watched her tighten the girth on Birdie's saddle. "What with Dad wanting to do some dehorning and vaccinating, I might be tied up for the next few days. I won't have a chance to see you again."

She glanced at him. "I understand. But you men have lots of things to do. I heard Hadley talking this morning at breakfast about the work he wanted done today. You don't need to be wasting your time on me."

He didn't know what had happened between the party last night and now, but something had caused her to revert to being the Clementine he'd first met at the Wagon Spoke. The woman who didn't have much to say and kept her face a closed book.

Last night he would've sworn she was having a great time eating, dancing and mingling with his family and friends. Could it be that she'd been putting on an act just to make him and his family believe she was friendly and sociable? Maybe she'd only come to the party because she'd felt it was a job requirement? But no, that wasn't the impression he'd taken from her kisses, he thought. He'd tasted desire and need on her lips. Surely those things couldn't vanish overnight.

Quint, you're so wet behind the ears. Clementine is running scared. She knows she was close to making love to you, and now that she's in the light of day, she realizes she doesn't want that to happen. She wants to keep to herself and play things safe.

The voice of reason going off in his head was far from what he wanted to hear and yet he believed there was some truth to the notion. Clementine hadn't gone through life alone for the past eight years just because she liked it that way. She didn't want to risk the pain and heartache she'd witnessed through her father.

"I wouldn't call it wasting time, Clem," he said. "But if you don't want my company—then go on alone."

After jerking the stirrup leather back into place, she turned to him and smiled. Even so, Quint could see there was nothing genuine behind the expression. He wanted to press her to explain her feelings, but something told him now wasn't the time. He figured she needed to get back into her element, where she felt comfortable, before he began tossing questions at her.

"It's not that I don't want your company, Quint. But the partying is over. It's time for us to get back to doing what we're supposed to be doing."

Shrugging, he grinned and did his best to go along with her practical attitude. "Guess you're right. A guy and a girl can't dance all the time."

"Exactly." Stepping closer, she reached for his hand. "Thank you, Quint. I had a very nice time with you and your family. It was thoughtful of you to include me in the celebration."

Now she was making their evening together sound distant and formal. Hadn't those hot kisses they'd shared meant anything to her? Just thinking about them made Quint's head reel. Surely she'd been feeling something when she'd clasped her arms around him and opened her lips to his.

His fingers tightened around hers, and it was all he

could do to keep from yanking her into his arms and plastering a long, searching kiss on her lips. But his father and Jack were standing only a short distance away in a small corral, inspecting pregnant heifers. Quint didn't want to take the chance of embarrassing her with a public embrace.

Sighing, he said, "Yeah. A little thoughtful and a whole lot greedy."

Something flashed in her eyes, and then she eased her hand from his and turned and climbed into the saddle. "Bye, Quint. See you."

"Goodbye, Clem."

She nudged her heels to Birdie's sides, and Quint stood watching her and the mare until they disappeared behind the hill that lay on the west side of the ranch yard.

"Clementine already headed back to the sheep camp?" Jack asked as he strode up to Quint's side.

"Yes. She wanted to leave early enough to get there before dark. I imagine Ted will be relieved to see her."

"No doubt. He probably feels like he's been gone from civilization for a month." His amused expression turned serious. "Did you give her any orders to start moving the sheep back in this direction?"

"No. She knows more about that than I do. And anyway, she's already camped at the western boundary fence of the ranch. Once she's out of grass there, she has no choice but to head back in this direction. Why do you ask?"

"Only for weather reasons. The long-range forecast is predicting subfreezing temps and that might be too rough for living in a tent."

Quint stared thoughtfully at the spot where Clementine and Birdie had disappeared from sight. This time he was determined to not allow much time to pass before he rode out to see her. And once he was at her camp, he wasn't going to waste the occasion by discussing the weather.

"Clementine is tough. She says she can stand the cold, but when the snows hit and make it impossible for the sheep to graze, she'll head the flock back to the ranch."

Jack whistled under his breath. "Tough lady doesn't begin to describe her. Van was commenting last night at the party about how Clementine was a paradox. So lovely and graceful, yet so much of an outdoors woman. When you hired her, you really got yourself something, little brother."

Yeah, Quint thought. He'd hired himself a dandy sheepherder. Trouble was, he wanted her to be far more than a capable hand at tending his sheep. And he wasn't at all sure she'd ever want him to be more than her employer.

Quint glanced at his brother. "I'm glad you approve. From the very beginning I've wanted you and Dad to see how serious I am about Stone Creek sheep."

Smiling, Jack laid a hand on his shoulder. "We can see. And I have good news for you, brother. Dad and I have been going over the budget, and we've allotted a tidy sum for you to purchase the sheep you've been wanting."

Quint's mouth fell open, which promptly had Jack raising a hand. "But just because the money is there, we don't want you to go out and buy the first flock you can find," he said.

Grinning, Quint replied, "Are you kidding? I'm going to be damned picky. Nothing but the best for Stone Creek Ranch. I want to make Grandfather proud."

"Ironic that you mentioned him," Jack said. "Van

told me this morning that she thinks she might have a lead on where we might locate Scarlett."

"Oh, hell," Quint muttered. "Do you think the woman would tell us Hollisters anything? Especially if she thought the information was crucially needed. Somehow I doubt it."

"How could you know she'd refuse to give us info? You've never met her. In fact, us kids have only seen that one picture of her. The one that Dad hid away from Grandfather. She might have softened over the years. She might have regretted leaving Grandfather and her boys behind. No one really knows what goes through another person's mind—or heart. Time changes some people."

Quint grimaced while thinking of everything Clementine had told him about her father's divorce, his remarriage and ultimately his death. Yes, time changes people, he grimly decided. But was the change usually for the better?

"I wouldn't hold my breath that Scarlett developed a heart," Quint said with an abundance of sarcasm. "Just ask Hunter. He's still waiting on Willow."

Jack frowned at him. "Man, did you eat something sour this morning at breakfast?"

"No." He released a heavy breath. "I—to be honest, Jack, I wasn't ready for Clementine to leave. But she seemed more than ready to get out of here. And that—kind of hurts."

"Look, Quint, just because I'm married and deliriously happy with Van hardly means I'm an expert on romance and women. But from what I see, I think your problem is that you can't decide whether you want a girlfriend or a sheepherder."

He slanted Jack a hopeless look. "There's a big difference in what a man wants and what he needs."

Chuckling, Jack gave Quint's back an affectionate slap. "I have no doubt you're going to figure everything out for the best."

Quint could only pray that his brother was right.

Four days later, Clementine had just eaten a lunch of canned meat and peaches and was about to saddle Peanut and ride back east in search of a better grazing area, when Quint rode up. This time Jimmy barked at him. Not as if he'd spotted a stranger. More like the guy he wasn't a bit fond of was back in camp. Clementine didn't know whether to laugh at the dog or scold him. So she ended up doing neither.

"I wasn't expecting to see you this week," she said as he dismounted and tied the bridle reins to a juniper limb.

Once he had the horse secured, he walked over to where she stood. Clementine noticed he was wearing a heavy wool jacket of green and brown plaid to ward off the cold. A dark brown muffler was wrapped around his neck, while worn leather gloves protected his hands from the wind. One of those smiles that made her stomach do a flip-flop was on his face, and she decided it was sinful that any man could be so sexy and charming at the same time.

"I'd planned on coming yesterday," he told her. "But we didn't get finished with vaccinating the last of the cattle until close to sundown."

Once he'd stepped down from the horse, Jimmy had quit barking and had gone to sit by the side of the tent. She saw Quint eye the dog before he glanced out at the milling sheep.

"They look quiet. No problems with more sniffles?"

"All the lambs have recovered, and I've not seen any more cases. I'm sorry you felt the need to check on them. There was really no need for you to make such a long ride out here," she said.

The weather had turned exceptionally cold today with a steady wind blowing down from the north and heavy gray clouds blanketing the sky. Each time Clementine looked up she expected to see flakes of snow in the air. Which meant her days here in the foothills would quickly end. And she didn't want that to happen. She felt safe here. At least, when she was alone.

However, when Quint invaded her private space, a part of her felt trapped and vulnerable, while the other part hummed with joy. Her reaction to the man didn't make sense. But then, there was nothing logical about her feelings for him, she thought.

A frown on his face, he took her by the arm and urged her across the rough ground until they reached the campfire. She'd built a fire earlier to boil coffee and ward off the cold. Now most of the dead limbs had turned to glowing coals. He retrieved a couple of big limbs from a nearby pile where she stashed her firewood, then tossed them onto the coals. In a matter of moments, the pine burst into flames.

Once he was satisfied with the fire, he said to her, "There was plenty of need to ride out here. I wanted to talk with you."

"I'm watching the weather, Quint. In fact, just before you rode up I was about to saddle Peanut and search for a lower meadow east of here. That way if snow hits and gets deep, I can begin to move the flock toward ranch headquarters."

He frowned at her. "Is that all you think about? The sheep? The weather?"

Her mouth fell open as she stared at him in wonder. "Isn't that what you hired me to do?" she asked after a moment. "You think I'm going to sit around on my butt and not take notice of what needs to be done? What's the matter with you?"

His expression regrettable, he gazed morosely at the low flames. "Sorry, Clem. I shouldn't have said any of that."

"No. You shouldn't have. Not watching the weather would be putting me and the sheep in danger. That's basic sheepherding. You ought to know it."

"I ought to know a lot of things, Clem, but right now I'm only concerned about one thing."

There was something on his face and embedded in the tone of his voice that told her he was in a mood she'd never seen before. Her heart began to thud with dread. Maybe he was going to fire her. Maybe he'd decided he didn't want a sheepherder year-round. Especially a woman. But what would that matter? she asked herself. She'd never told him she'd take the job, anyway.

"Okay. You're concerned how to tell me I'm out of a job. Don't worry," she said. "I won't fall apart if you do. I never expected to work to the end of December, anyway."

"Oh, damn it, Clem! There you go again talking about your work. I'm not here for that. I've already told you that I wanted you to stay on."

She took a few steps until she was standing at his side. "Then—you said you were concerned about one thing. What is it?"

Groaning, he turned to face her. "You, Clem. I— when you left the ranch yard last Sunday you were like a stranger. I've been racking my brain, trying to figure out what I'd said or done to make you so distant and—"

Whatever else he'd been about to say came to a halt as she placed a hand on his forearm. "You didn't do anything, Quint. You've been—" she sucked in a deep breath and blew it out "—kind and sweet and everything I could want in a man. The problem is with me."

As he studied her face, a crease slashed the middle of his forehead. "I guess you're trying to tell me you don't feel anything for me. Is that it?"

Oh, God help her, she silently prayed. She didn't have the emotional strength to resist this man, much less explain her fears of loving and losing.

"Of course I feel something for you, Quint. But I'm not one to stick my head in the sand and pretend. It's obvious. I'm not the right woman for you."

His frown deepened. "Obvious? That's crazy talk. You couldn't know whether you're right or wrong for me! We're just now getting to really know each other."

"Right, we are getting to know each other. And the more I'm with you, the more convinced I am that we need to keep our hands off of each other."

He muttered a curse word under his breath. "You're not going to convince me of any such thing!"

Groaning with frustration, she said, "Look, Quint, the next morning after your sister's reception, I woke up and wondered what I was doing lying in that beautiful bed, beneath a lush down comforter, in a warm room. And I was especially wondering what I was doing with you—letting myself believe that you could be anything more to me than—well, than what you are now."

Turning toward her, he wrapped his hands around her upper arms. "Why can't I be more? Why can't we be more to each other? There's nothing stopping us," he argued.

Because looking into his sky blue eyes was shaking everything inside her to the breaking point, she turned her gaze on the sheep. "You're not listening to me, Quint! We're not right for each other. We never will be. And in the hay barn, when we were kissing so passionately, I almost let myself forget that."

"What do you mean we're not right for each other? We're perfect for each other."

Her head moved from side to side. "Oh, Quint, I'm seven years older than you! You need to stick with your young girlfriends."

"Who's been telling you I have young girlfriends? Jett or Ted? They don't know anything about anything," he said crossly. "Yeah, I've dated plenty of girls in the past. But they mean nothing to me."

The intensity in his voice took her by surprise. "And I do? No. You need to forget about me. This—whatever it is you think you feel for me—will pass."

He tugged her forward until the front of her body was pressed to his. "You're wrong, Clem. I aim to show you how wrong. You—"

"I don't need a long speech from you, or a show-and-tell demonstration!" she interrupted. "All I need is—"

Her words broke off as his head dipped and his lips hovered above hers. "This. Me and you together. That's all you need," he muttered.

"Quint," she whispered in a helpless rush. "Why are you doing this to me—making me want you?"

"To show you that you need me as much as I need you."

He closed the fraction of space between their lips, and like every other time he'd kissed her, she felt herself melting. A couple of seconds was all it took for him to demolish her self-control and make her forget she was supposed to be convincing him she didn't want him. Instead, she responded hungrily to his searching lips and drew herself even tighter against him.

When they finally broke apart for air, he clasped her face between his hands and gazed deep into her eyes. "This time we're all alone, Clem. This time there won't be any interruptions."

She was fighting a losing battle and he knew it.

"No. No interruptions," she whispered.

His gaze pierced hers. "Do you want to run? Do you want to signal for Jimmy to save you?"

Jimmy couldn't save her now, she thought. Nothing or no one could stop her from making love to this man.

Her arms slipped around his neck. "No. I'm not going to run, Quint," she spoke against his cheek. "I think you need this as much as I do. You need to learn that the only thing you're feeling is—temporary infatuation."

With a mocking grunt, he bent and scooped her up and into his arms. "You've gone from not talking at all to talking too damned much, Clem."

She didn't say anything as he carried her over to the tent and set her down at the door. Actually, there was nothing left to say, she thought, as she reached for his hand and pulled him inside her little domed hut. He wanted her and she wanted him. There was no grand scheme about it or a future past this day. There was no place beyond this mountain sheep camp. Better he learned that now than later.

Two unzipped sleeping bags formed a double layer of blankets that were spread smoothly over the thin foam mattress that served as her bed. With his head hunkered to avoid hitting the ceiling of the tent, he tossed his hat and gloves aside, then joined her on the makeshift bed.

There was just enough room for him to stretch his legs to full length and leave space for her to join him. She removed her hat and heavy jacket, then lying next to him, she snugged herself to his side. He raised up on one elbow, and as he gazed down at her there was something in his eyes that caused a lump of emotion to lodge in her throat.

"You looked so beautiful the night of the party, Clem. But the way you look right now, this very moment, is taking my breath away." His hand moved to her face, where his fingertips tenderly explored the dips and angles of her features. "Do you think I see the years between our ages when I look at you?"

"You should," she whispered, while trying not to wince at the odd little pain in her chest.

"You're so wrong, Clem. I see nothing but the woman I want. The woman who's changed my life."

His name was all she could manage to speak before his lips came down on hers, and suddenly nothing else mattered except that the two of them were together. For however long it took to turn the fire inside of them to ashes.

He kissed her for another long moment, before he raised up enough to remove his jacket, which he folded and placed at the top of the mattress above her head.

"It's cold in here," she said. "You might need your jacket."

He grinned at her. "Cold? It feels like July in here to me. You're like a bed of hot coals lying next to me."

She pushed his shoulders down against the bed, then positioned her upper body so that she could look down at him. "I confess, Quint. Every night I've thought of having you here beside me—just like this. And now that I do—I..."

As her words trailed away, a knowing smile tilted his lips. "You don't know where to start. Well, I have a confession, too. I've thought of having you in my arms like this a hundred times or more. And each time I did, I imagined myself getting you naked and joining our bodies as fast as I could. But now—there's too much to look at, to feel and touch, to rush through this. I want to stop and savor every moment."

While he spoke, his hands had removed the elastic band holding the end of her braid. Now his fingers were threading through her hair, spreading the strands across her back, and she decided he made the simple act feel as intimate as a kiss from his lips.

"Quint," she murmured. "All I want is for you to make love to me."

"Beautiful Clem, that's all I want. For us to be together—completely."

As Quint drew Clementine's lips down to his, he had to keep asking himself if he was really in her bed, really about to make love to her. It seemed like a dream, and yet as he pulled her down and shifted her so that her back was against the mattress, everything about it felt very real. So real in fact that his hands were shaking as he fumbled with the buttons on the front of her shirt.

"Sorry. I'm used to snaps. Just pull and everything comes loose," he said as he finally managed to undo the button directly between her breasts.

"Hmm. You said you wanted to go slowly, remember?"

He darted a look at her face, and the desire he saw there caused his loins to clench with longing. "Yeah.

I remember. But now—I don't know if going slow is possible."

Finished with the final button, he pushed the fronts of her shirt aside to find her breasts encased in white lace. The color was a vivid contrast against her olive skin, and he feasted his eyes on the sight before he dropped his head and touched his lips to the flesh just above her bra.

She tasted sweet and salty at the same time, and in spite of the cold air inside the tent, her skin was like a scalding drink passing over his lips. He couldn't resist tasting more and more, until finally he slipped a hand beneath her back and fumbled with the hooks on her bra.

Once the fasteners came undone, he immediately pushed the fabric off her breasts, then cupped his hands around both soft orbs. The nipples were the color of milk chocolate and currently puckered into tight buds. To even think of putting his tongue on them made his shaft ache.

"Perfect." His throat was so clogged with emotion, he barely managed to get the word out, but that hardly mattered as her hand snaked around the back of his neck and pulled until his mouth was centered on one breast.

As soon as he drew the small bud between his teeth, she let out a groan of pleasure and the sound caused something to click inside of Quint. After that, everything around him began to fade as desire swiftly took control of his mind and his body.

He didn't know how long his mouth lingered at her breasts, or exactly when his lips returned to hers, but at some point he was drawn into a whirlwind, making it impossible for him to think or even hear. Touch and feel were the only things that registered in his foggy brain, and he was doing plenty of both as he quickly began to do away with her boots and the rest of her clothing.

After he'd covered her with one of the sleeping bags to shield her from the cold, he dealt with his own clothing, and all the while, he could feel her gaze roaming over him, watching him with an almost innocent fascination. The idea that she'd not seen a naked man in a long time rattled him a bit. He didn't know what kind of lovers she'd had in her past, and he was suddenly struck by the idea that he might fall short of what she wanted or needed.

He looked at her and tried to stem the unease coursing through him. "Clem, I—I'm getting cold feet."

"That's because you need to get under the cover with me."

Groaning, he shook his head. "Not that kind of cold. I mean—I think you have this idea that I'm some experienced playboy. And I'm not. And I—I'm not sure if I'll do any of this right."

She reached for his hand and tugged until he was lying next to her under the warm sleeping bag and her cheek was pressed against his. "You're not going to do this alone, Quint," she said softly. "We're going to do it together."

He pulled his head back to look at her, and as their eyes met, he knew everything was going to be right and perfect, because she was with him and he with her, and that was all that really mattered.

"Yes, darling, Clem. Together."

He kissed her then, and instantly he was consumed with a desire that burned from the soles of his feet all the way to his scalp. In his arms, he heard her moans and felt the lower part of her body arching hungrily toward his.

It took all his willpower to pull away from her long enough to collect a condom from his wallet, and even after he'd opened the packet, his hands shook so badly, he wasn't sure he could dress himself for the task ahead.

Seeing he was struggling, she raised up and took the piece of latex from his hands. "Lie back and let me do this," she whispered.

If she touched him, he wasn't sure his self-control would hold. But he couldn't admit such a thing to her. No. He'd have to grit his teeth and think of something else. Like Jimmy sitting outside the tent, growling with disapproval.

Her hands were soft and gentle as she rolled the condom onto his erection, but he didn't give her fingers a chance to linger. Instead he flipped her onto her back and parted her thighs with his knee.

"I'm sorry, Clem. I can't keep waiting."

Her lips curved into a provocative smile. "I'm sorry, but I can't keep waiting, either."

Air whooshed from his lungs as her hands clamped onto his buttocks and pulled him down and directly into her womanhood.

The incredible sensation caused his head to snap back, his senses to splinter. Several seconds passed before he finally found the wherewithal to push himself deeper into her hot, velvety folds.

Immediately, her legs wrapped around his and her arms slipped around the lower part of his back. And then suddenly she was moving, arching her hips and drawing him ever so deeper inside. After that, Quint began to thrust. Slowly at first and then faster as the hot desire between them began to build.

They stayed in that same rhythm for what seemed like forever. Each of them giving and taking until his breaths were short and ragged and she was moaning for relief. And all the while, his hands were straining to touch every inch of her, to glide over each curve and valley until the contours of her body were burned into his brain.

This wasn't sex, he thought. This was a wild journey he'd never been on before. He was an out-of-control train with no brakes. No way to stop himself from crashing. But the crazy thing about it, he didn't care if he crashed. In fact, he was waiting for the end. For the relief he'd no doubt find in the ruins.

She was repeating his name and gripping his hipbones when he suddenly felt as if a part of him was leaving the bed and floating around the tiny interior of the tent. The sensation caused him to cry out and clasp her upper body tightly to his. If he was going to soar away, he thought, he was determined not to go without her.

Long moments ticked away before his senses returned to earth, and it wasn't until then that he realized his body had collapsed on top of hers, and he opened his eyes to see strands of her hair had fallen across his face, while his nose was buried against the side of her neck.

Rolling onto his back, he cradled her head against his shoulder and stroked a hand over her tangled hair. She draped an arm across his chest, and the warm weight of it had him thinking how precious it was to have her touching him, loving him.

Love. Yes. Now he understood why Jack and Cordell were changed men. He'd finally learned the difference between sex and making love. A moment ago, he'd given everything to Clementine. Even his heart. And without her, he'd be empty. That was the simple reality.

But was she feeling the same way? Had her caresses and kisses, her sighs, actually been saying I love you?

He had to believe everything she'd just shared with him was real.

Tilting his head downward, he pressed a kiss against her damp forehead. "I love you, Clementine. I want to be with you for the rest of our lives. To love and protect you. To share everything with you."

She was silent for so long that Quint raised up on one elbow and was totally stunned to see tears slipping down her cheeks.

"Aw, Clem, why are you crying? Was I really all that bad?"

The question caused a sob to burst past her lips, and she twisted her head so that her face was partially hidden from his view. "Oh, Quint, please—you were wonderful—too wonderful."

Spoken against his shoulder, her broken words were muffled, but even if he'd heard them clearly it wouldn't have helped him to understand her tears.

Beneath the cover, his hand glided tenderly up and down her arm. "Then why are you crying?"

Tilting her head back, she looked up at him with tears brimming in her eyes. "Because now I have to give up my job and leave Stone Creek Ranch."

Chapter Eleven

The look on his face was worse than if she'd slapped him, and the idea that she was hurting him in any way left her sick inside. Yet she knew it was better to hurt him now than later. As for herself, she felt numb from the mix of emotions swirling through her.

She should have known making love to Quint would be earthshaking. That connecting her heart and soul to him would be a forever sort of thing. But she'd wanted him so badly, she'd tried to convince herself that being in his arms just one time wouldn't change anything. She'd been wrong. And now she was going to have to pay for her mistake in the worst kind of way. Like the rest of her life, she thought, as she tried to blink the tears from her eyes.

"What is that supposed to mean? Give up your job? Leave the ranch? That's crazy talk, Clementine."

"No. Not crazy. It's the only way," she said in a defeated voice. "I can see that if I stay here this will continue to happen over and over with us. I just can't do it, Quint."

"But why? If you love me why would you want to leave?" His eyes were suddenly full of shadows. "Is that what you're trying to tell me? That you don't care that deeply for me?"

She wanted to burst into sobs. She wanted to run out of the tent, jump onto Birdie's back and ride until the darkness of night swallowed them up and she'd no longer have to see the pain on his face.

"Listen to me. I can't love you or anyone. I lost my ability to feel that much a long time ago. And you rate more than half a woman, Quint. You deserve one who isn't afraid to live in the real world."

His hand came up to gently cradle the side of her face, and it was all Clementine could do to keep from reaching for him, from pulling his mouth down to hers and forgetting everything but the sweetness of his love. But there was always tomorrow to consider. And she loved him too much to hurt him.

Yes. Telling him she was incapable of loving him hadn't been the truth, she thought. But it had been the only way to make him see reason.

"Afraid to be in the real world," he thoughtfully repeated. "I can understand why you'd feel that way—up to a point. You've lost a lot in your life. You feel like you can't trust anyone or anything to be constant. Your father and…"

His words halted as she sat up and reached for her clothing. "I've lost more than you know, Quint. I lost a man I truly cared about. Marty walked out of my life and never looked back. He couldn't handle having Dad constantly putting him down and interfering in our relationship. Eventually, Marty decided I wasn't worth the fight."

Behind her, Quint snorted. "You think I could be like him? If so, then you'd better think again. I'm not going to give up on you and walk away!"

Determined to keep her tears at bay, she looked over her shoulder at him. Somehow she managed to keep the tears at bay, but she couldn't stop the painful lump that suddenly lodged in her throat.

"I'm giving you two weeks—three at the most," she said hoarsely, "for you to find a sheepherder to take my place. And during that time I don't want you coming back to my camp, expecting me to jump in bed with you. Having sex with you isn't going to happen again! Ever!"

"Sex!" He very nearly spat the word. "Why are you so determined to lie to me? To put on an act like you don't care? Because you're afraid? Well, here's a news flash for you, Clem. I'm damned scared, too. I saw my grandfather brood over a woman who hurt him so badly he refused to speak her name. I saw Grace agonize over the man she'd always loved and the one she tried to replace him with. And now I watch Hunter, still lost and alone and afraid to let himself even think of marrying again. You think those things have made it easy for me to trust? To want to give my heart to a woman? When it comes to love I've been a coward. Until I met you. I don't intend to be a coward anymore."

Throwing back the sleeping bag, he snatched up his boots and clothes and left the tent. Clementine stared after him, but only for a moment. She had to get dressed and see him off. She had to pretend that her world wasn't coming to an end.

Five minutes later, dressed and bundled in a heavy work coat, with her hat pulled low over her forehead, she watched him untether his horse.

Leading the horse behind him, he walked over to where she stood, and Clementine trembled inside her boots as he gave her face a long, last search.

"Jett will be out with your supplies in a few days," he said crisply. "If snow comes anytime soon, he and I will be out to move the sheep back to lower ground."

Her gaze traveled over to the flock. The ewes and lambs, the rams, they'd all become dear to her. She thought of them as hers. But soon she'd never see them again. The idea tore at her, but it didn't compare to the hard reality of leaving Quint. A hollow hole was already spreading through her chest, making it hard to breathe.

"I can manage to do that without either of you," she said stiffly. "Of course, if I'm already gone, you'll have to do it."

His jaw grew tight. "Christmas is less than three weeks away. I'm sure you know that it's highly unlikely I'll be able to find anyone to tend the sheep. But I guess you don't care."

She really wanted to slap him for that, but that would only give her a moment's satisfaction. And anyway, if he didn't know by now how much she loved the sheep, he was a blind man.

"I care," she said. "But I have to consider my own survival."

His lips twisted into a sneer. "And the only way you can do that is to run away, right?"

"I'm a nomad, Quint. You knew that from the very beginning. Don't hate me for being what I am."

The tautness of his features suddenly softened, and before she guessed his intentions, he lowered his head and placed a kiss on her cheek. "I don't hate you, Clem. That isn't going to happen. But now I have to go home and disappoint my mother. She has the belief that miracles come with the Christmas season. Now I have to tell her they do happen, but just not on Stone Creek Ranch."

With that, he turned and mounted his horse. This time, he didn't lift a hand in farewell. And even if he had, Clementine couldn't have seen it for the wall of tears in her eyes.

"Goodbye, Quint."

It wasn't until Jimmy let out a bark behind her that she realized she'd spoken the words out loud, and she turned to see the dog's gaze going from Clementine to Quint, then back to her as though he was trying to figure out what was going on between them.

Her heart hurting too much to care about showing her affection, she squatted on her heels and signaled for the dog to come to her. When he reached her, she hugged him close, and burying her face in his fur, she silently sobbed.

The next evening Quint was still so upset about Clementine's rejection, he wanted to escape to his bedroom after supper and not have to sit through family talk. But unbeknownst to him, his mother had sent Jett out earlier in the day to chop down a spruce and erect the tree in the den. Since then Bonnie had fetched numerous boxes of Christmas decorations down from the attic and part of the family had gathered to watch the tree being trimmed.

Out of her eight children, Quint had never understood why Claire always wanted him and Cordell to do most of the tree decorating. And because Quint never wanted to let his mother down, he went along with the festive occasion and tried to put on his best happy face.

"Look at the pretty lights, Bridget. Santa and his reindeer are going to see them twinkling through the windows," Cordell said to his little daughter as he carried her around the partially decorated tree.

The redheaded toddler reached toward one of the shiny ornaments and very nearly managed to get her fingers around it.

"Cord, watch out! She'll have the whole tree toppled over if you give her the chance," Maggie called out the warning from where she stood on the hearth, watching her husband and daughter.

"This is Bridget's first Christmas," Cordell told Maggie. "She needs to experience everything up close to get all the fun out of it."

With Bridget fastened to one hip, Cordell continued to drape tinsel around the upper branches of the tree, while Bonnie and Quint hung the ornaments.

"You should hang this ornament, Quint," Bonnie said, handing him a lamb with a tinkling bell around its neck. "This is your department."

"Thanks, Bonnie. I'll try to put him in a safe place."

The bell tinkled as he hung the furry ornament on a sturdy bough, and the sound was like knife pricks to his heart. As he'd lain on Clementine's bed, with her snug and warm in his arms, the sound of the sheep bells had been soothing and joyful. Like Christmas bells ringing out the promise of love everlasting.

Would he ever experience those precious moments with her again? If it was left up to her, he wouldn't. But he wasn't going to leave things totally up to her. Because like it or not, he loved her. And she needed to see she was looking at the world through a dirty window. Still, how was he going to prove to her that they truly belonged together? Not just for a few weeks or months, but until their dying days?

He must have been standing there staring off into space

for much longer than he'd thought, because Cordell's hand suddenly came down on his shoulder.

"Let's go take a break. We have plenty of time to finish this later," he said.

Quint looked at his brother. "I'm okay. I was just— thinking."

"Yeah, I know." He gave Quint's shoulder a nudge. "Bea has made hot chocolate. Let's go have a cup."

Moments later, after serving themselves from a thermos sitting on the coffee table, the two brothers sat down on a small sofa with their cups in hand.

The day had been an exceptionally long one for both men, and Quint didn't try to hide his weariness as he stretched his legs out in front of him.

"I appreciate your help with the water well pump today," Cordell told him. "I'm not nearly as good with mechanics as you are."

"It was either fix the pump or move the cattle. Fixing the pump was the easiest solution."

"Yeah, that range is fairly brushy. Moving cattle from it is never easy," Cord said.

Quint didn't reply. Instead he wiped a hand over his face and wondered whether he'd be able to sleep tonight. Last night was a disaster with him staring at the dark walls of his bedroom and making love to Clementine over and over in his mind.

"So what happened?"

Quint sipped the hot chocolate before turning a blank look on his brother. "About what? The sheep sale? Nothing. I'm considering a different flock."

Cordell rolled his eyes. "I'm not talking about sheep. I mean with Clementine. I know you rode out to see her yesterday and came back looking like a zombie. In fact, you look even worse today."

"Thanks. Nice of you to notice," Quint said sarcastically.

Shaking his head, Cordell said, "Sarcasm won't make me or the problem go away."

Staring glumly into his cup, he said, "Clementine has given me her notice to quit."

It took a lot to surprise Cordell, but this sent his brows shooting straight up. "Quit? Are you kidding? I thought she loved her job. What brought this about?"

Quint blew out a heavy breath. "I told her how I feel about her. And she—she can't deal with it."

"And how do you feel about her?" Cordell asked.

"I love her. But she refuses to give us a chance."

Regarding him thoughtfully, Cordell asked, "Because she's older than you?"

Quint made a frustrated sound. "Oh, she uses that as one excuse. But it's not the main reason. She's mostly afraid. Because she doesn't believe she could ever live like regular folks. She thinks as long as she's off to herself, sheepherding in the mountains, there won't be any danger of anyone hurting her. Not emotionally, that is."

Frowning, Cordell said, "Man, she must be carrying scars from some sort of tragedy."

"Some ugly things have happened to her in her past, Cord. It's a long story."

"We have plenty of time before we get back to the Christmas tree."

Quint glanced across the room to where their parents were playing with Bridget and the twins were keeping Maggie company. All of them were relaxed and happy, and he thought how wonderful it would be if Clementine could be a part of the family, if she would let, not only him, but all of the Hollisters love her as she deserved to be loved.

Turning back to Cordell, he said, "All right. Just keep this to yourself, though. I don't want her to ever think I'm talking about her behind her back. I'm only telling you because I think you care."

"You damn well know I care."

Quint nodded, then quickly related the whole story of Clementine's parents divorcing, her mother leaving, her father remarrying and the stepmother moving in, followed by Trent Starr's suspicious death. Which eventually led to Clementine and her brother, Kipp, losing their ranch.

Once he'd finished the story, Cordell whistled lowly under his breath. "Dear God, no wonder she wants to be alone. After all that, I wouldn't trust anybody."

"Oh, that's not the end of it, Cord. Wedged somewhere between all those disappointments, Clem lost a boyfriend. One she was apparently thinking about marrying. Seems he couldn't deal with her domineering father."

Cordell shook his head in dismay. "That's a load of baggage, Quint. And frankly, I don't think giving her more time will help matters. She's already had eight years and that hasn't fixed her. Maybe she needs some sort of closure with her father's death and losing the ranch. Then she might be able to move on. She might see that making a life with you is what she wants. Although, I don't have a clue as to how you might go about giving her those things."

Closure. Yes, Quint thought, before Clementine could ever start a new life she was going to need to shut the book on those chapters of her past life. Getting that done wouldn't be easy, he thought. But he had to try. Because he couldn't envision his future without her.

"Thanks, Cord."

Cordell grinned. "I haven't done anything yet. Except got you off your feet and put a cup of hot chocolate in your hand."

"Wrong. You've made me believe in Christmas miracles again."

Chuckling, Cordell said, "Gee, and Mom always called me her little Christmas grinch. So can I expect to find a special gift from you under the tree this year?"

"Not unless we finish the decorations."

Cordell drained the last of his hot chocolate, then made a thumbs-up sign to Quint. "Ho! Ho! Ho! It's off to work we go!"

Clementine dropped an armload of dead limbs onto the pile of firewood and trudged back up the mountainside to the fallen aspen to gather another load. She'd been fortunate to find the hardwood to use for her fire. Pine limbs were plentiful, but they burned up rapidly and produced far more smoke. With the cold weather persisting, she'd been forced to keep the fire going from early morning until she crawled into her sleeping bag at night. At least this aspen wood would last somewhat longer.

Yesterday, she'd moved the flock and her camp down from the foothills and onto the western mouth of the valley. She'd been relieved to find a substantial amount of winter grasses at the lower elevation, so there'd be plenty of grazing for the next several days.

Surprisingly, the snows that normally hit this area by now hadn't yet appeared. She didn't know whether that was a good omen or just Mother Nature's way of adding to her agony. Either way, she and the flock were a long distance from the ranch yard. When the snows did come, Quint would be forced to send a man, or come himself, to help her push the flock homeward.

Yes, she'd told him she could manage the task on her own, and if necessary, she could. But he wasn't the type to leave her to do a major job without supplying her with extra help. Still, a week and a half had already passed without any sign of him, and she wondered how much longer it would be before he showed up to end her employment.

Isn't that what you wanted, Clementine? You told him not to come back. You told him you'd never have sex with him again. You're getting exactly what you asked for. So why are you moping around like a sick lamb?

Shoving at the grim questions rolling through her mind, she gathered up another armload of fallen limbs. As she carried the load back to camp, she realized it was fruitless for her to try to deny the love she felt for Quint. She did love him. With everything inside her she loved him. That's why it hurt so much to give him up. That's why she was cursing the day she'd ever come to Utah and Stone Creek Ranch. Yet she couldn't roll back time and change anything. She simply had to get on with her life. Somewhere far away from Quint.

She and the four dogs were strolling through the flock when Zina let out a warning yip. The alert sent the dogs in a protective circle around the sheep, while Clementine peered toward the east. Throughout the long weeks that she'd been on the ranch, she'd not encountered a pack of coyotes or a wandering bear or mountain lion. Therefore, she'd gotten somewhat lax about carrying her rifle when she ventured on foot from camp. But then, she'd gotten careless about many things since she'd met Quint and his family, she thought. She'd let the iron curtain around her heart crack just enough to give more pain a chance to seep inside. She'd been behaving like a fool and now she was paying for it.

Zina let out another yip, and this time Clementine spotted the reason for the dog's agitation. A rider was approaching from the east, and judging from his stature and the way he sat the horse, it wasn't Quint. The knowledge filled her with disappointment.

Slowly, she walked through the sheep until she was standing at the edge of the herd. As the rider grew closer, she recognized Jett and immediately felt a spurt of relief. Hopefully he could answer some of the questions that were eating at her.

"Hello, Clementine. How's it going?"

The casual greeting grated on her raw nerves. How the hell did he think it was going with her? Surely Quint had already told Jett she was leaving Stone Creek Ranch. That she was counting the days until she packed up and headed back to Idaho. Counting the hours, even the minutes to when she'd be gone and never see Quint again. The reality was killing her and yet she had to pretend that everything was normal.

"Everything is okay," she said. "How about you?"

"Good," he said with a happy grin. "Christmas is coming. It's a fun time to be on the ranch. The Hollisters always go all out for the holiday. Claire sent sugar cookies over to the work barn this morning. I brought you some."

Christmas with the Hollisters. Yes, she could imagine the huge family gathering to celebrate the occasion. The house would be beautifully decorated and sugary treats and rich food would be everywhere. Kisses and hugs would be exchanged along with gifts. Most of all, the house would be filled with love. At one time, before her parents had divorced, the ranch house on the

Rising Starr had been that same way. But those happy days had been gone for years.

Shaking away the memories, she said, "Thanks. That was thoughtful of you, Jett."

"I brought a few supplies. Not enough to bring the pack horse, though," he told her. "I guess if you're still here later next week, Quint will send me out with more."

"If? He's supposed to be finding another sheepherder to take my place," Clementine said with a measure of frustration. "Has he mentioned if he's hired anyone yet?"

Jett glanced away from her, but not before Clementine spotted the awkward look on his face. Apparently he didn't want to be caught in the middle of a sticky situation, and Clementine couldn't blame him. Like her, he was just a hired hand trying to do his job.

"No. Haven't heard him mention anything about hiring a sheepherder. Guess you'll have to speak with him about that," he said, then turned his attention back to her. "Course that would be kinda hard to do seeing that he's been away from the ranch. Been gone for a few days now."

Rattled by this news, she frowned at him. "Gone? Away from the ranch, where?"

Jett shrugged both shoulders, but his eyes dropped to the ground, and Clementine got the impression the man knew much more than he'd ever tell.

"I don't know. I just heard him telling Cord something about going after a Christmas gift. Guess it's taking him a few days to get that done."

She stared at him in disbelief. If she knew one thing about Quint, it would be that he'd never leave the ranch for any length of time. Not unless he had something important to tend to.

"That's the lamest thing I've ever heard, Jett. Can't you come up with something better?"

He threw up both hands in a helpless gesture. "I swear, Clementine, I'm in the dark. I don't know where he is. But I'd bet my life savings, which ain't much, but I'd bet it, that you'll be seeing him soon."

No, Jett. You don't know the awful things I said to him. You didn't see the hurt and anger on his face when he rode away.

"Only because of the sheep," Clementine replied.

Jett frowned. "Well, not just because of the sheep. It's nearly Christmas. He wouldn't leave you out here alone for the holidays."

Biting back a sigh, Clementine looked over her shoulder at the flock. Nearly all of the ewes were growing heavy with babies. She'd miss seeing the newborn lambs that would begin arriving next month, along with many more things on Stone Creek Ranch.

"The sheep won't know it's Christmas."

"No. But you will," he said, then gestured to his horse. "I'll ride on up to camp and unload your supplies. By the way, you have some mail. I tried not to crinkle it too much."

He fished an envelope from inside his sherpa-lined jacket and handed it to her. Without looking at the address, she stuffed the letter into her pocket. "Thanks, Jett. I'll meet you up at camp."

He rode off, and Clementine walked slowly through the sheep and scrubby sage brush until she reached the campsite. Jett was already there, placing the supplies on a makeshift table she'd made from rolling two boulders together with the flat sides up.

"There's plenty of coffee, Jett, if you'd like a cup before you leave."

He tossed the empty saddlebags over one shoulder. "Thanks, but I need to head on back. Cord wants me to take the new ranch hands up to the C Bar C land and show them around. We need more cattle up there. You know, Stone Creek just keeps growing. One of these days it might be as big as that Hollister place down in Arizona. Wouldn't that be something?"

It would be something, all right, Clementine thought. But she'd never see the hundreds more sheep that Quint wanted, or the barns he planned to build for winter sheltering and spring shearing.

"Yes, it's growing."

With the supplies unloaded, Jett mounted his horse, but before he reined the animal back down the valley, he said, "You know, Clementine, you should hang a sheep bell near your tent or a sprig of mistletoe over the door flap. Christmas is coming. You ought to get in the mood."

She wanted to cry, not celebrate. "I'll think about it."

He nudged the horse's sides, and as it walked away, he called back to her. "See you next time."

No. There wasn't going to be any next time. She wasn't going to keep sitting here, agonizing over whether Quint was going to find the time or the decency to relieve her of a job that had basically been over as soon as they'd made love.

The idea caused her eyes to grow misty, and she pressed her lips tightly together and stared up at the sky. Thankfully it was covered with clouds and she couldn't see the exact color of Quint's blue eyes.

...I think you'll be happy to hear I've agreed to go with Buck to a Christmas party at the VFW next week. There'll be dancing. Just another reason for him to put his hands on me. But I've been think-

*ing and I have to admit it's nice to be touched by
a man again. A good man, that is.*

*Charlie is flying down from Alaska for the holi-
days. In a couple of days I'll drive over and pick
him up at the Pocatello airport. I'll be glad to see
him. Though, it would be nicer if he would have a
wife and kids with him. But I've given up on him
ever having a family.*

*The town has put up new Christmas decora-
tions this year. At night the lights look like Las
Vegas. I wish you could see them. It doesn't feel
right with you not being here in December. Is
the weather getting bad there yet? I hope you
are staying warm and your young boss is taking
good care of you.*
Your loving Nuttah.

Clementine's hands shook ever so slightly as she
folded the letter Jett had delivered to her four days ago
and pushed it down in the pocket of her jeans.

During the weeks she'd been here, she'd received a
few other letters from Nuttah, but something about this
one had struck her deep. Especially the very last line.
Clementine had read it over and over and each time
she reached the end, a lump of emotions started burning in her throat.

I hope your young boss is taking good care of you.

Yes, Quint had tried to protect and shelter her. He
tried to love her. But she'd kept pushing him away and
trying to pretend she could continue with the life she'd
made for herself these past eight years. But these past
two weeks without him had been a hellish revelation. No
matter how deep into the mountains she ran, she knew
the pain would follow her. She couldn't go on as she'd

been doing—trying to hide from life. She loved Quint with all her heart. Without him her skies were always cloudy. The joy of her job was gone, and as she looked toward the future, she saw nothing but more heartache.

It doesn't have to be that way, Clementine. All you have to do is find the courage to tell Quint how much you love him and want the two of you to be together for always.

But she'd not seen him in over two weeks. Maybe during all those days he'd decided he was truly finished with her. Even if she confessed her feelings, he might not even care anymore. And then what would she do? Run. Like she'd been running for the past eight years? No, she thought. This time she had to be like Kipp. She had to stand and fight and vow to never give up on the things she wanted most. Even if it meant taking risks.

With that decision made, she felt a surge of hope and a sense of purpose.

Tomorrow, she'd saddle Birdie and ride to the ranch yard. With any luck, Quint would be there, and one way or the other, she'd make him listen to everything she had to say.

Almost two hours later, the evening was growing late, sending purple shadows across the valley floor. As she walked the perimeter of the flock, making sure all the sheep were accounted for, the sound of popping brush and ringing bells sounded above the nearby trickle of Bird Creek.

As she turned and attempted to gaze around a thick stand of sage and juniper, all four dogs took off in a run toward the noise that sounded incredibly to Clementine like sheep.

Jimmy was the last to go, and Clementine called

loudly to the excited dog. "Jimmy! Here, boy! Stay with the sheep."

Just as he came trotting back to her, she spotted the Merino sheep spilling into the meadow and merging with her flock. Dear heaven, no wonder the dogs were distracted!

Where had these sheep come from? Just guessing, there appeared to be over a hundred! Quint had talked about purchasing more sheep, but she'd not expected to see any animals on her watch. Apparently in the past weeks he'd been away, he'd found the flock he wanted. Which probably meant he'd also found a herder to take her place. The reality left her sick with regret.

The idea was swirling through her brain when she spotted two riders in the distance. The sorrel with a blaze on its face resembled Quint's horse, but she didn't recognize the gray traveling along at its side.

Her heart thumping with uncertainty, she walked slowly to an open area and watched as the two men grew closer. When they were finally close enough to recognize their faces, her mouth fell open with shock.

Quint! And Kipp! Her brother was with Quint! What was he doing here in Utah? And why was Quint smiling at her as though she was still his darling Clementine? Was she dreaming this whole scene?

Her brother was the first to dismount, and before she could say a word, he grabbed her into a tight hug.

"Sis! It's so good to see you!" He ended the hug, then smacked several kisses to her cheek. "I should've known you'd be as beautiful as ever!"

Holding on to his hands, she stared at him in wonder. "Kipp, what are you doing here? Have you left the Rising Starr?"

Shaking his head, he glanced at Quint. "I'm here

to help my soon-to-be brother-in-law with a problem. And no, I'm still at the Rising Starr. I told Andrea I was taking a few days off to spend the holiday with you."

"Help? Brother-in-law? You're going to have to explain what all of this means."

Laughing at the confusion on her face, Kipp hugged her again, then grinned at Quint who was standing patiently to one side.

He said, "Since Quint found me, and I thank God that he did, we've had several long talks. He's promised to help me get the Rising Starr back, and I've promised to help talk you into marrying him."

Stunned, Clementine darted a glance at Quint. He was still smiling at her, a smile so tender that tears sprouted to her eyes.

"Marry?" she repeated in an incredulous voice. "After everything I said to you?"

Kipp chuckled. "I believe Quint is going to give you the chance to unsay all those words. So if you love the man, you'd better go tell him so. At the moment, I've got a date with your coffeepot."

Her brother grabbed up his horse's reins and began walking toward the rise where her camp was located. For a brief second, Clementine watched him go and then she looked anxiously at Quint. Without hesitation, he held his arms out to her, and with a little cry she ran to him.

"Oh, Quint! Quint!" With her arms pressed tight around his waist, she buried her face against his chest and wept with joy and relief. "I've been so very, very miserable without you. I thought—you've been gone so long. And I knew I'd probably ruined things for us. But I—"

"My darling Clem, it's okay now. Everything is going

to be good—the best—because we have each other. You understand that now, don't you?"

His arms held her so tightly she could scarcely breathe, but she didn't care. To be able to drink in his familiar scent and feel the warmth of his strong body seeping into hers was like sunshine breaking through the storm. She'd never get enough of him.

"I understand that I love you, Quint. I think I've loved you from the very beginning. But I've been so afraid. It's been so long since I've lived a normal life. I wasn't sure I could. But over these past three weeks, I've come to realize I can't live without you, and that's all that really matters, isn't it?"

Laughing now, he swept off her hat, then with a finger beneath her chin, he tilted her head up. "Don't worry, Clem. I'll help you get adjusted to living like a normal person—as my wife. And the mother of the children I hope we'll have together. How does that sound?"

She smiled at him through happy tears. "Like how I imagine heaven will be. And yes, yes, I'll marry you!"

He lowered his lips to hers and let his kiss convey all the love and joy he was feeling. "Well, I should tell you that we have a hundred and twenty-five more sheep now to go with the flock we already had. Kipp helped me locate the perfect flock up in Idaho, and I've spent the past week getting them transported here to the ranch."

She asked in a wondrous voice, "We? You're calling it *our* flock?"

He continued to hold her tight. "Of course it will be *our* flock. So if you get to feeling the urge to do some sheepherding from time to time, we'll come out here to the mountains and do it together. But there's only one problem with that."

Her expression quizzical, she asked, "What's the problem?"

"Jimmy. I've got to make friends with that dog or he's going to make my life miserable."

Chuckling, she said, "Look behind you. I think he's already decided he can't get rid of you."

Quint glanced over his shoulder to see Jimmy sitting on his haunches watching them with a big dog grin on his face.

Laughing, Quint turned back to her and pressed another long kiss to her lips. "You know," he murmured against her cheek. "Mom was right after all. Christmas is a time for miracles."

Epilogue

Clementine couldn't remember the last time she'd seen her brother look so happy, and the sight of him laughing with the twins over something one of them had said put a smile on her face.

Sitting next to her, on a couch directly across from Kipp and the twins, Quint spoke near her ear. "Poor Kipp. Bea and Bonnie have monopolized him for the better part of the evening. His head is going to be spinning before this Christmas night is over."

The day had been a long one, starting early with gift giving and breakfast for anyone who dared to eat and run the risk of ruining their appetite for the huge dinner that had come later in the afternoon. The meal had gone on and on with laughter and talk and endless toasts of goodwill. Once everyone was filled to the brim with the rich food, the group had migrated to the den where the children had been playing with new toys and the adults sipped hot drinks.

Now, as Clementine sat with the warm weight of Quint's arm resting across the back of her shoulders, contentment and peace poured through her. Finally accepting his love had given her courage and strength, and it amazed her at how calm and certain she felt about returning to a regular life where necessities weren't considered luxuries and the walls of a house would keep her warm. There were no guarantees that her life with Quint would always be a bed of roses. But with him at her side, she knew she could deal with any situation, whether it be good or bad.

She gave Quint a knowing little smile. "Does my brother look miserable to you?" she asked, then sighed at the gratifying sight of a room filled with a loving family. "I've never seen Kipp so carefree. Believe me, he's lapping up all the attention the twins are giving him. And he's enjoying every minute here on Stone Creek Ranch, too."

"I'm glad. To be honest, all of us wish Kipp would stay here," Quint remarked. "We could certainly use his experience and knowledge of raising cattle and sheep. And we already consider him a part of the family. But I understand he has to go back to Idaho. He wants to undo the wrongs done to him and you."

Clementine reached over and squeezed Quint's hand. "I'm so grateful to you and Flint for offering to help him. Although, I'm not sure what any of you can do to get the ranch back into Starr hands."

He gave her an encouraging smile. "We're not sure yet. But with Flint working as a law official, he has connections that can help. I assure you, Clem, we'll never give up on this. Not until things get righted for you and your brother."

For the first time since her father had died, Clementine felt encouraged about Kipp getting the ranch back. For her brother's sake she wanted him to have what was rightly his. As for herself, spending her life with Quint was all she'd ever need to make her happy.

"And speaking of going to Idaho," Quint went on, "I'm not sure if you overheard Van talking about the information she's gathered concerning Grandfather's birth information. It doesn't sound promising."

"I wasn't in the room when Van brought up the subject, but Claire told me later that Scarlett has been located in an assisted living home up in Coeur d'Alene," she replied.

Quint grimaced. "Right. But according to the director of the facility, the woman is suffering with some type of dementia. It's unlikely she can tell us anything. And even if she does, the information might be way off base."

"Maybe not. Usually people with memory problems tend to recall the past much better than short-term happenings. And by the way, I once worked near Coeur d'Alene for a sheep farmer. The countryside was gorgeous, but the weather could get really brutal," she said, then cast him a thoughtful glance. "I wonder how your grandfather's ex-wife ended up in Coeur d'Alene? It's a long distance from here. I'm wondering, too, if she might have any relatives in the area?"

"Dad has been asking that same question. After the holidays, I expect he'll be sending someone from the family up there to investigate. But it won't be me." He touched a forefinger to her cheek. "You and I have important things to tend to."

"Oh, what kind of things?" she asked curiously.

Quint was about to answer when Cord and Hunter strolled up to them, and, giving her a promising wink, he said, "I'll tell you later."

* * *

Later didn't come until everyone had left the den to retire for the night. Once the room was quiet and the two were finally alone, Quint took Clementine by the hand and ushered her over to the fireplace. Low flames were still burning from the stack of red coals, emitting a delicious warmth over the rock hearth where they were standing.

As his parents had been the last to leave the room, Hadley had turned off most of the lights. Whether his dad had done it to conserve electricity or make the den more romantic, Quint had no idea. Either way he was grateful that this end of the room was only illuminated from the soft glow of the fire. It reminded him of the first time he'd sat with Clementine at her campfire and he'd watched the golden light flicker on her face.

"Are you not ready for bed?" Clementine asked.

"Not quite. We were going to talk about what we'll be doing after the holidays. Remember?"

"Vaguely," she teased, then rising on her tiptoes, she pressed a kiss to his cheek. "But I'm fairly sure I can guess what you and I are going to be doing in the coming weeks. Helping all the lambs be safely born. And maybe laying out the barn you're planning."

Grinning, he snapped his fingers. "Darn it, I can't surprise you with anything, can I?"

She lovingly touched a finger to the diamond pin fashioned in the shape of a lamb that he'd pinned to her dress early this morning. "I was more than surprised with this gift, Quint. I'm still reeling over what it probably cost you. It's outlandish—especially for a girl who doesn't wear diamonds."

Laughing softly, he planted a kiss on her temple. "I'm going to be changing that. You know, diamonds are one of the toughest materials on earth. You can wear them while you're tending sheep and not have to worry about scratching or cracking a stone."

She slipped her arms around his waist and hugged him closer. "That's good to know. I can wear my pin while I'm in the sheep pen. Get it? A pin in the pen."

Chuckling again, he reached into the pocket of his jeans and pulled out a small jewelry box. "I get it. But those aren't the only diamonds you'll be wearing, Clem."

"What?" Easing slightly back from him, she spotted the velvet box. "Oh, Quint! If that's another gift, you're going to be in trouble."

"Yeah. In trouble for the rest of my life—hopefully." He flipped the lid open and watched her brown eyes grow wide at the sight of the diamond engagement ring.

"A ring?" she whispered huskily. "Isn't this a little fast? Don't you want to think on it a bit longer?"

"As far as I'm concerned, I wish it was all happening faster." His smile tender, he said, "I realize I've already told you how much I want you to be my wife. But you deserve a proper proposal. I love you, Clementine. Will you marry me? Soon? Like really soon?"

The sound that passed her lips was somewhere between a laugh and a sob. "Oh, Quint, I love you so much. Yes! Yes!"

He slipped the platinum band holding a square cluster of diamonds onto her finger, then lowering his lips to hers, he kissed her deeply and tenderly.

When he finally eased his mouth from hers, he said, "You know, each time I kiss you something magical happens. Will it always be that way?"

Her eyes were glowing as she gazed up at him. "Love is magical, Quint. You taught me that."

He kissed her again, and then as he lifted his head, he caught a glimpse of the windows facing the backyard.

"Clem, I believe I see snowflakes! Want to go outside and have a look?"

"I'd love to."

After pulling on coats, they walked outside on the patio and hand in hand stood peering at the western horizon. The night sky was already thick with fat white snowflakes, some of which were already sticking to the brown grass in the yard.

"This means we'll be hauling alfalfa out to the flock tomorrow or the next day," Quint mused out loud.

"I'm glad," she said. "I'm anxious to get a good look at the new sheep and see how they're all faring."

Squeezing her hand, he looked down at her. Although she was still the lovely woman who'd walked into the Wagon Spoke that fateful afternoon, there was an obvious difference in the way she looked now. Sadness had disappeared from her face, and for the rest of his life Quint was going to make sure it never returned.

"We're going to have a great life," he murmured. "Raising our children and our sheep together."

"Together, yes." With a sigh, she gazed up at the wintry sky. "The only thing that would have made this night more perfect would be for us to be able to see the Christmas star. But even though we can't see it through the clouds and snow, we know it's up there—shining down on us."

Circling his arms around her, he pressed his cheek to hers. "My darling Clem, you're my Christmas star. Tonight and always."

* * * * *

SPECIAL EXCERPT FROM

HARLEQUIN
SPECIAL
EDITION

Divorced rancher Hutch Dawson has one heck of a
Christmas wish: find a nanny for his baby triplets.
And Savannah Walsh is his only applicant! Who
knew that his high school nemesis would be the
perfect solution to his very busy—and lonely—
holiday season...

Read on for a sneak preview of
Triplets Under the Tree
by Melissa Senate.

Chapter One

Hutch Dawson's new nanny stood in the doorway of his home office with his squirming, screeching baby daughter in her arms. "Sorry, but this just isn't working out," she said.

He inwardly sighed but completely understood. His triplets were *a lot*. But maybe if he didn't look up from his computer screen, she'd take pity on him and go back into the living room where he could hear his other two babies crying. It was four thirty and her day ended at five. If he could just have this last half hour to deal with his to-do list.

He had three texts from his cowboys to return. Two important calls, including one from the vet with a steer's test results. And he was in the middle of responding to his brother's passive-aggressive email about the needs of the Dueling Dawsons Ranch.

The woman marched in, holding Chloe out with her legs dangling as though she were a bomb about to explode. Given the sight of the baby's clenched fists and red face, she was about to let out one hell of a wail.

She did, grabbing on to the nanny's ear too.

Mrs. Philpot, with her disheveled bun and shirt full of spit-up stains, grimaced and pried tiny fingers from her ear. "I won't be back tomorrow." She stood at the side of his desk and held out the baby.

This wasn't a big surprise. The previous nanny had quit two days ago, also lasting two days. But Hutch had to have childcare. He had ten days to go before his ex-wife was due back from her honeymoon—he could still barely wrap his mind around the fact that they were divorced with six-month-old triplets and that she'd re-married practically five minutes later. With two of his cowboys away for the holidays, his prickly brother— and new business partner—constantly calling or texting or demanding a meeting, a fifteen hundred acre ranch to run and way too many things to think about, Hutch *needed* a nanny.

Chloe let out a whimper between her shrieks, and Hutch snapped to attention, her plaintive cry going straight to his heart. He stood and took his baby girl, Daddy's arms calming her some. The moment Mrs. Philpot was free, she turned and hurried from the room. By the time he'd shifted Chloe against him and went after Mrs. Philpot to talk, use his powers of persuasion, to *beg*, she had on her coat and boots, her hand on the doorknob.

Noooo, he thought. *Wait!*

"I'll double your salary!" he called as she opened the door and raced out to her car in the gravel drive.

Then again, her salary, like the two nannies before her, had already been doubled. The director of the nanny agency had assured him that Mrs. Philpot, who'd raised triplets of her own, wouldn't be scared off by a little crying in triplicate.

A little. Was there any such thing?

"They're just too much for me, dear," Mrs. Philpot called back. She smoothed a hanging swath of her silver hair back into the bun, rubbed her yanked-on ear, then got into her car and peeled away, leaving him staring at the red taillights disappearing down the long drive.

And hoping for a miracle. Like that she'd turn back. At least finish the day. Even that would be a big help.

He did not see the car returning.

The other two babies were screaming their little heads off in their swings in the living room. Hutch was lucky he was hundreds of acres and many miles away from his nearest neighbor in any direction. This morning, before his workday, before the nanny was due to arrive, he'd dared take the trio into town because he'd discovered he was out of coffee and needed some and fast. He'd taken them to Java House, and two of the babies started shrieking. Compassionate glances of commiseration from those sitting at the café tables with their lattes and treats turned into annoyed glares. One woman came up to him and said, "They could really benefit from pacifiers and so could we."

He'd been about to explain that his ex-wife had gotten him to agree to wean the triplets off their pacifiers now that they were six months old. He truly tried to adhere to Allison's lists and rules and schedules since she really was better at all of it than he was, than he'd been since day one. Even her new husband, a very nice, calm optometrist named Ted, was better at caring for the triplets than Hutch was.

He shifted Chloe again, grateful that she, at least, had stopped crying. Whether from being in her daddy's arms or the blast of cold December air, flurries swirling, or both, he didn't know. She wore just cotton PJs, so he stepped back inside and closed the door. In the living room, Carson and Caleb were crying, the gentle rocking motion, their swings with the soft lullabies and pastel-mobile with little stuffed animals spinning having no effect. Little arms were raised, faces miserable.

What Hutch really needed was to turn into an octopus. He could cuddle each baby, make a bottle and down a huge mug of strong coffee all at the same time. He might have been chased out of Java House but not before he'd bought himself an espresso to go and two pounds of Holiday Blend dark beans.

"Hang on, guys," he told the boys, and put Chloe in her swing. She immediately started crying again, which he should have seen coming. "Kiddos, let me make a quick call. Then I'll be back and we'll see what the schedule says."

He lived by the schedule. His ex-wife was a stickler for it, and Hutch, truly no expert on how to care for triplet babies, regarded it as a bible. Between the trio's general disposition, which was crotchety, to use a favorite word of his late mother, and the three-page schedule, complete with sticky notes and addendums, it was no wonder Hutch had gone through six nannies in six months.

And he really was no better at caring for his own children than he was when they were born. He might be making excuses, but he blamed his lack of skills on the fact that he'd been relegated to part-time father from the moment they'd arrived into the world. His ex had left him for another man—her "soulmate"—when she was five months pregnant. He and Allison had joint fifty-fifty custody, so Hutch had the triplets three and a half days a week, which meant half the time to figure out how to care for them, to discover who they were becoming with each passing day, who liked and disliked what, what worked on which triplet. On his ex's custody days, he'd miss little firsts or milestones, and though just last week she'd Facetimed the trio trying their first taste of solids—jarred baby cereal—it wasn't the same as being there and experiencing it with them.

With his ex away for the next ten days, Hutch was actually very happy to have them to himself. The triplets were here, in his home, on his turf. Hutch's life might have been upended by the breakup of his marriage and the loss of his father just months ago and then everything going on with the ranch, but for the next week and a half his babies would be here when he woke up in the morning and here when he went to sleep. That made everything better, gave him peace, made all the other stuff going on trivial. Almost trivial.

He hurried into his office and grabbed his phone and pressed the contact button for the nanny agency, then went back into the living room, trying to gently shush the triplets, hoping his presence would calm them.

"I'm sorry, I can't hear you over the crying," the agency director said, her tone a bit strained. He had a feeling she'd already heard from Mrs. Philpot that she would not be back tomorrow. The woman had gotten *that* call four times before.

Hutch hurried to his office, closing the door till it was just ajar. He explained his predicament. "I'll *triple* the salary of whoever can start tomorrow morning," he said. "I'll even double the salary of *two* nannies so that the big job isn't heaped on one person at such a busy time." Emergency times meant emergency measures.

"That's quite generous, Mr. Dawson, but I'm sorry

to say that we're plumb out of nannies until after the new year." His heart sank as he glanced at his computer, the blinking cursor on his half-finished email to his brother, his to-do list running in his head. "If I may make a suggestion," she added—kindly Hutch thought, hope flaring.

"Please do," he said.

"You have quite a big family here in town—all those Dawsons with babies and young children and therefore tons of experience. Call in the cavalry."

Just what his cousins wanted to do when they had families, jobs, and responsibilities of their own and right in the middle of the holiday season. He'd leaned on the generosity and expertise of various Dawsons for the past six months. He needed a dedicated nanny—even part-time.

As he disconnected from the disappointing call with the agency and went back out into the living room, his gaze landed on the tilted, bare Christmas tree he'd ordered from a nearby farm the other day when one of those Dawson cousins noted there *was* no tree. Not a half hour after it was delivered, Hutch had accidentally backed into it while rocking Carson in one arm and trying to push Chloe in the triple stroller since that usually helped her stop crying. Two bare branches hung down pathetically. He'd meant to decorate the tree, but between running the ranch and caring for the triplets once the nanny left, the box of ornaments and garland remained in the basement.

He looked at his precious babies. He needed to do better—for them. No matter what else, it was Christmas. They deserved *better*.

Caleb was crying harder now. Chloe looked spitting mad. Carson just looked...sad. Very sad. *Please pick me up, Daddy*, his big blue tearful eyes and woeful frown said.

"All right, kiddos, I'm coming," he said, rallying himself. He went for very sad Carson, undid the harness and scooped him out. This time, just holding the little guy seemed to help. But no, it was just a momentary curiosity in the change of position because Carson started crying again. He carefully held the baby against him with one firm arm, then got Chloe out and gave them both a rocking bounce, which seemed to help for two seconds. Now Caleb was wailing harder.

Hutch needed a minute to think—what time it was, what the schedule said. He wasn't *off*-schedule; he knew that. He put both babies in the playpen and turned on the lullaby player, then he consulted his phone for the schedule.

6:00 p.m.: Dinner. Offer a jar of vegetable baby food. Caleb and Chloe love sweet potatoes. Carson's favorite is string beans. Burp each baby. 6:30: Tummy time. 6:45: Baths, cornstarch and ointment as needed before diapers and P.Js. 7:00 p.m.: Story time. 7:45: Bedtime.

It was five forty-five. Clearly the babies needed something *now*. But what? Were they hungry a little early? Had soggy diapers? Tummy aches—gas? He tried to remember what he'd read in last night's chapter of *Your Baby's First Year* for month six. But Chloe had awakened at just after midnight as he'd been about to drift off with month six milestones in his head, and then everything went out of his brain as he'd gotten up to tend to her. The moment he'd laid her back down in her bassinet in the nursery, Caleb's eyes popped open. At least Carson had slept through.

The schedule went out of his head as he remembered he still had to return the texts from one of his cowboys and had mini fires to put out. He stood in the middle of his living room, his head about to explode. He had to get on top of everything—the triplets' needs and the to-do list.

Maybe someone would magically respond to his ongoing ad for a nanny in the *Bear Ridge Weekly*. Just days ago he'd updated the half-page boxed ad, which ran both online and in the print edition with an optional border of tiny santas and candy canes to make the job seem more…festive. He quickly typed *Bear Ridge Weekly* classifieds into his phone's search bar to make sure his ad was indeed running. Yup. There it was. The holiday border did help, in his opinion.

Loving, patient nanny needed for six-month-old triplets from now till December 23rd. M-F, 8:00 a.m. to 5:00 p.m. Highly paid position, one hour for lunch, plus two half-hour breaks. See Hutch Dawson at the Dueling Dawsons Ranch.

He'd gotten several responses from the general ad over the past six months, but some candidates had seemed too rigid or unsmiling, and the few he'd tried out in between the agency nannies had also quit. One lasted three days. Now, everyone in town seemed to know not to respond to his ad. *It's those crotchety triplets!*

Caleb was suddenly shrieking so loud that Hutch was surprised the big round mirror over the console table by the front door didn't shatter. He quickly scooped up the baby boy and rubbed his back, which seemed to quiet him for a second. Chloe had her arms up again. Carson was still crying—but not wailing like Caleb. A small blessing there, at least.

The doorbell rang. Thank God, that had to be Mrs. Philpot with a change of heart because it was the Christmas season! Or maybe it was one of those wonderful Dawson cousins, any number of whom often stopped by with a lasagna—for him, not the babies—or outgrown baby items. They could strategize, make a nanny materialize out of thin, cold air. Mary Poppins, please.

He went to the door. It was neither Mrs. Philpot nor a Dawson.

It was someone he hadn't laid eyes on in seventeen years, since high school graduation. She was instantly recognizable. Very tall. The long red wavy hair. The sharp, assessing brown eyes. Plus there had always been something a little fancy about her. Like the cashmere emerald green coat and polished black cowboy boots she wore.

It was Savannah Walsh, his old high school nemesis—really, his enemy since kindergarten—standing there on his porch. In her hand was the updated ad from the *Bear Ridge Weekly*.

It might have been almost twenty years since he'd seen her, but he doubted she was anything like Mary Poppins.

"You might not remember me," Savannah said in a rush of words, her heart hammering away so loud she was surprised he didn't hear it over all the wailing. "Savannah Walsh? We were in school together." *I had an intense crush on you since the first time I saw you—kindergarten. And every year I secretly loved you more...*

"I'd recognize you anywhere," he said, giving the baby in his arms a bounce. "Even without eyeglasses."

For a split second, Savannah was uncharacteristically speechless. She always had something to say. He *remembered* her. He even remembered that she wore glasses. She wasn't sure he would. Then again, she'd been the ole thorn in his side for years so she was probably unforgettable for that reason.

He looked surprised to see her—and dammit, as gorgeous as ever. The last time she'd seen him up close was seventeen years ago. But the warm blue eyes, almost black tousled hair, the slight cleft in his chin were all the same except for a few squint lines, a handsome maturity to his thirty-five-year-old face. He had to be six-two and was cowboy-muscular, his broad shoulders defined in a navy Henley, his slim hips and long legs in faded denim.

She'd seen him around town several times over the years, always at a distance, when she'd be back in Bear Ridge for the holidays or a family party, and any time she'd spot him on Main Street or in the grocery store or some shop, her stomach would get those little butterflies and she'd turn tail or hide behind a rack like a sixteen-year-old who couldn't yet handle her emotions.

Amazing. Savannah Walsh had never been afraid of anything in her life—except for how she'd always felt about this man.

His head tilted a bit, his gaze going to the ad in her hand. "You're here to apply for the nanny position?" He looked confused; he'd probably heard along the way that she was a manager of rodeo performers—even had a few famous clients.

She peered behind him, where the crying of two more babies could be heard. "Sort of," she said. "We may be able to help each other out."

His eyes lit up for a moment, and she knew right then and there that he was truly desperate for help. Then his gaze narrowed on her, as if he was trying to figure out what she could possibly mean by "sort of" or "help each other out." That had always been their thing back in school, really; both trying to read the other's mind and strategy, one-up and come out victorious.

They'd been rivals whether for class treasurer, the better grade in biology, or rodeo classes and competitions. They'd always been tied—she'd beat him at something, then he'd beat her. She'd had his grudging respect, if not his interest in her romantically. She'd been in his arms exactly once, for two and a half minutes at the senior prom, when she'd dared to ask him to dance and he'd said, *Okay*. A slow song by Beyoncé. But he'd stood back a bit, their bodies not touching, except for his hands at her waist and hers on his shoulders, and he'd barely looked at her except to awkwardly smile. Savannah, five foot ten and gangly with frizzy red hair, oversized crystal-framed eyeglasses and a big personality, had been no one's type back then.

"Well, come on in," he said, stepping back and letting her enter.

The baby he held reached out and grabbed her hair, clutching a swath in his tiny fist. Ooh, that yank hurt. Rookie mistake, clearly.

She smiled at the little rascal and covered her eyes with her hands, then took them away. "Peekaboo!" she said. "Peekaboo, I see you!"

The baby stopped crying and stared at her, the tiny fist releasing her hair. Ah, much better. She took a step away.

He looked impressed. "You must have babies of your own to have handled that so well and fast."

For a moment she was stunned that she *had* done so
well and she smiled, feeling a bit more confident about
the reason she was here. But then the first part of what
he'd said echoed in her head—about babies of her own.

"Actually, I don't. Not even one," she added, and
wished she hadn't. *Do not call attention to your lack
of experience.* Though, really, that was why she was
here. To *gain* experience. "I have a three-year-old niece.
Clara. She was a grabby one too. In fact, that's why I
knew to put in my contact lenses to come see you. Clara
taught me that babies love to grab glasses off my face
and break the ear piece in the process."

He smiled. "Ah. I thought all my pint-sized relatives would have better prepared me for parenthood,
but nope." Before she could respond, not that she knew
what to even say since he looked crestfallen, he added,
"So you said you're *sort of* here about the nanny job?"

Her explanation would take a while so she took off
her coat, even though he didn't invite her to, and hung
it on the wrought-iron coat rack. For a moment all the
little snowsuits and fleece buntings and man-size jackets on the various hooks mesmerized her. Then she realized Hutch was watching her, waiting for her to explain
herself. Thing was, as she turned to face him, she really didn't want to explain herself. What was that saying, *all talk and no action*? Act, she told herself, like
she had with the peekaboo game to free her hair from
the itty fist. Then talk.

She turned her focus to the baby who'd resumed crying in Hutch's arms. Even red-faced and squawking,
the little boy was beautiful. That very kind of observa-
tion was among the main reasons she was here. "Well,
aren't you just the cutest," she said to the baby. "Hutch,
why don't I take this little guy, and you go deal with

the loudest of the other two and then we'll able to talk without shouting." She smiled so it would be clear she wasn't judging the triplets for being so noisy. Or him.

He still had that look of confusion, but he let her take his son from his arms. As she cuddled the baby the way her sister had taught her when Clara was born three years ago, rubbing his little back in gentle, wide circles, he calmed down a bit and gazed up at her with big blue eyes.

"You wanna hear a song?" she asked him. "I'm no singer, but here goes." She broke into Santa Claus Is Coming to Town. "He's making a list, he's checking it twice, he's gonna find out who's naughty and nice…"

Hutch paused from where he'd been about to pluck a baby in pink-and-purple-striped PJs from the swing area by the sliding glass doors and stared at her in a kind of puzzled wonder.

But she barely glanced at him. Instead, her attention was riveted by the sweet, solid weight in her arms, the blue eyes gazing up at her with curiosity. As the baby grabbed her pinky and held on with one heck of a grip, something stirred inside her. She almost gasped.

She'd been right to come here. Right to propose her outlandish idea. If she ever got around to it. She was stalling, she realized, afraid he'd shut her down and show her the door.

It was really her sister Morgan's idea. And it had taken Savannah a good two hours to agree it was a *good* one. She had no idea what Hutch would think.

She glanced at the baby she held, then at the other two. "Is it their dinner time?" she asked. "Maybe they're hungry?"

"Dinner is at six but I suppose they could eat ten minutes early." He paused. "That sounds really dumb—

of course they should eat early if they're hungry. I'm just trying to follow the holy schedule."

Hmm, was that a swipe at the ex-wife she'd heard about from her sisters? "I know from my sister how important schedules are when it comes to children," she said with a nod. She'd once babysat Clara when she was turning one, and the list of what to do when was two pages long. "I'm happy to help out since I'm here."

His gaze shot to her, and he seemed about to say, *Why are you here*, but what came out of his mouth was, "I appreciate that. Their high chairs are in the kitchen."

She followed him into the big, sunny room, a country kitchen but with modern appliances. A round wood table was by the window, three high chairs around it. She'd put her niece in a high chair a time or two, so she slid the baby in and did up the straps. The little guy must know the high chair meant food or Cheerios because he instantly got happier. "What's this cutie's name?" she asked.

With his free hand, Hutch gave himself a knock on the forehead. "I didn't even introduce them. That's Caleb. I have Chloe," he said, putting her in the middle chair. "And I'm about to go get Carson." In twenty seconds he was back with a squawking third baby, who also immediately calmed down once he was in the chair. Hutch went to the counter and opened a ceramic container and scooped out some Cheerios on each tray. The babies all picked one up and examined it before dropping it on their tongues.

"Are they on solids?" she asked, remembering that was a thing at some point.

He nodded. "Jarred baby food. Their schedule has their favorites." He pulled out his phone and held it so she could see the list, then went to the cabinet and got out three jars and then three spoons from the drawer.

"Bibs?" she asked, recalling seeing it on the schedule next to dinner: *Don't forget the bibs or their good PJs will get stained.*

"Oh right," he said, and pulled three bibs from a drawer. He handed her one and quickly put on the other two. "Since you've made buddies with Caleb, maybe you could feed him while I do double duty with these two."

She smiled and took the jar he handed her. Sweet potato. And the tiny purple spoon. He sat back down and opened up two other jars, spoon in each hand, dipped and into each little mouth they went at the same time.

The kitchen was suddenly remarkably quiet. No crying.

She quickly opened up the sweet potato and gave Caleb a spoonful. He gobbled it up and tried to grab the spoon. "Ooh, you like your dinner. Here's another bite." She could feel Hutch's gaze on her as she kept feeding Caleb.

"I definitely recall hearing somewhere that you're a manager of rodeo performers?" Hutch said, dabbing Chloe's mouth with her bib.

"Yes. I'm off till just after Christmas, taking a much-needed vacation. I'm staying with my sister Morgan while I'm in town."

"But you're sort of here about the nanny job?" he asked, pausing from feeding the babies. Chloe banged a hand on the tray, sending two Cheerios flying.

"I...yes," she said. "I'll get this guy fed and burped and then I'll explain."

He nodded and turned his attention back to Chloe and Carson.

As she slipped another spoonful of sweet potato puree into the open tiny mouth, she wondered how to explain herself without revealing her most personal thoughts and questions that consumed her lately and kept her up at night.

She could just launch into the truth, how she'd been at her youngest sister's bridal shower earlier today, which she would have enjoyed immensely were it not for her least favorite cousin, Charlotte. Charlotte, also younger than Savannah and a mom of three, had peppered her with questions about being single—long divorced—at age thirty-five. *Don't you want a baby? And don't you want to give that baby a sibling? Aren't you afraid you'll run out of time?*

Savannah's middle sister, Morgan, happily married with a three-year-old and a baby on the way, had protectively and thankfully pulled Savannah away from their busybody cousin. And what Savannah had admitted, almost tearfully, and she was no crier, was that yes, she *was* afraid—because she didn't know what she wanted. She'd been divorced since she was twenty-five. Ten years was a long time to be on her own with every subsequent relationship not working out. She'd put her heart into her career and had long figured that maybe not every woman found their guy.

Over the years she'd wondered if she measured her feelings for her dates and relationships against the schoolgirl longing she'd felt for Hutch Dawson. No one had ever touched it, not even the man she'd been briefly married to. That longing, from grade school till she left Bear Ridge at eighteen, was part of the reason Morgan had shown her Hutch's ad in the *Bear Ridge Weekly*.

The other part, the main part, was about the babies. The family.

She just had to explain it all to Hutch in a way that wouldn't mortify her and would get him to say: *the job is yours*.

"I have a proposal for you," she said.

Chapter Two

Savannah held her breath as Hutch looked over at her, spoonfuls of applesauce and oatmeal midway to Chloe's and Carson's mouths.

"A proposal," he repeated, sliding a glance at her. "I'm listening."

Since no words were coming out of her mouth, he turned his attention back to the babies, giving them their final bites of dinner. Then he stood and lifted Chloe out of the high chair, cuddling her against him and gently patting her back. One good burp later, he did the same with Carson.

Maybe Hutch realized she could use a minute before she blurted out her innermost burning thoughts. She definitely did, so she focused on Caleb and his after-dinner needs. She'd never been able to get a good burp out of her niece when she was a baby. Savannah was on the road so often, traveling with her clients, or at home three hours away in Blue Smoke, where one of the biggest annual rodeos was held every summer, that she didn't really see Clara as much as she wanted. Savannah had a bit of experience at childcare. But it was just that. A bit. And when it came to babies, that experience was three years old.

She'd watched how Hutch had handled burp time, so she stood and took Caleb from the high chair, put him against her shoulder and gently patted his back. Nothing. She patted a little harder. Still nothing.

Her shoulders sagged. How could she expect Hutch to give her a job involving baby care when she couldn't even get a baby to burp!

"Caleb likes three fast pats dead center on his back," Hutch said. "Try that."

She did.

BURP!

Savannah grinned. "Yes!" The little boy then spit up on her fawn-colored cashmere sweater, which probably wasn't the best choice in a top for the occasion of coming to propose he let her be his nanny till Christmas. At least she wore her dark denim and cowboy boots, which seemed perfectly casual.

Hutch handed her a wet paper towel. "Sorry."

"No worries. That I don't mind is actually an important element of why I'm here."

"Right," he said. "The proposal." He stared at her for a moment. "Let's take these guys into the living room and let them crawl around. They're not actually crawling yet but they like to try. Then I want to hear all about this proposal of yours."

She had Caleb and he took both Carson and Chloe. She followed him into the living room, and they sat down on the huge soft foam play mat decorated with letters and numbers. The babies were on their hands and knees and sort of rocked but didn't crawl. They were definitely content.

She sucked in a breath. *Okay*, she told herself. *Come out with it*. "I'm kind of at a crossroads, Hutch."

He glanced at her. "What kind of crossroads?"

"The kind where I'm not sure if I want to keep doing what I'm doing or…something else."

"Like what?" he asked, pushing a stuffed rattle in the shape of a candy cane closer to where Carson was rocking back and forth. The boy's big eyes stared at the toy.

Here goes, she thought. "I'm thirty-five and long divorced. Married life, motherhood has all sort of passed me by. I have a great job and I'm suited to it. But lately, I've had these…feelings. Like maybe I do want a family. I'm not the least bit *sure* how I feel, what I truly want."

His head had tilted a bit, and he waited for her to continue.

Why was it so hard to say all this? "My sister happened to see your ad while she was looking for a date-night sitter in the local paper's help wanted section. She thought maybe I could get a little clarity, find out what family life is like by helping you out with the triplets till Christmas."

"I see," he said. And that was all he said. She held her breath again.

For a moment they just watched the babies, Carson batting the stuffed rattle on the mat, Chloe still rocking on her hands and knees, Caleb now on his back trying to chew his toe.

"I don't have any experience as a nanny," she rushed to say, the uncomfortable silence putting her a bit off balance. Clearly, since she wasn't exactly selling herself here. "I've cared for my niece, as I've said, here and there over the past three years. More there than here. I want to see what it feels like to care for a baby—babies. To be involved in a family."

"Like an experiment," he said.

"I guess so." Her heart sank. She was sure *experimenting* with his children wasn't going to be okay with him. Why had she thought he might consider this?

"And no need to pay me for the ten days, of course, since we'd be helping each other out." Savannah was very successful and didn't look at this as a temporary job; it was a chance to find out if motherhood really was what she wanted. For that, *she'd* pay. Her heart hammered again, and she took a fast breath to calm down a bit. "I'm sure you want you want to think it over." She hurried over to the coat rack and pulled her wallet from her coat pocket, taking out a business card. She walked back over and knelt down to hand it to him. "My contact info is on there."

He looked at it, then put it in his back pocket. "Can you start immediately?" he asked. "Like now?"

She felt her eyes widen—and hope soar. "I'm hired?" Had she heard him correctly?

"I can't do this alone," he said. "And I can't take off the next several days from the ranch. I need help. And here you are, Savannah Walsh. If there's one thing I remember about you it's that you get things done. And—" He cut himself off.

Well, now she had to know what that *and* was about. "And?" she prompted gently.

"And…okay, I'm just going to say it. I used to think, man, that Savannah Walsh is all business, works her tail off, but then I experienced firsthand that you have a big heart too. That combination qualifies you for the job. And like I said, the fact that you're here. Wanting the job. Many nannies have given up. I insist on paying you, though. And a lot."

She was still caught on the middle part of what he'd said. About his experiencing that she had a big heart. There could only be one instance he was referring to— that bad day at a rodeo competition when he'd come in third and his father had gone off on him, and she— who'd come in second—had tried to comfort him. She was surprised it had stuck with him all these years later, but she supposed those kinds of things did stick with people. When you were going through something awful and someone was in your corner.

"Of course, we were big-time rivals back then," he rushed to say. "So we might not get along even now."

She smiled. "I'm sure we won't, if it's like old times."

He smiled too. "Though we had a couple of moments, didn't we?"

She almost gasped. So he remembered the other incident too. The dance at the prom. All two and half minutes of it. Had *that* stuck with him?

"Plus it's been a long time," she said. They were different people now; they'd lived entire lives, full of ups and downs.

"A long time," he repeated.

"I can't promise I'll be great at the job," she said, probably too honestly. "But I'll try hard. I'll be responsible. I'll put my heart and brains into everything I do when I'm with your children, Hutch."

"I appreciate that," he said. "And you have two hands. That's what I need most of all."

Happy, excited chills ran up and down her spine. "Well, then. You've got yourself your holiday season nanny."

A relief came over his expression, and she could see

his shoulders relax. He was desperate. But in this case, it worked in her favor.

"Look, Savannah," he said. "Because I know you, I mean, we go way back, and this is a learning experience for you and a severe need for me, would you consider being live-in for the ten days? The triplets are pretty much sleeping through the night, if you consider midnight to five thirty 'the night.'"

Live-in. Even better. "That would certainly show me true family life with babies," she said. "So yes. I'll just get my bags from my sister's and be back in a half hour."

"Just in time for the bedtime routine," he said. "I'm pretty bad at that. And I have a lot of unfinished business from today that I still need to get to, so having your help will make it go much faster. I can't tell you how lucky I feel that you knocked on the door, Savannah."

Ha. We'll see if you're still feeling lucky tomorrow when it's clear I don't know a thing about babies. Times three.

She extended her hand. "And truly, I won't accept pay."

"How about this—I'll donate what I'd pay you to the town's holiday fundraiser for families who need help with meals and gifts and travel expenses."

She smiled. "Perfect."

He gave her hand a shake, holding on for a moment and then covering her hand with his other. "Thank you."

"And thank you," she said a little too breathlessly, too aware from the electric zap that went straight to her toes that her crush on Hutch Dawson was far from over.

"Well, guys," Hutch said to the triplets, each in their own little baby tub in the empty bathtub. "That is what's known as a Christmas miracle."

He still could barely believe he'd gotten so lucky—

though lucky was of course relative. Savannah Walsh might not have experience with babies but she was here. Or would be in about ten minutes. To help. And oh man, did Hutch need help.

Carson banged his rubber duckie, and Chloe chewed her waterproof book with the chewable edges as Hutch poured warm water over the shampoo on Caleb's head, careful not to let it get in his eyes. A minute ago, Chloe had dropped her head back at the moment Hutch had gone to rinse the shampoo from her hair, and water and suds had streamed down her face. She'd wailed for a good half minute until Hutch had distracted with peekaboo—Savannah's earlier go-to. One of his cousins—Maisey, who ran the childcare center at the Dawson Family Guest Ranch, had given him five pairs of goofy glasses to make peekaboo work even faster. He'd grabbed the plastic glasses with their springy cartoon puppy cutouts, and Chloe was indeed transfixed and had stopped crying. He had a pair in practically every room in the house.

Carson batted his hands down, splashing lukewarm water all over his siblings, who giggled.

"All right, you little rug rats, bath time is over. Let's get you dry and changed."

He lifted each baby with one hand, drained their tub with the other, then wrapped them in their adorable hooded towels, a giraffe for Caleb, a lion for Chloe and a bear for Carson. He plopped them down in the portable playpen he'd bought just for this purpose—to get all three babies from the bathtub to the nursery at the same time. It was probably the baby item he used most often; he transported them all over the one-story ranch house with ease.

He got each baby into a fresh diaper and PJs, and

now it was time for their bottles. Then it would be story time, then bedtime. Hopefully Savannah really would be back to help with that.

The doorbell rang. Perfect. She was back a little early and could help with bottles. He'd gotten okay at feeding two babies at once, but he didn't have *three* hands.

He wheeled the playpen to the door, but it wasn't Savannah, after all. It was Daniel, his brother. Or his *half* brother, as Daniel always corrected him. Tall like Hutch, with light brown hair and the Dawson blue eyes, Daniel lived in town with Olivia, his wife of twenty years. When he and his brother inherited the ranch from their father three months ago, Daniel had surprised Hutch by taking down his CPA shingle in town and coming aboard full-time as chief financial officer, which Hutch had been initially glad about since it freed him up to focus on the day-to-day of managing the ranch. But his brother disagreed with a lot of Hutch's plans for the Dueling Dawsons Ranch—too apt a name, as always. Hutch had been the foreman for a decade—he knew the fifteen hundred acre ranch inside and out—but family feuds had plagued the Dawsons on this property since his great-grandfather and great-uncle had bought the land more than a century ago. He and Daniel did not break the pattern.

The one thing Daniel did not seem interested in was pursuing the list of "Unfinished Business" that Lincoln Dawson had left tacked up on his bulletin board. There were only two items, both doozies. But Hutch intended to cross them off by Christmas. Somehow, he thought his father would truly rest in peace that way. And Hutch by association. God knew, Daniel needed some peace.

"I'm leaving for the day," Daniel said, shoving his silver-framed square eyeglasses up on his nose. "And still no response to my email about your list of costly initiatives for the ranch," he added, shoving his hands into the pockets of his thick flannel barn coat. He wore a brown Stetson, flurries collecting on top and the brim.

"I was actually in the middle of answering when disaster struck," Hutch said, stepping back so Daniel could come in out of the cold. "The new nanny quit on me."

"Another one?" Daniel raised an eyebrow, stopping on the doormat, which indicated he wasn't staying long—good thing. "Is it you or the triplets? Probably both," he said with a nod, answering that for himself.

Ah, Daniel. So supportive, as always.

"I was just about to make up their bottles," Hutch said, angling his head toward the playpen. "If you can feed one of the babies, I can do two and we can talk."

Daniel scowled. "I'm long done feeding a baby." Hutch mentally shook his head. Daniel and Olivia were empty nesters; their eighteen-year-old son was in college two hours away near the Colorado border. "We'll talk in the morning. Or are you going to be trapped here with them and not out on the ranch, taking care of business?"

Keep your cool, hold your tongue. That was Hutch's motto when it came to dealing with his brother. His half brother.

"Trapped isn't the word I'd use," he said, narrowing a glare on Daniel. "And I have a new nanny already. She's staring tonight, as a matter of fact. She'll be a live-in through Christmas Eve."

"Good. Because you need to get your share of the work done."

Keep your cool, hold your tongue...

"I'll see you at 6:00 a.m. in the barn," Hutch said. "We can talk about the email and the sheep while taking on Mick's and Davis's chores."

"I don't see why cowboys had to get ten days off," Daniel groused.

Had Hutch ever met someone more begrudging than Daniel Dawson? "Because they've worked hard all year and get two weeks off. They both had the time coming to them."

"It's bad timing with our father being gone."

"Yeah," Hutch said, picturing Lincoln Dawson. He'd been sixty-two when an undiagnosed heart condition took him from them. Maybe he'd hidden the symptoms; Hutch wasn't sure, and Daniel had kept his distance from their dad as he had his entire life. Lincoln had worked hard, done the job of a cowboy half his age. He'd hated administrative work and trusted few people so he'd offered Hutch the foreman job ten years ago, when Hutch had been fresh out of an MBA in agricultural business, about to take a high-paying job at a big cattle ranch across town. Hutch had shocked himself by saying yes to his father's offer at half the salary and fewer perks. *Maybe I'll finally figure you out*, Lincoln Dawson, he'd thought.

But he hadn't. And Daniel hated talking about their father, so he'd never been any help.

Daniel reached for the doorknob. "Six sharp."

"You could acknowledge your niece and nephews," Hutch said unexpectedly, surprised it had come out of his mouth. But he supposed it did bother him that his brother barely paid them any attention. He was their uncle.

"Don't make this something it's not," Daniel said, without a glance at the triplets, and left.

Hutch sighed and rolled his eyes. "Your uncle is something, huh, guys?" he directed to his children. "*A piece of work* as your late grandmother would have

said. Or as your late grandfather would have said suc-
cinctly, *difficult*."

His brother had always been that. When Daniel was
four, Lincoln had walked away from his family to marry
his mistress—Hutch's mother. A year after their marriage, Hutch was born, and Hutch could recall his brother
spending every other Saturday at the ranch for years,
until Daniel was twelve or thirteen and said he was done
with that. Their dad hadn't insisted, which had still in-
furiated Daniel and also his mother; Hutch had known
that from screaming phone calls and slammed doors
between the exes.

What Hutch did know about his father was that he'd
loved his second wife, Hutch's mom, deeply. The two of
them had held hands while eating dinner at the dining
table. They'd danced in the living room to weird eight-
ies new wave music. They'd gotten dressed up and had
gone out to a fancy meal every Saturday night without
fail. The way his father had looked at his mother had
always softened Hutch's ire at very-difficult-himself
Lincoln Dawson; Hutch had given him something of
a pass for what a hardcase he'd been with Hutch and
Daniel and anyone else besides his wife. Hutch's mother
had died when he was eighteen, and in almost twenty
years, Lincoln had never looked at another woman as
far as Hutch knew. But the loss had turned his father
even more gruff and impatient, and Hutch had threatened to quit, had quit, about ten times.

*Your mother wouldn't like the way I handled things
earlier*, Lincoln would say by way of apology. *She'd
want you to come back.*

Hutch always had. He loved the Dueling Dawsons
Ranch. The land. The work. The livestock. And he'd
loved his father. He'd been gone three months now, and

sometimes his absence, the lack of his outsize presence on the ranch, gripped Hutch with an aching grief.

There were just some things that stayed with a person—the good and the bad. When Hutch's ex-wife had sat him down last year and tearfully told him she was leaving him for Ted, a distraught, confused, scared Hutch had packed a suitcase and turned up at the ranch. His father had taken one look at his face, at the suitcase, and had asked him what happened. Lincoln had called Allison a vile name that Hutch had tried to put out of his memory, then told his son he could stay at the ranch in his old room, take some time off work as the foreman if he needed and went to make them spaghetti and garlic bread, which Hutch had barely been able to eat but appreciated. They'd sat at the table in near silence, also appreciated, except for his father twice putting his hand on Hutch's shoulder with a, *You'll get through this.*

Whenever things with his dad had gotten rough, he'd remember that Lincoln Dawson had been there for him when it really mattered. He also liked how his father had bought the triplets a gift every Monday, the same for each, whether tiny cowboy hats or rattles or books, when Allison would drop them off. Lincoln would give her the death stare, then dote on the triplets, talking to them about ranch life. Then in another breath, he'd flip out on Hutch for how he handled something with a vendor or which pasture he'd moved the herd to.

He's never going to be any different, Daniel had said a few times the past couple of years when Lincoln must have started feeling sick or weakened but had refused to see a doctor and had brushed off questions about this health. *Stop chasing his approval already.*

Hutch often wanted to slug his brother, but never so much as during those times when he'd accuse Hutch of exactly that. Chasing his approval. He'd had it—his father had made him his foreman, hadn't he? Daniel would say it was more than that, deeper, but Hutch would shut that down fast.

Five minutes later, the doorbell rang again, and he shook off the memories, shook off his brother's visit and attitude. Savannah was back. His shoulders instantly unbunched. There was something calming about her presence, a quiet confidence, and he liked the way she looked at the triplets. With wonder and affection.

He liked the way she looked, period. Had she always been so pretty? He hadn't really thought of her that way back in school, given their rivalry. But he did remember being surprised by his reaction when she'd taken his hand in solidarity after that rodeo competition their senior year. A touch he'd felt *everywhere*. His father had screamed his head off at Hutch about a minor mistake he'd made that had cost him first and second place, and Savannah had heard the whole thing. She'd walked up to him and took his hand and just held it and said, *You didn't deserve that. You were great out there as always.* The reverberation of that touch had distracted him for a moment, and he wanted to pull her to him and just hold her, his rival turned suddenly very attractive *friend*. But he'd been seventeen and humiliated by his father's tirade and wanted the ground to swallow him so he'd run off without a word, shaking off her hand like it had meant nothing to him.

He wondered if she even remembered that. Probably not. It was a long time ago.

He went to the door and there she was, her long red hair twisted into a bun—smart move—her face scrubbed free of the glamorous makeup she'd worn earlier. She wore a down jacket over a T-shirt with a rodeo logo and faded low-slung jeans. He swallowed at the sight of her. Damn, she was beautiful.

"The doorbell reminded me that I need to give you a key," he said, reaching for her bags. He took her suitcase and duffel and set them down by the door, then reached into his pocket for his key ring and took off one of the extra house keys. "I'll give you a quick tour and show you your room, and then we can give the triplets their bottles."

She smiled and put the key on her own ring, looking past him for the triplets, first at their swings, then at the playpen, in which the three were sitting and contentedly playing with toys. "Let me at those adorable littles." She rushed over to the playpen and knelt down beside it, chatting away to the babies about how she was here to help take care of them.

As she stood and turned back to him, she seemed so truly happy, her face flushed with excitement, that he found himself touched. This was a completely different setup than he was used to; she wasn't working for him, he wasn't paying her. She was here to get experience, to have some questions answered for herself.

It occurred to him that they should probably talk about that setup—expectations on both sides, how she wanted to structure the "job," the hours he'd need to devote to the ranch, the triplets' schedule, details about each of them, such as their different personalities, likes and dislikes, what worked on which baby. They should also talk about nighttime wakings; at least one triplet woke up at least once a night and would likely wake her up. He wanted to ensure that he wouldn't be taking advantage of her being a live-in.

He suddenly envisioned Savannah coming out of her room at 2:00 a.m. to soothe a crier in nothing but a long

T-shirt. He blinked to get the image out of his head. He seemed to be drawn to her—there was just something about her, something winsome, something both tough and vulnerable—and they did go back a ways, which made her seem more familiar than she actually was. But Hutch had had his entire world turned upside down and sideways and shaken—by the divorce, by being a father of three babies that he loved so much he thought he might burst sometimes, by his father's loss and the sudden onslaught of his brother. He couldn't imagine wanting anything to do with the opposite sex.

Or maybe I could, he amended as a flash of Savannah in just a long T-shirt floated into his mind again.

Nah, he thought. He really doubted that even sex could tempt him to step back into the romance ring. Not after what he'd been through.

Suuure, said a very low voice in the back of his mind where reality reigned.

Chapter Three

Savannah liked her room. It was a guest room next door to the nursery. There were two big windows, soothing off-white walls with an abstract watercolor of the Wyoming wilderness, a queen-size bed with a fluffy blue-and-white down comforter and lots of pillows, a dresser with a round mirror, a beautiful kilim rug, and a glider by the window. Perfect for taking a crying baby into her room in the middle of the night to soothe without waking up the other two.

Hutch, with the baby monitor in his back pocket, was putting her suitcase and duffel by the closet. Being in here, her room for the ten days, with him so close was doing funny things to her belly. "This was my room growing up. The furniture was different then, but that's the window I stared out every day, wondering where my life would take me." He walked over and looked out. He'd had a view of a stand of evergreens and the woods beyond and part of the fields.

"It took you right here," she said, thinking about that for a moment. Full circle. "Did you even consider that then? That you'd be the foreman on this ranch?"

"Absolutely not. My father wasn't the easiest man to get along with. But not long after I left for college to study agricultural business—with the intention of having my own ranch someday—I lost my mom. When my dad offered me the foreman's job, the idea of coming home called to me. She loved this ranch. I always did too."

"I grew up in town," she said. "But I've always wanted to live on a ranch. I'm a rodeo gal at heart."

"Well, for the next week and a half, you'll be woken up by a crowing rooster long before a crying baby or two or three, so that might get old fast. You should visit the barn. We have six beautiful horses."

She smiled. "I'll plan to. So what's on the schedule? I'm excited to jump right into my first official task as Christmas season nanny."

"It's time for their last bottles. Usually I feed two at once, then the third, but now we can split that up."

"I see what you mean about needing an extra set of hands," she said. "It must have been really hard these past six months, being on your own once the nannies were done for the day. I guess you had to figure it out as you went?"

"Yup, exactly. I'm a pretty good multitasker, though, something necessary to be a good ranch foreman. You know what the hardest part has been? When I don't know how to soothe one or two or all three, when they're crying like they were earlier when the former nanny quit on me. When I don't know how to make it better and nothing works. I feel like a failure as a dad." He frowned, and it was clear how deep the cuts could go with him.

"Oh Hutch," she said, her heart flying out to him. "I'll bet it's like that for any parent of even just one baby. They don't talk, they can't tell you where it hurts or what they want, and you love them so much that it just kills you."

"Exactly," he said. "For someone who doesn't have experience with babies, you definitely get it."

She felt herself beam. She wasn't entirely sure how she "got it"; she supposed it was just human nature to feel that way about something so precious and dependent on you.

"Let's go feed them, and we can talk about how to arrange this," he said, wagging a finger between them. "How it'll all work. I really don't want to take advantage of you being here, living here, and the *reason* you're here. It's a tough job, Savannah."

"I'm a tough woman," she said. Except she didn't feel that way here in Hutch's house, in his presence. She felt...very vulnerable.

"You were a tough girl," he said. "Kept me on my toes."

She laughed. "Well, tough might have kept me from—" Ugh, she clammed up in the nick of time. Was she honestly about to tell Hutch Dawson that she was afraid her cousin Charlotte's assessment of her earlier at the bridal shower was right, that who Savannah was made her unappealing to men—*intimidating* and *too successful* were the actual words her cousin had used today.

Oh please, Savannah had thought, but she'd heard that her entire life. She'd been five foot ten since she was thirteen and no slouch, literally or figuratively, so she'd been standing tall a long time. And yes, she was straightforward and could be barky, and she was damned good at her job. It was true that she could make some people quake because of her stature in the industry at this point. But that was business, and her profession demanded *tough*. She'd never gotten very far with men, though. She'd get ghosted or told it just wasn't working out after a week or two of dating.

Or seven months of marriage. *I'm not one of your clients*, her new husband had said so many times that she'd started doubting herself—who she was, particularly. *You're trying to manage me*, he'd toss at her. *Maybe if you didn't work such long hours or travel so much, I wouldn't have cheated.*

With a friend, among others, no less. Savannah hadn't been sure he had been cheating until her "friend" had confirmed it and said the same thing her husband had: *If you devoted yourself to your marriage instead of your career...* At twenty-five she'd had an ex-husband, an ex-friend and dealt with her doubly broken heart by devoting herself even more to her career. She was in a male-dominated industry, but her voice, drive and determination had carried her to the top. She took reasonable risks, demanded the best of her clients and for them, but cared deeply about each one. Yeah, she was tough.

To a point, she reminded herself. Lately, she'd find herself tearing up. She'd been in a grocery store a few days ago and the sight of a young family, a dad pushing the cart with a toddler in the seat, the mom walking beside him with a little girl on her shoulders and letting the child take items off the high shelves for her— Savannah had almost burst into tears in the bread aisle of Safeway.

Do I want that? she'd asked herself, perplexed by her reaction. Why else would she have been so affected? She'd written off remarriage and happily-ever-after, having lost her belief and faith in either, in the fairy tale. Her parents had had a wonderful, long marriage.

One sister was happily married and the other was engaged and madly in love with her fiancé. Savannah knew there were good men out there, good marriages. But she'd always been…tough. And maybe meant to be on her own.

She didn't know how to be any different. It was her natural personality that put the fear of God into the men and women rodeo performers she managed, from up-and-comers with great potential to superstars, like her most famous client, a bull rider who'd quit fame and fortune to settle down with the woman he loved and the child he'd only recently discovered was his. She'd spent some time with the happy family the past few months, and Logan Winston's happiness, a joy she hadn't seen in him ever before, made her acknowledge a few hard truths about herself. That she was lonely. That she did have a serious hankering for something more—she just wasn't sure what, exactly. A change, but what change? She should talk to Logan about it while she was in town.

Hutch was leaving the room so she shook off her thoughts and followed, excited to get started on her new role—for the time being, anyway. A life of babies and Hutch Dawson.

In the kitchen, she stood beside him as he made up the bottles, watching carefully how he went about it so she could do it herself. Back in the living room, he set the three bottles on the coffee table, then grabbed a bunch of bibs and burp cloths from the basket on the shelf under the table, and finally, wheeled the playpen over to the sofa.

"I'll watch you for a moment," she said, sitting down. "See how you hold the baby, hold the bottle, just so I know how to do it all properly."

"It's a cinch. Maybe the easiest part of all fatherhood—and the most relaxing, well, except for watching them sleep. There's just something about feeding a baby, giving him or her what they need, all in the grand comfort of your arms."

"I always felt that way when I watched my sister feed Clara," she said, recalling how truly cozy it looked, how content mama and baby had always appeared.

He picked up Carson and settled him slightly reclined along one arm, then reached for a bottle and tilted it into the little bow-shaped mouth. Carson put his hands on the bottle and suckled away, Hutch's gaze loving on his son.

"Got it," she said. "Should I grab another baby for you?"

"Sure, take your pick."

"I'll save Chloe for myself since I got time with Caleb earlier." She scooped the little guy from the playpen and settled him on Hutch's right side. When he shifted Caleb just right, she handed him a bottle. In no time, he was feeding both babies.

My turn! She picked up Chloe, who stared at her with huge blue eyes. *Oh, aren't you precious*, she thought, putting Chloe along her arm and grabbing the third bottle. "Hungry?" she asked. She slipped the nipple into the baby's mouth, and it was so satisfying as Chloe started drinking, her little hands on the sides of the bottle. Savannah gazed down at her, mesmerized. When she glanced up, she realized Hutch was watching her. Her. Not how she was holding Chloe or the bottle. *Her.*

Could he be interested? Hutch Dawson, guy of her dreams since she was five, star of her fantasies since middle school? He was the one thing she'd ever wanted that she hadn't gone for, her fear—of rejection and how bad it would hurt—and lack of confidence when it came to personal relationships making her anything but tough.

"This is great," he said with a warm smile. "Having the extra two hands."

Oh. That was what the look of wonder was about. How helpful she was. He wasn't suddenly attracted to her. It wasn't like she'd changed all that much physically since high school, and he'd never given her a second glance back then.

"Having you here for the bedtime routine will be a huge help," he added. "I've really never been good at it. One of the triplets always fights their drooping eyes and fusses, then another fusses, then one starts crying... What takes Allison and Ted fifteen minutes takes me an hour."

"Allison and Ted?" she asked, glancing at him. She darn well knew who Allison was—his ex-wife. Savannah remembered her from school. Petite, pretty, strawberry blonde and blue eyed. A cheerleader. Hutch Dawson's type. They'd dated on and off but had always been more off as Savannah recalled. She knew a little bit about the divorce from her sister. Apparently Allison had reconnected with an old flame from college on Facebook. And actually walked away from her marriage at five months pregnant. According to Morgan, Allison had been shunned by some and lauded by others—*How could you*? vs *Life is too short not to follow your heart*.

All Savannah could think was how absolutely awful it must have been for Hutch.

"My ex-wife," he said. "And her new husband. You might remember Allison Windham from school. Then she was Allison Dawson for three years but now she'll be Allison Russo. Sometimes I can't wait until the triplets are old enough for people to stop gossiping about how I'm divorced with babies. Some folks know the sob story but most assume *I* left, even though my ex is the one living in my former house with another man. You should see some of the stare downs I get in the grocery store."

"Ugh, that's terrible," she said. "How unfair. To have your life turned upside down and to get the blame."

He shot her something of a smile. "Small town, big gossip."

"Yeah, I remember. It's one of the reasons why I was excited to leave for bigger pastures. I do love Bear Ridge, though."

"Yeah, me too." They glanced at each other for a moment, and she felt so connected to him. They came from the same place, had the same beginning history in terms of school and downtown and the Santa hut on the town green. She'd passed it several times since she'd arrived, her heart warmed by the sight of the majestic holiday tree all decorated and lit up in the center of the small park, the red Santa hut with the big candy cane chimney, the families lined up so that the kids could give Santa their lists.

She wondered if Hutch had envisioned himself standing with his family in line, the triplets in the choo choo train of a stroller she'd seen by the door, his wife beside him. Had he been blindsided by her affair? In any case, he must have been devastated when his ex had told him she was leaving.

She glanced down at Chloe, just a tiny bit left in her bottle, and then the baby turned her head slightly.

"That means she's done," Hutch said. "You can burp her and set her in the playpen, and then grab Carson—he's done too."

Savannah stood and held Chloe up vertically against her, about to pat her back.

"I'd set a burp cloth on your shoulder and chest," he said. "You don't want spit up all over that cool shirt."

She glanced down at her *Blue Smoke Summer Rodeo 2019* jersey. Years old and soft and faded. She'd worn it specifically for the job—no worries in getting dirty and grabbed and pulled out of shape. But she'd still prefer spit up on the burp cloth and not her. She shifted Chloe and bent a little to pick up a cloth, arranging it on her shoulder, hanging down on her chest.

She gave Chloe's back a good three pats and a big burp came out. "Success!" Savannah said. "What a great baby you are," she whispered to Chloe. "An excellent burper."

She set Chloe in the playpen and reached for Carson. Was it her imagination or did Hutch's gaze go to the sliver of belly exposed by her shirt lifting up as she leaned over? He handed over Carson and she repeated what she'd just done, but getting a burp out of this guy was taking longer.

How many times had she told her clients—and in talks to various groups and schools—not to think one great performance meant another? You had to work for it—always. She adjusted Carson in her arms and gave up two more pats with a bit more force, and out came a big, satisfying burp.

"I've got this!" she said, unable to contain her excitement. "I was afraid you'd regret taking me on as a student nanny, but I'm feeling a lot more confident."

He smiled. "Good. Because you're doing great."

"You hear that, Carson?" she said, running a finger down the baby's impossibly soft cheek. "I'm doing great!"

Once all three babies were in the playpen, Hutch stood. "If you'll keep watch over them, I could use a solid twenty minutes to finish up today's work—just some administrative stuff, texts and calls and emails."

"Sure thing," she said.

As he left the room, she felt the lack of him immediately.

My crush on your daddy will never go away, I guess, she said silently to the triplets as she wheeled the playpen over to the sliding glass door. There was a pretty pathetic Christmas tree with one strand of garland hanging down along with two branches. The entire tree was tilted as though someone had backed into it. She had a feeling that someone was Hutch with two babies in his arms. She'd help him get the tree decked out. Since the babies weren't crawling, there were no worries about safety-proofing for Christmas yet.

"Well, guys," she said. "How am I doing so far? Not too bad, right?"

Carson gave her a big gummy smile, two tiny teeth poking up.

I sure do like you three, she thought, giving Caleb's soft hair a caress. She'd been here, on the job, for barely an hour and she was falling in serious like with everything to do with the triplets. And Hutch Dawson all over again.

Hutch sat at his desk in his home office, half expecting Savannah to appear in the doorway with a crying baby with a firm grip on her hair or ear and say, *Sorry, but I've already realized that this isn't the life for me, buh-bye*—and go running out the door.

But he'd gotten through three calls, returned all the texts and had made himself mental notes for tomorrow's early-morning meeting with his brother in the barn—and no appearance in the doorway. No quitting. No *crying*.

Blessed silence.

His office door was ajar and every now and then he could hear Savannah's running commentary. She'd wheeled the babies in the playpen into the nursery and changed them one by one, choosing fresh PJs, which he knew because she was chatting away. *Stripes for you, Caleb. Polka dots for Chloe, and tiny bears for Carson. Oooh, another rookie mistake, guys, Caleb almost sprayed me!* She'd laughed and then continued her commentary all the way back down the hall to the living room.

Now she was talking to the triplets about the Christmas tree and how she and her sisters used to make a lot of their ornaments when they were little as family tradition. From what he could tell, she'd wheeled the playpen over by the tree and was picking up each twin to give them turns at being held and seeing the lonely, bare branches.

"Oooh, that's what I get for letting you get too close to my ear," he heard her say on a laugh to one of the triplets. "Strong girl," she added. "Peekaboo! I see you!"

He smiled as he envisioned her playing peekaboo with one hand to get her ear back. He'd have to tell her about the goofy glasses.

"Okay, now it's Carson's turn," she said.

This was going to work out just fine, he thought, turning his attention back to his brother's email. Ten minutes later, he was done, turned off his desk lamp and went to find Savannah and the babies.

They were sitting on the play mat, and she was telling them a story about a fir tree named Branchy who no one picked for their home at Christmastime.

"Buh!" Caleb said, batting his thigh.

Carson shook his stuffed rattle in the shape of a bunny.

Chloe was giggling her big baby laugh that always made Hutch laugh too.

Savannah turned and grinned. "They like me! Babies like me!"

He realized just then how nervous she'd probably been about how they'd respond to her. They'd managed to chase off professional nannies, including one who'd raised her own triplets. So he understood why a woman who'd never spent much time around babies would worry how she'd fare with three "crotchety" six-month-olds. She'd probably expected them to cry constantly and bat at her nose.

They did do a lot of that kind of thing. But they were also like this. Sitting contentedly, giggling, shaking rattles. If not exactly listening to her story, hearing it around them, enjoying her melodic voice.

"I'd say so," he confirmed, and she beamed, her delight going straight to his heart. "It's bedtime for these guys."

As if on cue, Carson started rubbing his eyes.

Then Caleb did.

Chloe's face crumpled and she let out a loud shriek, then started crying.

Savannah picked up Chloe and held her against her chest, rubbing her back, which helped calm the baby.

Hutch picked up both boys, Carson leaning his head against his father's neck, one of Hutch's favorite things in the world, and Caleb rubbed his eyes.

Savannah's phone rang, and she shifted Chloe to

pull it from her back pocket. She glanced at the screen. "Ugh, business," she said, continuing to rub Chloe's back as she bounced her a little. "Savannah Walsh," she said into the phone. "Ah, I've been waiting for your call. No, those terms are *not* acceptable. That's right. No again. Oh well, no deal then. Have a nice night. What's that? You'll come up the five thousand? Wonderful. I'll expect the contract by end of business tomorrow." Click.

He watched her turn the ringer off and then chuck the phone on the sofa.

"Sorry," she said. "I just realized I shouldn't have taken that call. I'm on duty here."

"Of course you should have taken it. Your life off this ranch still exists. You do what you need to. And that was very impressive to listen to. Hopefully you'll rub off on me and I'll be tougher when it comes to negotiating at cattle and equipment auctions."

She eyed him. "Were you always a nice guy? I don't remember that."

Hutch laughed. "Nice enough. But competitive with you. Now, I'm just relieved we're both Team Triplets."

She grinned. "Team Triplets. I like it. And I don't want my life to interfere with my time here. In fact, I just realized that for certain. I'll have my assistant, who already has a few clients of her own and is ready to be an agent in her right, handle that contract. I want to focus on the reason I'm here."

Chloe rubbed her eyes and her face started scrunching.

Savannah cuddled Chloe closer. "You better watch out, you better not cry," she sang softly. "You better not pout I'm telling you why. Though, that is what babies do, isn't it, you little dumpling. But Santa Claus *is* coming to town, and he's making a list."

Chloe made a little sound, like "ba," her gaze sweet on Savannah's face, then her eyes drooped. She let out a tiny sigh and her eyes closed, her little chest rising and falling.

"Aww, she fell asleep!" Savannah said. "Huh. I'm not too shabby at this, after all. They're all changed and ready for their bassinets."

"You really are a Christmas miracle," he said.

Her face, already lit up, sparkled even more. He led the way into the large, airy nursery with its silver walls decorated with tiny moons and stars, a big round rug on the polished wood floor, the bookcase full of children's titles, two gliders by the window. His father had ordered the three sleigh-shaped wooden bassinets, each baby's name stenciled and painted on it. Every time he looked at the bassinets, at the names, he'd forget all the crud that Daniel kept bringing up and he'd miss his dad, his grief catching him by surprise. People were never just one thing.

Savannah was a good example of that. If he'd seen her walking down Main Street yesterday in her cashmere coat, barking a negotiation into her cell phone, he'd never imagine her as someone who'd sing Christmas carols to a crying baby, whose eyes would light up at a crabby little girl falling asleep in her arms. People could always surprise you, he knew.

"I'm praying for my own Christmas miracle that I can transfer Chloe to her crib without waking her," she said. "What are my odds?"

"She's iffy," he said. "You just never know. Carson's more a sure bet—heavy sleeper. Caleb always wakes up the minute his head touches a mattress. At my house, anyway."

Savannah glanced at him for a moment, seeming to

latch on to that part about "his house." She started quietly singing Santa Claus Is Coming to Town again, then carefully lowered Chloe down, gently swaying just a bit. The baby's lower lip quirked, and when she was on the mattress, she simply turned her head and lifted a fist up to her ear, eyes closed, chest rising and falling.

"I did it!" Savannah whispered.

But then Chloe's eyes popped open and she started fussing.

"Scratch that. I didn't do it." Savannah's shoulders sagged.

"Told you she's iffy," he said. "She likes having her forehead caressed from the eyebrows up toward her hairline. And she likes your song. You could try both."

Savannah brightened and reached down to caress Chloe's forehead, singing the carol, and the baby girl's eyes drooped, drooped some more, and then she was asleep. "Phew," she whispered.

A half hour later, both boys were finally asleep in their bassinets, Caleb indeed taking longer than Carson. Hutch had the urge to pull Savannah into his arms for a celebratory hug, but a fist bump seemed more appropriate.

"Our work here is done," he said, holding up his palm "I could use coffee. You?"

She grinned and did give him a fist bump. "Definitely. And we can talk about the grand plan for my time here."

As they tiptoed out of the nursery, the urge for that embrace only got stronger. Because they were Team Triplets, and it felt so good to have someone on his side, someone who wouldn't quit on him, someone he could talk to?

Or was it all of the above *and* because he was attracted to Savannah Walsh?

It was choice B that her made her just as scary as she'd been seventeen years ago.

Don't miss
Triplets Under the Tree
by Melissa Senate,
available November 2023 wherever
Harlequin® Special Edition
books and ebooks are sold.

www.Harlequin.com

COMING NEXT MONTH FROM

◆ HARLEQUIN
SPECIAL EDITION

#3019 A MAVERICK'S HOLIDAY HOMECOMING
Montana Mavericks: Lassoing Love • by Brenda Harlen
'Tis the season...for a holiday reunion? Rancher Billy Abernathy has no interest in romance; Charlotte Taylor's career keeps her far away from Montana. But when the recently divorced father of three crosses paths with his runaway bride from long ago, a little bit of mistletoe works magic...

#3020 HER BEST FRIEND'S WEDDING
Bravo Family Ties • by Christine Rimmer
Through the years Sadie McBride and Ty Bravo have been rivals, then enemies—and in recent years, buddies. But when a Vegas wedding party leads to a steamy no-holds-barred kiss, will they risk their perfectly good friendship with something as dangerous as love?

#3021 MARRY & BRIGHT
Love, Unveiled • by Teri Wilson
Editor Addison England is more than ready for a much-earned promotion. The problem? So is Carter Payne, her boss's annoyingly charming nephew. Competition, attraction and marriage mayhem collide when these two powerhouse pros vie for *Veil Magazine*'s top job!

#3022 ONCE UPON A CHARMING BOOKSHOP
Charming, Texas • by Heatherly Bell
Twyla Thompson has kept Noah Cahill in the friend zone for years, crushing instead on his older brother. But when a bookstore costume contest unites them as Mr. Darcy and Elizabeth Bennet—and brings unrealized attraction to light—Twyla wonders if Noah may be her greatest love after all.

#3023 A FAMILY-FIRST CHRISTMAS
Sierra's Web • by Tara Taylor Quinn
Sarah Williams will do anything to locate her baby sister—even go undercover at renowned investigation firm Sierra's Web. She knows her by-the-book boss, Winchester Holmes, would fire her if he knew the truth. So falling for each other is not an option—*right*?

#3024 MARRIED BY MISTAKE
Sutton's Place • By Shannon Stacey
For Chelsea Grey, the only thing worse than working next door to John Fletcher is waking up in Vegas married to him. And worse still? Their petition for annulment is denied! They'll keep fighting to fix their marriage mistake—unless knee-weakening kisses and undeniable attraction change their minds first!

YOU CAN FIND MORE INFORMATION ON UPCOMING HARLEQUIN TITLES, FREE EXCERPTS AND MORE AT HARLEQUIN.COM.

HSECNM1023

HARLEQUIN
PLUS

Try the best multimedia subscription service for romance readers like you!

Read, Watch and Play.

Experience the easiest way to get the romance content you crave.

Start your **FREE TRIAL** at
<u>www.harlequinplus.com/freetrial</u>.